THE PHARMACIST

GILLIAN JACKSON

www.bloodhoundbooks.com

Print ISBN 978-1-914614-49-1

For Mum
Enid Shaw, 1933 – 2019

PROLOGUE
THE CATALYST

'*And on that farm he had some pigs, e i e i o...*' The two little girls collapsed into the back seat of the car in fits of giggles as they snorted like pigs, their cheerful laughter drifting out of the open car windows into the heat of the August morning.

The woman in the front passenger seat drew in a deep breath and relaxed into the contours of the seat, briefly closing her eyes, a smile playing across her lips. It was good to get away, she thought, to enjoy some family time, and the day looked as if it was turning into an absolute scorcher. Perfect.

At the wheel of the bronze Ford Granada Scorpio, her husband concentrated on the road, well aware of his responsibility to his precious cargo. The rising temperature quickly burned off the surface water from the overnight rain and a heat haze ahead gave an ethereal feel to the landscape. Quietly humming along to the familiar children's song, he dropped down a gear as the incline steepened and they approached a bend.

Sadly, not everyone was as circumspect that day. Heading towards the Granada was a white Transit van, an ancient model that had seen better days and was travelling far too fast for such a notorious stretch of road. A brash seventeen-year-old, yet to gain his full driving licence, was at the wheel, an arrogant youth, lightheaded from three cans of lager already consumed that morning and egged on by his eighteen-year-old friend.

'Get the feel of the wheel,' his friend goaded him into putting his foot down, but the approaching bend was much sharper than he anticipated and the befuddled, inexperienced driver struggled to control the vehicle. The road narrowed without warning and in order to avoid colliding with a barrier on the near side, he yanked the wheel sharply to the right, taking the van across the central white lines and onto the right-hand side of the road.

The driver of the Granada, turning into the same bend from the opposite direction, was suddenly confronted with the Transit van and instinctively swerved to his left to avoid a head-on collision. Unfortunately, he didn't stand a chance and the Granada veered off the road through the flimsy weather-weakened crash barrier, which buckled immediately at the force of the impact, and the car plunged down a steep incline.

The vehicle bounced like a rubber ball as it gathered momentum, the occupants shocked and helpless, screaming in panic and wild fear without the slightest hope of being heard. Shattering glass and crunching metal coalesced with the occupants' screams, drowning out the children's CD, which still merrily played its tune. The airbags activated and the seat belts held, but nothing could save them. Four precious lives ended abruptly that day in such a cruel, violent and unnecessary way, the ugly reality of death incongruous on such a glorious summer day.

The trembling pale-faced driver of the van swung the wheel

to his left and narrowly avoided colliding with the near-side barrier. He was well aware of what had happened, as was his passenger, but he drove on shakily, fear and guilt washing over him in equal measures. He stopped the van in a passing place about half a mile down the road, exited his vehicle, and vomited violently at the side of the road.

His friend jumped out too. 'What the hell happened?'

'It was your fault. You told me to put my bloody foot down!' He wiped his mouth with his sleeve and spat more foul-tasting bile onto the roadside.

Their angry words were stilled by the sudden, unmistakable, sound of an explosion. Turning, they looked back. Plumes of black smoke were already belching into the sky, the perfect summer day marred by the ugliness of the crash.

The pair were as sure as they could be that no one else witnessed the incident. It all happened so quickly that any passing vehicle would barely have time to register their mistake, least of all, remember their number plate. As other vehicles stopped, their occupants climbing out to stare impotently over the edge at the burning wreckage, the youths jumped back into their van and drove away.

The two made a pact never to speak of the incident again, and the only other people who knew the truth were, by then, forever silent.

PART I

THE MOTHER

1

Alice Roberts rolled over in bed, surprised to find an empty space at her side. It was only 7am, but already Tom was up. She supposed the habits of a lifetime were hard to break and wondered, not for the first time, if her husband would find adjusting to retirement challenging. Tom was such an active man, never still, his body always in motion.

The chance of more sleep was inviting but proved impossible. Thoughts of the day ahead and the many tasks awaiting her filled Alice's mind – there were still several finishing touches she wished to make to complete their new home, a task she relished and would enjoy.

As Alice pushed the duvet back and padded to the en suite for a shower, a somewhat disorientated feeling washed over her. Perhaps she'd consumed too much wine the evening before, she couldn't remember, but it would come back to her when she was fully awake and her head stopped throbbing.

Silence hung heavily in the house. Only the unfamiliar plumbing noises interrupted the stillness, sounds to which Alice was becoming accustomed and which barely registered in her consciousness. It was strange how every house created its peculiar noises, creaks and groans, which you ceased to notice over time. Tom's voice, singing along to the radio, would have been welcome, but he must have taken Barney for a walk. It was such a lovely morning and he'd probably be back by the time Alice showered and dressed.

Twenty minutes later, with the kettle full and starting to boil, Alice gazed from the kitchen window for signs of her husband's return. There was something niggling at the back of her mind, something she and Tom wanted to discuss with their daughter, Rachel, but Alice couldn't recall what it was. Snatches of a half-finished conversation drifted into her head and then out again, but the details eluded her. Was it something to do with them moving here? No, not that. Alice's mind felt quite woolly. She hated being unable to remember. Tom would remind her when he came home. She did feel a little strange this morning; perhaps the stress of the recent move was catching up on her.

The view from the kitchen window was nothing short of spectacular. Open countryside stretched over the lush green Eden valley and a narrow wooded path offered a pretty circular route of about two miles. It was perfect for walking their little mongrel dog and for keeping them fit. It was this view and the near-perfect situation of Melkinthorpe which initially attracted them to the cottage. The village, or perhaps it was best described as a hamlet, was home to a popular garden centre and tea rooms, as well as a smattering of chocolate-box cottages. The proximity of the Lake District and the sprawling gardens and woodland of nearby Lowther Castle guaranteed that there would be plenty of exploring to fill their retirement hours. June was turning out to be warm and the forecasters promised a hot summer ahead, the first of many, Alice hoped, in their new home.

Alice knew that not being in Penrith itself suited their daughter more than them. Rachel would not have cared for them to be living too close to her, Tom and Alice were in no doubt of that and saddened by it, but it was a fact they'd come to accept and another reason why Melkinthorpe was so perfect for their retirement home.

Alice hadn't yet met any of their neighbours, but now they were finally in residence and retirement was becoming a reality, she intended to remedy this by inviting them around for coffee to get to know them. Perhaps she might even join in some of the village activities. It would be interesting to see what was on offer. A WI maybe, Alice would enjoy the opportunity to make new friends, perhaps even become part of the jam and Jerusalem brigade. She smiled at the thought.

An hour later, there was still no sign of her husband, and Alice was starting to worry. She was also feeling nauseous and dizzy. Surely Tom would have left a note if he'd intended being this long? Alice could see her beloved Mini Cooper parked in the drive from the front window of the house and decided to check the garage to see if Tom had taken his car to go further afield. It was an effort; she felt a strong desire to return to bed to sleep off this awful sickly feeling but the need to know where Tom was spurred her on.

The garage was empty, which was more of a puzzle than the comfort for which she'd hoped. If Tom planned to go any distance, he would have told her the night before or woken her before leaving. Going back inside, Alice picked up the phone to ring Rachel. If her husband were anywhere, surely it would be with her. She could think of nowhere else that Tom could be.

'Hi, Rachel, sorry to ring so early but is Dad with you?'

'Mother?' Her daughter, usually brusque and business like asked, 'Are you okay?' Alice hoped she hadn't woken her.

'Yes, fine, thanks, love. It's just that your dad's taken Barney out and hasn't come back yet. He's taken the car too, so I thought perhaps he'd popped over to see you?' Even as she formed the words, Alice knew it was irrational that Tom would be at their daughter's so early in the morning; they rarely visited uninvited. Something felt strangely amiss and Alice was beginning to feel decidedly ill.

'Stay there. I'll be over in a few minutes.'

'But there's no need. If Dad's not with you, I'm sure he'll be back soon, although there was something we wanted to talk to you about – no, never mind that now. I'd ring his mobile, but you know he never has it switched on and the signal here's a bit iffy.' Alice's voice began to break as she spoke, her head still ached and she felt increasingly dizzy.

'Stay there,' Rachel repeated. 'I'll be with you soon.' Rachel ended the call before there was time for further protest. Feeling foolish about causing such a fuss, Alice hoped their daughter wouldn't be angry. Tom would surely be back before Rachel arrived. It was only 9.30am, he'd hardly been gone long enough for her to worry, but if Rachel wanted to come round, she would. Alice learned a long time ago that their only child would do precisely as she wanted to do in life. Moving slowly back into the kitchen, Alice made herself a coffee, hoping it would revive her and banish the throbbing headache.

It was in the kitchen that Alice noticed the red coat hanging on the rack beside the door. How strange – it wasn't her coat and she couldn't remember seeing Rachel wearing it either. Whatever was going on? A heavy, uncomfortable, knot was forming in the pit of Alice's stomach and she felt suddenly quite queasy and more than a little afraid. Sitting down, she looked around the room, taking in everything that was there and that wasn't. Barney's lead was missing from the coat rack, Tom must have taken him, yet his food and water bowls were gone too. Her eyes travelled through to the lounge where the dog's bed nestled in the corner, but no, that also was no longer there. Turning her head back to the coat rack, Tom's old parka was missing, but if he'd left early, it would still have been cool so he could be wearing it. Nothing unusual there.

Unsteadily, Alice got to her feet and went into the hall. Opening the cloakroom door revealed only her two everyday coats hanging up, with a few pairs of shoes underneath, her shoes. All of Tom's things were missing. She made her way back to the kitchen and sat down, her legs suddenly weak, unable to support her.

The crazy idea that Tom had left her popped unbidden into her head. He must have left in the night and taken Barney with him, but why? Life couldn't have been better for them. They were happy – weren't they? On the cusp of retirement, while they were still young enough to enjoy themselves, financially secure, well off even – what could possibly be wrong? And Tom wasn't a coward; surely, if he wanted to leave her, he'd have said so to her face and not just slunk off into the night without a word.

Was there another woman? The very thought was unbearably painful. Tom was the bright spot in her life, her soulmate. But if there was another woman, could the red coat be hers? No, that was crazy. Why would it be hanging in their kitchen? It was all wrong and all very unsettling. Tom would soon walk through the front door, Barney at his heels, and explain everything to her. They would laugh about it in time, wouldn't they?

The sensible thing to do would be to check the bedroom, Tom's wardrobe, his toiletries. Seeing those things would reassure her, but before she could summon up the strength to move, the sound of the front door closing startled her. Alice looked up to see Rachel hurrying through the hall.

'Are you okay?' Rachel approached her mother, a frown etched on her face.

'No, I'm not. Your dad's not here. I think he's left me! I can't find his things and he's taken Barney too.' Tears were rolling down Alice's cheeks as she looked hopefully to her daughter for an explanation.

'Let me get you a fresh coffee, and then we'll talk.'

'I don't want another coffee; I want to know what's happening!'

'Okay, well, at least take these. They'll help to calm you down.' Rachel took a small brown bottle from her bag and shook out a couple of white pills.

Alice took the two tablets her daughter offered and swallowed them with a gulp of cold coffee. She then stared intently at Rachel, willing her to explain what she couldn't comprehend.

'Did you know that your dad was going to leave me?'

'No, Dad hasn't left you... not in the way you mean. But, look, Mum, you're confused about things, so I'm going to call the doctor.'

'I don't need a doctor. I need to know what's going on. Where's your father?'

'Why don't you go back to bed and I'll ring the surgery?'

'No, why won't you tell me, Rachel, where is your father?'

'But, Mum... Dad died nearly four years ago, don't you remember?'

'No! Of course he didn't die. I'd know that! He was here last night, and you were too, but this morning he's gone. I thought he'd just taken Barney for his walk. What are you talking about?'

'You're obviously not well. Let me call the doctor. You've got some kind of delirium and your mind's not working properly. Try not to worry, we'll get it sorted and you'll be fine.' Rachel pulled out her phone while Alice struggled to take in her daughter's words. *It couldn't be true. Tom had been with them both last night – hadn't he?*

Rachel left the kitchen to make the call. When she returned, she told Alice that the doctor was coming soon.

'Why are you telling me that Tom's dead? It's a wicked thing to say. Is this some sort of sick joke?'

'No, Mum, it's true, I'm sorry. Don't you remember? Dad had a heart attack nearly four years ago; it was very sudden, but for some reason, you seem to have forgotten all about it.'

'But there are other things too, the red coat over there.' Alice nodded towards the door, 'Whose is that? And what about Barney, his bed is gone and his bowl...'

'The coat's yours. We chose it last Christmas on one of our shopping trips, don't you remember?'

'No, I never wear red. Don't lie to me, Rachel, and what about the dog?'

'Barney's gone too, I'm afraid. He died a couple of years ago, long before you moved here. He was old and there was nothing we could do.'

'Stop it! You're making it all up. Let me try Tom's phone, he might have switched it on by now.'

'I'm not making it up... Why would I do that? Look, the doctor will be here soon. Why don't you go to bed and try to sleep some more?'

Alice was feeling sleepy. Her mind was swimming too. Reluctantly she allowed her daughter to guide her to the bedroom, where she lay down on the bed and very soon succumbed to the welcome oblivion of sleep.

'Thank you for coming so quickly, doctor. My mother rang me this morning, asking if I knew where Dad was, but my father died four years ago. She seems totally confused; do you think it could be an infection? That can cause delirium, can't it?'

'It could be, we can do some tests to see, but if you'd like to wake her for me now, I'll examine her and have a chat with her.'

Alice half heard the conversation through an increasingly foggy mind and opened her eyes as Rachel gently shook her arm. The feeling of disorientation had increased, and as she tried to sit up, dizziness made her reel and Alice flopped back down. The unfamiliar doctor smiled as he introduced himself. Since the move, she'd not had cause to visit the surgery, not even to register as a patient.

'How are you feeling, Mrs Roberts?' He was already taking out his stethoscope to sound her chest. Tears welled in Alice's eyes as she discovered that she couldn't form the words she wanted to speak. What was happening to her? Was she going mad? The doctor continued his examination and asked his questions, but her mouth refused to work and she found herself making deep guttural noises rather than forming complete words. Alice was terrified, she wanted Tom, but Rachel said that Tom was dead. Was he? If so, why couldn't she remember?

Rachel and the doctor left her and moved into the lounge. Alice could hear muffled voices but was unable to hear much of what they were saying.

'You may be right about an infection, but I'm a little concerned about her speech.' The doctor spoke kindly. 'It could be that she's had a mild stroke. But then, it could also be dementia; it's too early to say definitively. Have you noticed any unusual behaviour recently, memory loss or confusion perhaps?'

'Now you come to mention it, she has been a little confused lately, but I put it down to the stress of moving house and she's never really coped well since my father died. She's been a bit forgetful of late too, but again, I assumed it was stress.' Rachel looked thoughtful as the doctor continued.

'I'd like your mother to be admitted to hospital for a CT scan to rule out a stroke. So I'll send for an ambulance and we'll get her to hospital straight away for that brain scan. Is that all right with you?'

'Of course, whatever's best for Mum, thank you, doctor.'

The ambulance arrived within the hour and took a confused Alice to the local hospital with Rachel following in her car. The rest of the day passed by in a round of tests and a brain scan until finally, they received the news that she'd not suffered a stroke or a brain haemorrhage. Alice was relieved but still felt unwell. Thankfully, her speech had returned, if still a little slurred, enabling her to protest that she wanted to go home.

'But, Mum you're still very confused and I'm concerned about you. If you go home, you could worsen. Can you remember what you thought was happening this morning?' Rachel's tone was kind but firm.

'I remember you telling me some ridiculous story about your dad being dead. I don't know what's going on with you, but I want to go home. Tom will probably be there by now, waiting for me.'

'I'm sorry, but that proves you're in no fit state to go home. I'm going to have a word with the sister and try to see the doctor about finding somewhere safe to help you get better.' Rachel left the room and Alice sighed. She didn't want to fall out with her daughter, but why was Rachel doing this and making up this fantasy about Tom? If Alice had the strength and didn't feel so woolly-headed and disorientated, she would have discharged herself and got a taxi to take her home. However, not having her bag or any money with her, she was entirely in the hands of her daughter.

When Rachel returned, it was with the news that Alice was to be transferred to a 'step down bed' in a nursing home. Alice's heart sank as if weighted with lead, but she acquiesced in the hope that Tom would soon come to find her, and this whole surreal situation would be over and relegated to history.

2

A slice of early morning sunlight fell across the bed, intruding into Alice's dreams. Turning over under the warmth of the duvet and pulling it tighter around her was useless, as the tinny clatter of the cleaning trolley nudged her reluctantly into wakefulness. Suddenly Mavis was shaking her shoulder and the reality dawned on Alice that she was still an unwilling resident of The Elms – a nursing home – a place where people went to await death.

'Come on, wakey wakey, Alice, time to get up now.' The woman sounded like a relic from a bygone holiday camp. Alice didn't want to 'wakey, wakey'. She didn't want this obnoxious woman as her 'carer'. Mavis so obviously didn't care – and she most certainly didn't want to be in this awful place, a hybrid of a prison camp and a mental hospital.

As Alice's feet touched the cold wooden floor, Mavis reached for the buttons on her nightdress.

'I can manage!' Alice snapped, shrugging her off, sick of being treated like a child.

'Suit yourself.' Mavis smirked and straightened the bed

while Alice hurried into the small shower room, her only place of escape, even though the door didn't have a lock.

As hot water cascaded over her body, so did the all-too-regular hot tears and familiar despondency which marked this confusing period in her life. She hardly noticed Mavis enter the room and did not attempt to cover her nakedness. Her dignity had been the first thing to go, or was it her sanity?

Alice had always assumed that dementia – or madness – or whatever affliction this was, would overtake her, unawares, that should such awful misfortune strike, there would be no knowledge of losing her mind and therefore no pain or regret at the loss. But this was a living nightmare. She was deemed no longer safe to live independently or make her own decisions, but it was such a struggle to accept this new reality and Alice hardly recognised the woman she'd become.

A cocktail of drugs was served to Alice with each meal and monitored by a carer to ensure she took them. Unfortunately, taking the medication appeared to have no benefit and served only to elicit feelings of constant woolly headedness, confusion and exhaustion.

'Clean clothes,' Mavis shouted above the noise of the running water, placing a small pile on the toilet seat, 'and breakfast's here.'

After drying herself off, Alice struggled into the shapeless clothes she didn't recognise. She'd given up trying to tell them that they weren't her clothes as everyone insisted they were.

The breakfast tray held one banana, one slice of toast and a dish of yoghurt, the same fare every morning and apparently her choice.

Mavis hovered in the room, a spy for her jailers, but precisely who those jailers were, was still unclear to Alice. Deliberately taking her time, she sensed the other woman's growing annoyance, but as this was one of the few things over which she was still in control, Alice was determined to exercise it.

Alice still couldn't recall exactly how long she'd been in The Elms. The first few days had passed in a haze of sleep, only waking for meals and visits from staff, and Alice struggled to differentiate between being awake and dreaming. During those days, as she was helped to her feet, dizziness washed over her and her eyes struggled to focus. She ascribed these feelings to the side effects of the drugs they continued to give her — and Alice loathed taking medication of any description. The idea of all those chemicals swimming around in her bloodstream was abhorrent to her.

As the days dragged by, Alice's memories tormented her. Vague recollections robbed her of peace, or could they be dreams? At times it seemed that she was back in the hospital, the distinctive clinical smells in her nostrils – and there was a CT scan. They said she needed a brain scan. Alice remembered being pushed on a trolley towards a vast doughnut-shaped machine flanked by two smiling nurses. The machine moved towards her enveloping her head. Her heart pounded and it became an effort to breathe. She wanted to get out of the monstrous contraption.

Grinding noises filled her ears and she strained to hear the nurse's voice in the distance, attempting to reassure her, urging her to remain still. And there were the blood samples; they seemed to take so much blood that Alice wondered if she would become anaemic. Her fear was almost tangible, yet still, Alice couldn't speak up for herself, it was like being trapped in a bad dream, one of those awful experiences when your legs feel like lead and you can't run away, when someone is chasing you — and that someone seemed to resemble Rachel. Tom drifted in and out of her mind too. Could he be dead, as her daughter insisted? Surely not, please God no!

By the third or fourth day at The Elms, Alice's awareness of her surroundings increased, her brain cleared enough to assess the situation and know exactly where she was. But with clarity came despair and an unsettling degree of anger at being at the mercy of others. A constant smell of incontinence and disinfectant vied for dominance in the atmosphere, making her feel quite nauseous. While meals were cooked, other odours invaded her space and she longed for her own home. Televisions blared from the day room or other residents' bedrooms, the inevitable backdrop to latter years.

Alice always hated visiting nursing homes, the whiff of despair, the residents wandering aimlessly up and down corridors with no goal to their lives, no hope of a better future, merely waiting to die. But here she was, in just such a place, where she most certainly didn't belong. It was for old people, and Alice was only fifty-five. Surely that was still middle-aged?

It was all Rachel's doing, her fault that she was here. It was her daughter who'd insisted on calling a doctor in the first place — and who'd told her the vicious lie that Tom was dead.

As Alice's awareness increased, she was determined to leave The Elms as soon as possible. Needing answers and not knowing how long it would be until they allowed her to go home, she decided to take matters into her own hands.

Alice required a distraction to facilitate her escape; the opportunity for such was everywhere, and after breakfast would be the ideal time. The staff were busiest then – the dining room needed clearing, the medication trolley organised, and notes made. The carers made never-ending notes; it seemed that each resident's every move was to be recorded, for whose benefit Alice had yet to decide.

Alice's room was on the first floor, with the staircase only a few doors down and the day room opposite. She'd been taken downstairs on a couple of occasions and watched the carer tap numbers into the keypad, which opened the door. It was the gateway to freedom, so Alice held the numbers in her mind, knowing that this was the only exit; the lift required a key.

After breakfast, most residents were ushered into the day room where the television played continuously and yet more weak, milky, lukewarm tea served. Alice had noticed one particular lady who was prone to frenetic outbursts, the slightest incident prompting loud wails and hysteria. She felt sorry for the poor woman, who appeared to have lost all sense of reality, but she was the ideal target.

Reluctantly, despite her empathy, Alice approached the woman who sat at the far end of the day room, well away from the door. Then, using her own body to shield her target from view, Alice took the biscuit which the woman was holding, leaned in close enough for only her to hear, and in a loud whisper said, 'No more of these for you, ever!' It was totally against her character to do something so cruel to a poor soul who couldn't understand, but it resulted in the desired effect.

The woman shrieked as if physically assaulted, then began hyperventilating, throwing her body backwards and forwards in the seat, a frantic noisy rocking. Alice didn't stay to see what happened next and as every available staff member rushed into the day room to see what the commotion was about, she quickly walked, unobserved, towards the stairs.

With her heart pounding, she grabbed the handle, confident she could be down to ground level and out of the building before being spotted. Pulling with all her might on the heavy door, Alice gasped in frustration as it refused to open. Confusion washed over her until she remembered the keypad. Yes, she needed to tap in the numbers, and quickly before anyone came. Her fingers hovered over the buttons: she pressed three, five, seven, nine, but nothing happened. The door remained locked.

Certain that this was the right combination of numbers, she

tried again. Still, the door remained locked. Alice tried a different combination, with tears of frustration beginning to dampen her cheeks. Perhaps she'd remembered wrongly and it should be even numbers? Two, four, six, eight, still nothing moved.

'Alice?' A voice made her jump. 'What are you doing?' The carer was at her shoulder, moving her away from the door and steering her towards her room. 'Did Olive's outburst scare you? Don't worry, she's fine. I'll take you back to your room, shall I?'

The woman was kind, and Alice could do nothing other than allow the carer to return her to her room as if she were a piece of lost property. It seemed that they hadn't connected Olive's outburst to her escape attempt, which proved to be nothing more than pathetic.

'Can I get you anything?' The carer asked as they arrived at the room.

'Yes, I'd like to see a policeman.' Alice looked hopefully into the woman's eyes.

'Why would you need to see a policeman?'

'To ask them to find Tom.' Tears streamed unchecked down Alice's face.

The woman smiled. 'I'll fetch you a nice cup of tea.'

Alice closed her eyes, her brow furrowed – so much for her escape, her grand gesture – and so much for finding Tom, her real goal. In her heart, she knew he wouldn't have left her. Their marriage was strong. They'd been together for so many years, there must be a good reason preventing him from coming for her. She feared that something might have happened to him, and Rachel, for some reason, was telling everyone that he was dead. Behind Alice's closed eyes, Tom's face was clear in her mind, as if she'd been with him only yesterday. If Rachel was telling the truth, how was it that Alice could see her husband so distinctly in her mind's eye?

3

Jack Priestly studied his wife as she stacked the dishwasher in the kitchen of their new home. At forty-seven, Sarah was still a beautiful woman, slim and small framed with a pretty heart-shaped face, blue eyes and blonde hair. She was the first to admit that these days the hair colour received some help from a bottle, and her figure was maintained only through regular exercise and a good diet. Sarah was nothing short of Jack's ideal wife, and he was every bit as much in love with her now as when she'd first captured his heart over twenty years ago.

Being a policeman's wife wasn't always easy, but Sarah was supportive, accepting of his often unpredictable schedule, and a great listener whenever he needed to offload his feelings. Jack knew how fortunate he was in this regard; he'd seen too many colleagues' marriages fail through the job's pressure, too many wives feeling like second fiddle to the force and too many children used as pawns in bitter divorces.

Fulfilled by her role as a wife and mother, Jack knew that any ambitions Sarah may once have cherished in her youth were willingly superseded by her marriage to him and the birth of their two sons, Jake and Dan. With neither Jack nor Sarah driven by materialism, money was never a primary issue to the family, and as long as there was enough to live comfortably, they were content. Sarah delighted in being a 'stay at home mum' when the boys were young, and even as they grew and needed her less, homemaking was still her priority. When their sons attended primary school, she volunteered in the classroom, which she continued long after both the boys had left for senior school.

Even now, after only six weeks in their new home, Sarah was already involved in another voluntary position in a local nursing home, The Elms, a job she already loved. Jack was proud of her altruistic nature and often felt that she was too good for him, but he appreciated his good fortune and tried to care for her the same way she did for him.

Moving to Penrith was a huge step for Jack and Sarah, but one they'd carefully considered for many months beforehand and now embraced with enthusiasm, relishing the potential such a new beginning afforded. Of course, it was a whole world away from Leeds, where the couple had spent all of their married life. But then, that was one of the area's chief attractions and here they'd found the tranquillity they'd been seeking

Even the air in Penrith tasted different, cleaner and woodier somehow, a scent Jack was already beginning to appreciate. Leeds did, of course, hold its attractions, the nightlife was second to none, and Sarah loved to shop in the city centre, yet they were ready for a change of pace and Penrith certainly ticked the box on that score.

With an approximate population of 16,000, Penrith was far from a sleepy backwater and, in Jack's opinion, was located close to some of the UK's most stunning scenery. It was their long-held dream to move near the Lake District, escape the city's noise and grime and live at a more leisurely, pace, and now it had become a reality.

Their sons had also relocated further north in recent years, which became the deciding factor for Jack and Sarah. Jake, their elder son, lived in Carlisle with his girlfriend, Grace, and worked for the police as a civilian at divisional headquarters. He did something with computers that Jack couldn't even begin to understand, but which Jake found totally absorbing. Dan, a year younger, was at medical school in Edinburgh, both places so much more accessible from Penrith than Leeds.

Jack was a proud father. In a world he often viewed from the very lowest level, Jake and Dan had both turned out well. However, he did give credit for this to Sarah, their needs always took precedence over her own, and there was no doubt she was the glue that held their family together.

The cottage they'd discovered and subsequently bought on the town's outskirts was also a dream come true. It was a home with character and charm, stone floors, exposed beams – the whole package and a place which delighted them both. The downstairs rooms still boasted the original rough lime plaster, restored sympathetically over the years. Sarah loved the look and was unconcerned at the challenge it presented to her husband each time she asked him for more shelves or to hang pictures. Jack had already nearly ruined the chimney wall when attempting to hang a large oval mirror, one of Sarah's antique shop finds, as the plaster proved too fragile to hold the weight. An original inglenook fireplace was a feature they both loved and was now fitted out with a new log-burning stove, for convenience yet in keeping with the room.

Having worked tirelessly to restore the cottage in the few weeks they'd been in residence, only the garden was left to tackle. Sarah required nothing less than an old English cottage garden, which Jack knew would be amazing when his wife set to work. Their friends in Leeds joked that they would need masses of room for the many visitors they'd inevitably receive, and Jack countered that he'd keep their new address a secret.

Jack was in no doubt that their move was the right decision. At work, night time call-outs were much less frequent, allowing him to spend more time with Sarah, who appreciated his regular hours. When not visiting their sons, weekends off were spent exploring their new locality, long leisurely walks, discovering new places to eat and visiting local attractions.

At forty-eight, Jack was almost certain that this would be his last post in the police force, although he viewed impending retirement with mixed feelings. Sarah laughingly suggested he could become a private investigator. He quickly pointed out that there was minimal call for a PI in a town as small as Penrith or the surrounding area and that perhaps she read too many novels. Various hobbies were mooted by some of his new and helpful colleagues now that they'd got the measure of their new boss and discovered him to be approachable, with an effortless sense of humour. Pigeon racing, woodturning, and breeding ferrets were a few of the more repeatable suggestions – but Jack wasn't a hobby kind of man. He was a policeman through and through, devoted to the job, a devotion which only his family trumped.

For now, however, there was work to be done. Jack would worry about retirement in due course. He kissed his wife goodbye and set out on the short drive to Hunter's Lane, notching up the police station's proximity as another plus in his new life.

4

Alice had an 'appointment.' It was on the floor below her room and Mavis accompanied her, carefully shielding the keypad on the fire door while tapping in the numbers to freedom, on the off chance that her charge was still capable of memorising such things. Since her futile escape attempt, Alice learned that they changed the combination of numbers each week.

The scent of pine lingered in the air with other, more unsavoury, body odours as they walked down the stairs in stony silence. Mavis knocked on a door and opened it without waiting for a reply, steering Alice inside by the elbow before she could make a dash for it.

The room was small, warm and relatively comfortable, if a little stuffy, with neutral decor and absolutely no reflected personality. A man of about Alice's age sat behind a desk and looked up with a wide smile. He was new to her. She was quite sure they'd not met before, and that perplexed her somewhat. What kind of appointment was this?

'Hello, Alice, my name's Richard Edwards. How are you today?' His round brown eyes, set below a broad forehead, focused on her face. Then, when she didn't answer, he motioned for her to sit opposite him and she dutifully obeyed, patiently waiting while he read from a file on the desk and tapped a few keys on his computer.

'Are you a doctor or a policeman?' Alice broke the silence.

He raised his eyebrows. 'Why would you think I'm a policeman?'

'Because I asked to see one.'

Dr Edwards lowered his eyes and turned the page in the file, searching for something but not immediately answering.

'Why do you want to see a policeman, Alice? His tone was not unkind as he raised his head to meet her eyes.

'To report my husband as missing.'

He nodded as if he understood but made no further comment.

'Alice, I'm a doctor, not a policeman, and I'm here to see if I can help you. Firstly, I'm going to give you an address to remember, one that I'll ask you to repeat later. It's 27 Greenfield Close, do you understand?'

'Yes... and my date of birth is June seventh, 1964. Today is Thursday, and the month is–' She stopped, suddenly unsure of the month. They'd asked her the same questions so many times, nodding at her answers but not telling her if she was right or wrong. She'd been quizzed about where she lived, the time of year, the current prime minister, everything a sane person should know, and Alice had answered correctly, or so she thought. But was her brain playing tricks on her? Perhaps they were right and she was going mad? *If I am crazy*, she thought, *it could be 2030 and I'm living entirely in the past.* The thought was surreal and more than a bit scary, but she dismissed it. Her primary focus was on Tom. Why hadn't he come to see her, to take her home?

'Can you tell me your occupation, Alice?'

'I'm a teacher, or at least I was until I retired.'

'And where did you teach?'

'Hayfield Primary School in Matlock, I was there for fifteen years before Tom and I moved near Penrith to retire.'

'You're very young to be retired.' Dr Edwards seemed to expect an answer to his statement, but she didn't offer one.

'Can I use a telephone, please?'

'Perhaps later, Alice. What about your family? Do you have children?'

'Yes, a daughter, Rachel. Why isn't Tom coming to see me – or Rachel? You're keeping me here against my will – do my family even know I'm here?' Alice was worried, particularly about Tom. It wasn't like him not to come. She really needed his comforting presence, his strong arms around her.

'Your daughter was here yesterday, don't you remember?'

'Yes, yes, of course, I remember, I meant Tom! When's my husband coming to see me?' She'd made a mistake. *Stupid, stupid me! I remember Rachel visiting, but it seemed like days ago, not just yesterday. This thinking through fog is so hard. If only they'd let me go home, I'd be able to think clearly there.*

'When can I go home?' She tried to sound rational when she really wanted to beg and plead, anything to get them to let her go.

'We need to be sure you're well enough before that can happen. We want you to be safe, Alice. Do you remember why you came to The Elms in the first instance, or how long you've been with us?'

The short answer to both questions was no, but she couldn't admit that to this man. The last few days were more than a little hazy. She remembered Rachel telling her she was confused, but how she'd physically got to The Elms was a mystery. *Perhaps Tom was away*, she thought, *he's been winding up his business affairs ready for our retirement, but I can't understand why he hasn't been to see me yet. I must ask Rachel when she next comes.*

A vague recollection of being in hospital floated around in Alice's mind and she remembered feeling afraid because she couldn't speak. It was like being trapped in a bad dream, but when she awoke, it was in here, her prison, and she still didn't know why she was here.

Alice knew her silence was probably every bit as bad as admitting to having no recollection of the recent past, yet no sensible answer came to mind.

'Alice, can you remember the address I gave you when you came in?' Dr Edwards took her by surprise.

No, no! I meant to keep repeating it, to hold it in my mind, but thoughts of Tom and Rachel and home have distracted me. This man has confused me!

'It was somewhere green, Green Street? Number twenty-something?'

'Well done, Alice, I think that's all for today. Now, would you like to go back to your room, or perhaps to the day room with the others?'

'My room, please.' The 'others' were all mad and being with them created doubts about her own sanity.

'Have I got dementia?' She felt suddenly bold enough to ask the question which sat heavily on her mind, the answer to which she was unsure if she wanted to hear.

Dr Edwards raised an eyebrow. 'Truthfully, we're not sure. You're certainly confused about some facts, and that's why your social worker and the medical staff have decided on a Deprivation of Liberty Order.' Dr Edwards must have noticed her recoil at those last words, that awful label which sounded so final. And as for her social worker, Alice wasn't even aware she had one.

'It's nothing to worry about, just a precaution for your safety, and at this stage, it's not permanent. These little assessments are to monitor your progress and decide what the best way forward is for you. We're keeping Rachel informed. In fact, she's coming in shortly, so you'll be able to see her. The very fact that you're asking these questions shows an improvement in your cognitive capacity, which is certainly a good sign.'

Dr Edwards smiled again, a benign dismissive smile, probably reserved for the mentally ill. Yet, for the first time in goodness knows how long, Alice felt encouraged. Perhaps she wasn't going mad after all if this doctor seemed to think there was hope, or was that just a ploy to keep her compliant by offering a few drops of optimism as a sop?

The doctor stood up and opened the door. Mavis was waiting outside, no doubt she'd been listening to every word, her smile so obviously false as she walked ahead of Alice towards the stairs.

Back in her room, when Alice looked out of her window, rain was falling, darkening the summer skies and lashing against the window with a sudden, fierce strength. The battering raindrops sounded brutal, like hailstones, and Alice shuddered, afraid. The murky clouds obscured the morning sun, and summer was suddenly, cruelly, snatched away. *Like my life has been*, Alice thought as those frequent, crazy thoughts once again edged into her mind.

'You can have a nice cup of tea now, Alice.' Mavis might just as easily have given her a sweetie and a pat on the head for being a good girl – she was heartily sick of being treated like a child – or a madwoman.

Being in The Elms was nothing short of stifling. Time ceased to have meaning and the days were punctuated only by mealtimes, endless cups of tea, or 'little chats' with the doctor. So it was hardly surprising that Alice could barely remember what day it was. This place would deaden anyone's sensibilities. Her head constantly swirled with images which she was told were from the past, but they were so vivid, so clear. If Tom had died four years ago, Alice was convinced she'd not be able to recall his features with such clarity or summon up the feel of his touch as if it was only yesterday. Her mind appeared to be a maze through which she wandered, one minute seeing the way out but the next confronted with another obstacle to blur her vision and confuse reality with fantasy. Was this what dementia was like? All certainty gone, not knowing what reality was anymore?

Increasingly, Alice found herself looking back on her life, searching for those happy memories, the details of which grounded her, events for which she had complete certitude. But was this merely another sign of dementia – living in the past, confusing today with yesterday? Yes, there was pain in the past, immeasurable pain, but such comfort in the happy memories, a welcome escape to a place of safety and a time when Alice knew who she was again; a wife, a mother.

5

1988 Alice

Tom Roberts, tall and handsome with thick blond hair and deep blue eyes, was always the only man for me! Our parents were great friends and we grew up as childhood sweethearts in the beautiful Derbyshire countryside, always in and out of each other's houses and closer than if we'd been brother and sister. I did have a sister, Karen who was two years younger than me and she often tagged along with us, but as we grew into our teenage years, Karen seemed to drift away, still a child when we thought we were so grown up. My relationship with Tom inevitably changed and we looked at each other with new eyes as we grew older, our friendship blossoming into love. His broad smile and intense eyes melted my heart each time we met, and neither of us so much as considered going out with anyone else.

I remember our first magical kiss when we were sixteen. It marked the change in our relationship, the end of puppy love and the beginning of a relationship that I was confident would stand the test of time. Our love was a certainty. Even our parents could see the strength of our feelings and were delighted for us.

When Tom went to university, I studied locally at the technical college, but we still only had eyes for each other, our future destiny together never in doubt. Every weekend Tom travelled home from Manchester University so we could spend as much time together as possible. Tom's mother often hinted that she too would occasionally like to see her only son. There was never any doubt that we would eventually marry and live in Matlock, where we'd grown up, so when Tom completed his degree in business studies and secured his first job, we became engaged. Our families were delighted and began the exciting task of planning our wedding.

It was a spring wedding in 1985, a week before my twenty-first birthday – and the happiest day of my life. Walking up the gentle incline to St Giles Parish Church on my father's arm, the sun smiled down on us. Dad beamed with pride, and I almost floated, as if on a cloud, so happy that I thought it was a dream from which I would wake. Daffodils stood to attention on both sides of the path, nodding their approval as I walked between them towards the ancient picturesque church ahead. I felt like the most blessed woman on earth.

Karen was close behind me, lifting the train of my dress and halfway up the path, she tugged me back, laughing and warned me not to be in so much of a hurry, to make the moment last. But I could barely wait to be Tom's wife. Passing through the vast wooden doors and seeing my future husband waiting for me at the altar, I knew this was only the beginning of a life filled with love and joy. I stood on the threshold of all I'd ever wanted. With the spring sunshine casting shimmering prisms of colour through the stained-glass windows onto the aisle, I stepped into my new and brilliant life.

Perhaps I was naive to imagine that the road ahead would be a smooth and easy path, but that belief was strengthened over the following two years when it proved to be just so. We moved into a quaint stone cottage in Matlock near to my parents and Tom's widowed mother and set about fashioning it to suit our needs. An endless troupe of workmen shared our first few weeks of residence, encroaching into our privacy, but it was worth it. The kitchen and bathroom were updated, internal walls removed to give the space we wanted, and a new electrical wiring system installed. Tom and I spent every spare hour working to restore our home, helped by family and friends. We lovingly stripped off layer upon layer of paint, polishing the wood which lay beneath until finally, the old place could breathe again. It took most of the first year of our marriage and was a true labour of love, hardly seeming like work at all.

As we worked, we dreamed. The cottage boasted three large bedrooms and from the very day we married, we longed to start a family, to fill those empty rooms and the whole house with the laughter of children, yet for the first three years of our life together, that joy was denied to us.

As is so often typical of the young, we were impatient. Having so much to offer and longing to share it with a child, we decided to adopt, even though it was far too early to give up hope of ever having our own baby. Our love overflowed and we desperately wanted to share it, to encompass a child who needed the love and care of a family.

We eagerly embarked on the unavoidable official process, which seemed arduous and intrusive at times, but we were keen and complied with all that was asked of us to be approved. Eventually, the news we longed for arrived. There was a baby girl who the authorities thought to be a perfect match for us.

Rachel came into our lives. She was nine months old when we first met her, a tiny mite, undernourished and with a haunted look on her little face which no child should have. Her background was one of neglect and squalid conditions which we could hardly bear to contemplate, an injustice we so badly wanted to redress. Because she was so young, the process of settling her into our home was an unusually swift one, unprecedented because of Rachel's need for stability which we were eager to offer. We quickly took over from her temporary foster carers as her new parents, her forever family, and welcomed her with such love and anticipation, full of hope for the future.

As well as being small for her age, Rachel was unnaturally quiet and we found ourselves strangely longing to hear her cry, while most of the mothers I met at the clinic dearly wished for the opposite. Perhaps, we reasoned, her cries had gone unheard for so long that she'd simply given up trying, except for the odd occasions when she felt physical pain. It was almost a relief when, after a few months, our daughter tentatively tried to walk. On occasions, she fell and hurt herself and we welcomed her cries as a chance to hold and soothe her. But sadly, my arms were never a comfort to Rachel, she fought against physical contact, and I was distraught.

From the very beginning, she was not a baby to seek out cuddles, no matter how much Tom and I tried. When we did pick her up to hold her, her little body would stiffen, her back would arch, and she'd pull away from us with such strength, wriggling to be put down on the floor or into her cot, a stubborn expression of independence on her little cross face.

The social workers shared their suspicions that she'd spent most of her first few months in a cot and so it became her place of safety, rather like a dog retreats to its kennel. My heart ached to hold our daughter, but physical contact was alien to her, abhorrent almost. I longed to hear her laugh when we tried to play with her, but we knew it would take time and we would simply need to have patience.

In the end, it wasn't me or Tom who released the happy child inside of her, but the new baby who made her appearance almost a year to the day after Rachel became our daughter.

We were overjoyed to discover that I was pregnant, and suddenly the world looked a brighter place as we felt sure that a new baby would melt Rachel's heart.

It did indeed, and when Jenny was born, our prayers appeared to have been answered. Rachel became the baby's self-appointed guardian. At not yet two years old, she doted on her little sister, always by her side and wanting to help care for her. So naturally, I allowed her as much involvement as possible and Tom and I were thrilled that our elder daughter, at last, appeared to be happy.

Rachel's delight in her baby sister continued over the coming months and by the time Jenny was walking, the girls were inseparable and did everything together. Perhaps, as they grew, there were even occasions when I felt somewhat left out as our daughters' bond was strong and they appeared to need only each other. I berated myself for those petty feelings of jealousy at their closeness.

Generally, life was perfect, even with Tom working long hours to establish his business, and the Peak District was such a beautiful place to live. The girls and I would fill our days with picnics in Hall Leys Park, girly shopping trips to Derby with tea and cake in a cafe, or visiting my parents in Matlock Bath. Life was full and happy. Simple pleasures, like walking in the rain, became adventures, with the girls dressed in their bright yellow raincoats, duck-fashioned wellington boots and frilly umbrellas. Puddles became rivers to splodge in and the wet grass was a rain-forest to explore and hunt for wild animals.

My sister, Karen, and her family lived close by, in the village of Cromford, and we spent many happy times with them on the historic Birdswood narrowboat, lazily drifting along the Cromford Canal. By that time, Karen and her husband, James, a local GP, had their own daughter. Beth was born a year before Jenny, so the three girls were close in age and loved to spend time together. I couldn't have wished for a more charmed life and with Tom's business doing so well, I could stay at home with our daughters and concentrate solely on raising them.

By the time the girls were all at school, Karen and I could finally indulge our long-held dream of opening a tea shop in Matlock. We would meet each week at Scarthin Books, a delightful antiquarian bookshop in Cromford, housed in an ancient, atmospheric building with a narrow staircase leading to an upstairs coffee shop. After browsing the many hundreds of books and buying not a few, we would follow the tempting aroma of freshly ground coffee, treat ourselves to some of their irresistible cherry scones, and plan our future endeavour.

Karen was an excellent cook, her cakes and pastries were to die for, and I would enjoy working front of house and keeping the books, although Tom would undoubtedly help on that score. Those early days of planning were exciting and we looked forward to the day when our dream would become a reality. My life was as light, colourful and beautiful as a perfect soap bubble, but I was to learn, the hard way, that it was also every bit as fragile.

I was totally unprepared for the fallout when the bubble of my flawless life burst.

6

Parking the car in an allocated space in the Hunter's Lane car park, Jack paused outside Penrith police station and looked at the date above the doorway, 1904. Briefly, he wondered how much drama the grand old building had witnessed throughout the years before his mind jumped back to the present and his immediate future. Pushing open the heavy wooden doors, he stepped inside to continue this new phase in his life.

After only six weeks on the job, Jack had found his feet at the station and quickly got to know his colleagues.

It seemed reasonable to assume that the kind of crime Jack would encounter in Penrith would be far removed from his experiences working in Leeds city centre. Yes, there were still the modern-day evils of drugs, knife crime and abuse, but on a far lesser scale, and already it seemed to Jack that he had stepped back some thirty years. Indeed, the décor of his new working environment suggested age. It appeared sadly neglected, a low priority on the demands of an overstretched budget.

Perhaps crime in Penrith would also prove less complex than in Leeds and solved by good, old-fashioned, bobby on the beat stuff. That would be fine with Jack. He'd seen more than his fair share of vicious crimes and the inevitable heartache it left in its wake and would be delighted to spend the rest of his career solving more straightforward crimes, but was that even possible? He was assuming that a smaller town with a population living a relatively easy-going lifestyle wouldn't throw up the kind of deprived crime he'd encountered in Leeds, and he certainly hoped this would prove to be so.

Jack, never a man to waste time, had immersed himself in work at Hunter's Lane from day one of his new appointment, with his first couple of weeks spent familiarising himself with each of the station's active cases, as well as some of the more serious cold case files. His natural tenacity ensured that he would never give up on any of them, old or new. Initially, he did find a noticeable difference in the type of crime in Penrith, just as he'd assumed. Compared to his last post in Leeds city centre, the workload was much lighter too, but inevitably to counterbalance this, there was less manpower with which to work.

Jack's comprehensive review also presented him with the opportunity to get the measure of his new colleagues, in particular, DC Claire Swift and DS Owen Hardy, the two officers with whom he'd be working most closely. He made a point of talking through the active cases with them both.

Claire was young, smart as a whip, and ambitious. She arrived for work early each morning dressed immaculately in a dark tailored trouser suit over a clean fresh pastel blouse. An attractive girl, with her short elf-like haircut and sensible shoes, she certainly looked the part. Her given tasks were completed quickly and with accuracy and attention to detail which Jack appreciated. Claire's expression was one of eagerness to move on with the task in hand. She wasted no time and didn't quibble about working after hours. Jack found her more than capable of taking initiatives, yet wary of uncalculated risks. All considered, he was delighted to have such an officer on his team.

DS Owen Hardy wasn't quite as particular with his appearance, but Jack made allowances as the DS was a new father. Jack wasn't so old that he didn't remember the pressures of a new baby in the house. Owen had worked his way up from being a uniformed PC and served in the force for twelve years. He was of a wiry build and had been into long-distance running before his children arrived to usurp much of his free time, but he still attempted to keep fit when time allowed. His hair hung a little too long over his collar for Jack's liking, but Owen's mind was proving to be every bit as sharp as Claire's, and so far, Jack was pleased with his new colleagues. If he could pick fault, it would be the occasional tardiness that Owen had already displayed, but again, Jack made allowances for the baby and for the time being, would be lenient. The test would come when they worked on a serious case, which was always when character was tested and strengths and weaknesses proved.

So far, Jack was delighted with his move to Hunter's Lane. Stress levels seemed so much lower here than in Leeds, making for a lighter, less pressured working environment and his colleagues had already proved to be a welcoming bunch.

Should he have been privy to his colleagues' evaluations of their new DI, Jack would have learned that his team, taking less than a week to decide, marked him down as an okay kind of guy and a considerable improvement on his predecessor. His enthusiasm was infectious and his quiet, but rather droll, sense of humour was slowly appealing to them. They were unanimously impressed with their new DI's ability to absorb and retain every detail of the cases he reviewed, and they appreciated his even temperament, something they'd not been used to before.

All in all, the atmosphere at Hunter's Lane was on an all-time high since the arrival of the new DI. Yes, it was a good move for Jack, and all things considered, Detective Inspector Priestly was a very happy man.

7

R achel Roberts walked across the car park towards the entrance of The Elms. She was an attractive woman, tall and slim, with natural red hair falling in gentle waves to her shoulders. A narrow but pleasant face accommodated wide-set grey-green eyes, with a small slightly upturned nose and full lips combining to present a striking appearance. With an aura of confidence around her, she could certainly pass for a woman much younger than her thirty-two years.

As she entered The Elms, she nodded briefly to the receptionist. It was an excellent facility and housed a secure dementia unit, where Alice could be assessed in a safe environment, and Rachel was free to visit at any time.

Dr Richard Edwards smiled as he offered his hand, her look of concern not lost on him.

'I've seen your mother this morning, Rachel. Alice is still confused but perhaps a little better than previously.'

'Really? That's good to hear. Did she ask about Dad?'

'Yes, he seems to be her chief concern. She even asked if I was a policeman so she could report him as missing.' He paused as if to take in the pained expression which crossed Rachel's face. 'How long is it since your father died?'

'Over four years, but she doesn't seem to remember anything about it. Is this sort of thing usual?'

'Sadly, yes, it is. Patients with dementia often live in the past. It's a more comfortable existence for them. The memories of years gone by are generally clearer than those of yesterday.'

'But what do I do? Should I tell her that Dad's dead or let her live in her fantasy world, expecting him to come and visit at any time?'

'For the moment, perhaps, it would be better to try to avoid the subject altogether. It could be painful for Alice to find out her husband's dead; it's like suffering the bereavement all over again. On the other hand, if she insists on answers, and your mother does seem quite a determined lady, then you'll have to tell her the truth, and we'll deal with any fallout as it occurs. I know how distressing this must be, but it's still early days, too early to make any permanent decisions as Alice's cognitive capacity is fluctuating from one day to the next. We'll keep on with these short assessments for the time being and I'm always happy to answer any questions.'

'Did my mother know what day it is and how old she is? The last time I saw her, she couldn't even remember where she lived.'

Dr Edwards glanced at his notes. 'Alice told me her date of birth and she knew it was Thursday but not what month it was.' He looked back to his notes as Rachel nodded thoughtfully. 'Your mother talked a little about her retirement from her teaching job in Matlock–'

'Teaching?' Rachel interrupted. 'Mum's never been a teacher. She spent her working life in an office!'

'Ah, I see.'

He danced his fingers on the edge of the desk for a moment,

made a few more notes on his keyboard, then smiled as Rachel asked, 'Is it normal to invent such a story?'

'Oh yes, I've known patients to invent a whole new history for themselves, careers, partners and lifestyles completely different from the reality they've actually experienced. I know it's worrying, but as I said, it's still early days. You could help with our assessments by recalling any unusual behaviour Alice might have been exhibiting lately. Sometimes it's only with hindsight that we see the signs of dementia. It could be she's been deteriorating for some time and you haven't picked up on the signals.'

Rachel nodded again, tears welling in her eyes. 'Thank you, doctor. I'll give it some thought. I suppose there are signs I could have missed as she's only recently moved nearby. Now I'd like to go and see her if that's okay?'

'Certainly, you can visit at any time. I'm sure Alice will be pleased to see you.'

Rachel left the doctor's office and climbed thoughtfully up the stairs to her mother's room.

Rachel pasted on a bright smile which Alice met with an anxious stare. 'Hello, Mum.'

'Rachel! Thank goodness you're here. Please will you take me home? I don't know what's going on, but they seem to think I'm mad, and your father hasn't been yet. Where is he? I'm seriously worried about him.'

'Calm down, please. You're not well enough to go home yet, but I've just spoken to the doctor and he seems to think you're improving, so that's good news, isn't it?' Rachel perched on the edge of the bed next to her mother's chair, her hair still damp from the continuing rain outside, the smell of fresh air clinging to her clothes.

'Don't patronise me, Rachel. I want to go home! Surely they can't keep me here against my will?'

'It's for your own good, Mum. You don't seem to realise how poorly you've been and to be quite honest, if you went home now, you'd be vulnerable and probably back here in no time. Surely you can see that it's better all round if you just do what the doctor suggests?'

'But I won't be alone. Your dad will be there! I might have been a bit confused, but I'm certainly fit to go home now.'

'Oh, really?' Rachel's impatience took control. 'Don't you remember Dad died four years ago? He had a heart attack, I'm sorry, Mum, but you're living in the past...'

'No, that's a wicked lie! Tom's not dead. He's away sorting out his business affairs; you know that as well as I do!'

'I know that's what you want to believe and it's hard to accept that he's dead, but it's true! You'll just have to trust me on this. Your memory's playing tricks on you. You've lived alone since Dad died, but moved here a few weeks ago, don't you remember?'

'Yes, of course, I remember moving, we wanted to be nearer you, but your father's not dead! Don't you think I'd know if my own husband was dead?'

'It's all part of the illness, Mum, but it'll come back to you soon, so don't worry about it.' Rachel smiled what she hoped would be a reassuring smile, but it was evident that her mother still didn't believe what she was saying. Alice raised her voice, growing increasingly agitated and demanding to see Tom. The seemingly omnipresent Mavis appeared in the doorway, the last straw for Alice.

'Everything all right, is it?' Mavis asked with that fake smile on her face.

Alice picked up the water glass on the side table and threw it at the woman in sheer exasperation. 'No, it's not bloody all right! You're all liars. Why are you doing this to me?' She stood and made to run out of the door. Rachel jumped up too and grabbed her mother's arm while Mavis pressed the buzzer beside the bed, then caught hold of Alice's other arm.

'Let me go. I'm going home!' Alice screamed and struggled, trying to free herself from the two younger, stronger women. A nurse appeared in the doorway with a syringe which she quickly pressed into Alice's arm as Mavis held her still. Very soon, all was quiet as the medication took effect.

'She'll sleep it off now and most likely will have forgotten the whole incident when she wakes.' The nurse spoke kindly to Rachel, whose face was stained with tears.

'Can I see Dr Edwards again for a moment?'

'I think he's still in his office. Let's go and see if he's free, shall we?'

The two women went down the stairs.

Rachel sobbed as the doctor looked on sympathetically. 'Mum's insisting that Dad's still alive, she became quite aggressive.'

'I'm so sorry, dementia's such a cruel illness, but your mother might remember the truth tomorrow; we can never tell from one day to the next.' Richard Edwards again tapped into Alice's file and made more notes.

A few minutes later, Rachel left the residential home, her step brisk and purposeful as she crossed the car park, hurrying to get out of the rain. Starting her car, she pointed it in the direction of her mother's cottage, in Melkinthorpe, five miles south of Penrith, where there were a few things she needed to do before returning to work.

It really was the perfect retirement cottage, situated in a quiet leafy village with enough privacy to be comfortable but with neighbours near enough not to feel isolated. It was quite a find. Properties as desirable as this one rarely came onto the open market, and when they did, they were snapped up immediately. Alice had been in the right place at the right time to secure the sale, and as the property had undergone a complete refurbishment before being placed on the market, there'd been only minor, superficial, work to be done.

Rachel let herself into her mother's home and turned off the alarm. There would be decisions to make about the cottage, but not yet. It was too soon – she shouldn't let her mind race too far ahead. What transpired in the next few weeks would determine what she would do.

The house was quiet, almost eerie, as she moved from room to room, finally entering the kitchen to empty the fridge and see that everything was in order. Rachel hurriedly completed the chores she'd come to do and then paused to look at the red coat hanging on the peg next to the back door. It was a small piece of the jigsaw puzzle and perhaps the catalyst for what had recently transpired.

8

Alice opened her eyes and looked at the stranger tiptoeing from her room.

'Sorry, I didn't mean to wake you.' The woman turned and apologised.

'It's okay. I was only dozing. What time is it?'

'Nearly three, I came to see if you'd like a cup of tea?'

'Yes, please. You're new, aren't you? I've not seen you before?' Alice was unsure if she could trust her memory anymore. Perhaps she had met this woman previously?

'Yes, my name's Sarah Priestly. I usually work upstairs, but Mavis is on holiday for a fortnight, so I'm helping out on this floor. I'll just get that tea for you, Mrs Roberts, won't be a minute.' Sarah's smile lit up her face and Alice thought this pretty woman would certainly make a pleasant change from Mavis. When she returned with the tea a few minutes later, Sarah seemed in no hurry to leave and asked if there was anything else she could do for Alice.

'Apart from helping me to escape, no, not really.' She smiled so Sarah would see she was only half-serious.

'Are you in for respite, Mrs Roberts?'

'I'm not exactly sure why I'm here, and please call me Alice. It appears I'm deemed unsafe to live alone and I'm having trouble accepting certain facts, which to my mind, are not true. Even things which I'm certain about are apparently wrong, so I don't know how long I'll be here, but I do know that I'm being kept against my will, and I thought that was illegal.'

At such stark words, Sarah's eyes widened.

'Please don't look so shocked. I'm probably just rambling.'

'You don't sound like you're rambling to me, but the mind can play tricks on you at times, particularly after an illness or an infection. Hopefully, you'll feel better soon.'

'Thank you. You're very kind and a refreshing change from Mavis. How long have you worked here, Sarah?'

'Actually, I'm just a volunteer helping out wherever I'm needed, and I've only been here a couple of weeks. We only moved to Penrith six weeks ago.'

'Really? I'm new to the area too. Where did you live before?' Alice was warming to this newcomer who didn't seem to be in a hurry to get away, unlike most other staff.

'We lived in Leeds, my husband's a police officer and we've moved further north to be nearer to our sons.'

'How lovely for you. I lived in Matlock, do you know it?'

'Yes, it's such a beautiful part of the world. What did you do in Matlock, Alice?'

'I taught in a primary school, reception mainly, little ones are so rewarding.' A faint smile crossed her face at the memory.

'Which school did you teach at?'

'Hayfield Primary but I retired last year. My husband, Tom, is in the process of winding up his business interests before he retires, too, so he's been travelling a lot.' Alice's eyes suddenly clouded and a frown crossed her face,

'That is, I think he must be travelling – we were looking forward to settling down to a quiet retirement, but I'm not sure what's happening now. Rachel, that's my daughter, keeps insisting Tom's dead – yet I know he isn't. How would I forget something like that? Perhaps I am going mad after all.' Alice wasn't entirely sure of her facts but instinctively felt that Tom was alive and wondered why her daughter would tell such hateful lies. She looked towards the window and a longing to be outside stirred within her, to feel the rain on her face and know she was still alive. Alice almost forgot someone else was in her room until a voice intruded into her thoughts.

'Do you have any grandchildren?' Sarah asked.

'Yes. My daughter has a little girl, Millie. She's five now and such a gorgeous child. I don't see nearly enough of her, which is another reason why we moved here from Matlock. Rachel leads such a busy life, she's a single mum, and we thought we'd be able to help care for Millie in the school holidays while she works. She goes to a childminder now, but she'll be much better off with family.' Alice frowned. Something was niggling at the back of her mind, something concerning Millie that she wanted to discuss with Rachel. It was a terrible feeling, like when you knew a name but couldn't quite bring it to mind, yet Alice knew that whatever it was, it was important.

'There's something about Millie that I can't remember.' Her frown deepened.

'Illness can be cruel, Alice, but a little time in here will help you to get better. Is your daughter coming to visit today?'

'Maybe, but honestly, I'm not even sure what day it is today.' A tear escaped from her eye and slid down her cheek. Sarah passed her a tissue from the box on the bedside table.

'Please don't get upset. I'm sure everything will be fine soon. The doctors here are excellent.' She squeezed her hand. 'Look, is there anything else I can get you? There's bingo in the day-room later if you'd like to join in, or I could bring you a couple of books from the library downstairs?'

'You're very kind, but I don't fancy bingo. A book would be nice, though, if I can stay awake long enough to read it. All this medication they give me makes me so drowsy.' Alice made an effort to smile and Sarah left her to drink the tea, promising to bring her some books later.

Sarah didn't quite know what to make of Alice Roberts; she wasn't like the others in the unit. For a start, she wasn't old, probably not much older than herself. There was sadness in her eyes, too, a weariness, as if she was tired of fighting, her spirit almost broken and at the point of giving in to whatever her fate may be. As Sarah made her way to the day room, she popped her head around the office door to see if the sister-in-charge was there. Lynne was sitting close to the computer, grimacing at the screen as if there was something she didn't understand.

'Lynne?' Sarah interrupted.

The nurse looked around and smiled. 'Yes, what can I do for you?'

Like everyone else on the floor, Lynne liked Sarah. She was like a breath of fresh air after grumpy Mavis, pleasant, caring and willing to do anything they asked of her.

'Just wondered about Mrs Roberts in room twelve. What's she in for?'

'An assessment for dementia after exhibiting delirium and confusion. She's not giving you any trouble, is she? She can become a little agitated when she gets confused.'

'No, anything but, she seems a lovely lady. I feel a bit sorry for her, that's all. Is there anything else medically wrong?'

Lynne pressed a few buttons on the computer and brought up Alice's notes. 'No, it seems that she came to us from hospital after a suspected stroke, but they think the delirium is now dementia and a DOL, Deprivation of Liberty, order is in place. It's sad and seems to have come on rather suddenly, but she has all the classic symptoms: living in the past, false memories, all the usual signs.'

'False memories?' Sarah frowned.

'Yes, she thinks she was a teacher in her working life, but her daughter tells us she only ever worked in an office.'

'How sad, and she's such an intelligent woman, so I suppose everything she says could be wrong? Is the DOL order permanent?'

'No, the assessments will continue, but if there's no improvement, the order will probably stand and she could be with us permanently.'

'She seems so young to have dementia.'

Lynne glanced again at the screen. 'She's fifty-five, no age at all, is it? Now, would you be okay to go to the day room and help with the bingo?'

'Yes, no problem. I just wanted to know a little more about Alice. Thanks for the information, Lynne.'

Sarah smiled before hurrying from the office to help set up for the afternoon activities. She'd look out a few books for Alice later on or even bring some in from home. She'd probably have some titles that would interest her.

9

Sarah Priestly was searching through one of the many unpacked boxes at home in the spare bedroom, intent on finding some books that Alice Roberts might enjoy reading. True to her word, she'd taken her a couple of novels from the somewhat limited library at The Elms, but the selection was poor and Sarah was sure she'd find more suitable offerings in her own collection.

'Unpacking those books at last?' Jack poked his head around the door.

'I would if I could find the shelf space to put them, but no, I'm looking for some that will suit one of the residents at The Elms. Their library consists of some very ancient, dog-eared Mills and Boons, or westerns, which are hardly appropriate. I've got a couple of Kate Morton novels somewhere that she might enjoy.'

'You're on the dementia unit now, aren't you? Will she be up to reading?' Jack asked.

'Oh yes, Alice is an intelligent lady and although they suspect dementia, she seems quite lucid to me.'

'I hope you're not going to get too fond of your clients, love. You shouldn't get attached, you know.'

Sarah smiled, Jack always accused her of being too sentimental about the kind of work she chose to do, but she loved working with people. He'd already expressed concern that working with the elderly could be depressing and feared she might become attached to individuals who were in the latter days of their lives.

'Yes, so you keep telling me, but this lady's not old, only fifty-five.'

'Goodness, we're not far off that. Why's she in a residential facility at her age?'

'Just the dementia, I think. It's sad, as Alice doesn't appear to be confused and you can have quite an intelligent conversation with her, but Lynne says she's living in a kind of fantasy world. Alice told me all about her career as a teacher in Matlock, but apparently, it's all in her mind. The poor soul has never been a teacher. Most of the while, she's fine, yet occasionally she becomes agitated and asks to go home, but then most of the residents do that at times, I suppose.'

Jack grinned. 'You take her those books, take the whole box in if you like. It'll save me having to put up more shelves.' He'd just finished an early shift and was heading for his bed for a couple of hours while his wife was getting ready to go to The Elms for the afternoon. She kissed him goodbye and took her books with her, thinking of Alice and hoping she'd enjoy them.

Alice was sitting, staring out of the window when Sarah looked into her room.

'Hello, Alice, I've brought some books you might like.' She

placed three books on the table beside the bed and watched Alice's face transform from pensive to pleased.

'That's so kind of you. They look interesting.'

'I've enjoyed them, so thought maybe you would too. Is your daughter coming in today?'

'I think so. I'm not sure.'

'Perhaps she'll bring your granddaughter to visit. You must be missing her. What did you say her name was?' Sarah remembered the child's name but wondered if Alice could.

'Millie. She's such a sweet little thing and the image of her mother when she was that age, but I'm not sure Rachel will want to bring her here; it might be upsetting.'

'You could always use the visitors' lounge downstairs. It's quite cosy in there and near the front door. If we know when she's coming, you could have it to yourselves.'

'Oh really, I didn't know about that, but it sounds a good idea. I'll ask Rachel to bring her in if it can be arranged.'

'Great, if you tell someone when she's coming they'll book the lounge for you.' Sarah thought Alice seemed quite well. She offered her a cup of tea or coffee and then went off to get one. On her return with the tea, Rachel was with her mother, so Sarah went in, introduced herself to the younger woman and asked if she would like a drink too.

Rachel shook her head. 'No thanks, I only have a few minutes this afternoon.'

'I was just telling Alice that we have a small visitors' lounge available on the ground floor. If you wanted to bring your daughter in to see her grandma, you could use it. It's quite cosy and even has a few toys.' Sarah watched Alice's smile widen, but Rachel stared coldly at her.

'Can I have a word with you outside?' Rachel sounded annoyed and marched into the corridor away from earshot of Alice. Sarah followed but shrank back slightly as Rachel, who was a good six inches taller than her, towered over her and spoke in a half-whisper.

'I don't know what my mother's been telling you, but I don't have any children; therefore, she has no grandchildren. Please don't encourage her in these little illusions. Things are difficult enough as it is.' Her tone, although quiet, was sharp and determined. Sarah was at a loss to know what to say.

'I'm so sorry... she told me you had a five-year-old daughter called Millie and I assumed it was true.'

'Well, it's not. My mother's living in a fantasy world and I'd rather you didn't encourage her in these ramblings.' With that, Rachel turned abruptly and went back into the room, leaving Sarah embarrassed and upset that she'd inadvertently said the wrong thing. She thought she'd better tell the sister about the confrontation with Alice's daughter in case there were repercussions and so went straight to the ward office.

The duty sister was checking the medicine trolley ready for the afternoon rounds when Sarah found her.

'Lynne, I think I've just put my foot in it and upset one of the visitors!'

The sister looked surprised.

''Fess up then, what have you done?' She closed and locked the trolley to give Sarah her full attention.

'I'd asked Alice if her daughter was coming to visit and if she might be bringing her granddaughter. I mentioned the visitors' lounge and said that they could use it if they preferred, and just now, I repeated the offer to her daughter. Rachel took me outside to inform me that Alice has no grandchildren, it's another of her fantasies, but she seemed cross about it. I'm so sorry. I assumed there was a grandchild. Alice told me the little girl's name and age; there was no reason to doubt her...'

'Don't worry about it. I shouldn't think Rachel will complain about such a trivial incident, but if she does, you've done nothing wrong, and we'll back you up. I'll add the imagined 'granddaughter' to her notes, and I think in future we'll have to take everything Alice says with a rather large pinch of salt!'

'Poor Alice, I'd asked her about any grandchildren to try to cheer her up and lift her mood and she spoke so affectionately about the little girl. I almost wish for her sake that it wasn't simply her imagination.'

'Patients with dementia can be quite inventive with their delusions.' Lynne smiled reassuringly. 'I often wonder where their stories come from. Perhaps they choose a better version of their past, one they would have preferred to the reality their life actually was? But don't fret, Sarah, we'll put it down to experience, shall we?'

10

Alice was quite taken with Sarah Priestly; being treated like a grown woman instead of a child or an imbecile was gratifying and the volunteer made time to stop for a chat. Most of the staff were continually dashing away to attend to something else. She hoped to see more of Sarah; her company was quite refreshing.

As the days went by, Alice increasingly spent the time alone in her room, declining to join the other residents in the day room, where they sat around the walls as if in a queue, waiting to enter the Pearly Gates.

On fine days there was pleasure to be found in gazing from the window, not that the view was great, a courtyard housing the dustbins, but a Rowan tree reached up to the window, a mountain ash, incongruous amid the drab, concrete square. A female blackbird nested nearby and often sat in the branches, her little chest puffed out as she sang for all she was worth. It reminded Alice of summers gone by when she too was young and happy with a life of promise stretching out before her. But happiness was fleeting, a transitory emotion that couldn't be relied upon.

Alice. Summer 1996

Matlock Coffee & Cake became a reality for Karen and me when we rented a property on the main street, with a spectacular view of the river Derwent from the upstairs seating area. Our excitement was off the scale. We could hardly believe it was really happening.

The property was a dream of a place and needed only superficial work in the seating areas and the kitchen fitting out to Karen's exacting standards to allow us to open. We managed to do this in just a few weeks after the completion of the sale. Its bargain price was the icing on the cake.

Opening in spring afforded us sufficient time to learn our trade before the busy summer period was upon us, when hopefully we'd be rushed off our feet. With Karen's talent for baking, there was never any doubt that the coffee shop would be a success, and during that first summer, we needed to employ three seasonal workers to cope with the growing number of customers.

Part of the downstairs area was set aside as a gallery for artists to display their work, another of Karen's brilliant ideas. The walls swiftly filled up with stunning local scenes in oils and watercolours. The shelves groaned with pottery, jewellery and all manner of artefacts, attractively displayed to entice customers and enhance the downstairs space. As well as tourists, we gathered a loyal band of regulars, whatever the weather, some meeting friends, others out to enjoy the atmosphere and get away from the loneliness of their own homes.

My mother was only too keen to help out with the care of our three girls. She swore that having them all together was easier than one at a time, which I suppose was true, but we were careful not to put on her too much. As the business became successful, Karen and I took regular days off to spend time with our girls.

Life was full and exciting, but Rachel was still a concern to us, and sadly I never felt close to her, no matter how hard I tried. The only time she was anything near animated was when she was with Jenny, a reality I found hard to accept. Perhaps I was even a little envious of their closeness, the way they could communicate with a single look, the way Jenny could so easily elicit a smile from her sister when my efforts were fruitless. But I pushed those thoughts down inside of me. I had no right to feel that way. I was the adult here, wasn't I?

At school, Rachel became Jenny's self-appointed protector and although they were in different classes, she would seek her out at every play-time and stay with Jenny to the exclusion of any friends of her own. This in itself was a concern, but then came an incident in which Rachel intervened during a simple playground tussle. A boy in Jenny's class was teasing her. It amounted to nothing more serious than the usual pigtail pulling rather than out and out bullying, but our elder daughter took it upon herself to put the boy in his place, verbally at first. His response was to call her 'carrot top', a name to which she took exception and promptly punched him on the nose. The poor child wasn't seriously hurt. It was no more than a storm in a tea cup, with the only repercussion being a visit to the headteacher for Rachel and a letter home to us. Naturally, when we were made aware of the incident, we had stern words with our daughter about unacceptable behaviour, but secretly, in a perverse way, I was pleased. It seemed to prove that she wasn't entirely dispassionate.

When Rachel was nine, she contracted chickenpox during the school summer holidays. No great surprise as it had been going around the girls' school, but for my eldest daughter, it couldn't have come at a worse time. A day trip to one of our favourite places, Manor Park in Glossop, was planned by Karen and James, who invited my two girls to go with them and Beth. It was only an hour's drive through the beautiful Peak District, an area we adored and a place we visited often. Rachel was devastated when I decided she couldn't go and pleaded with me to relent, but it was impossible. She was covered in sore, weeping spots and running a temperature.

Jenny and Beth were upset for her, although not so much that they wanted to forgo the trip themselves, and so the outing went ahead without poor Rachel. Naturally, I tried to make it up to her, suggesting activities to capture her interest at home, but she was inconsolable for most of the day. It so obviously wasn't my company our daughter craved. All that morning, she stood with her nose pressed against the windowpane, waiting for Jenny's return, her eyes wide with sadness and anticipation, stubbornly refusing to end her self-imposed vigil. Tom was working at home that day, but even he couldn't cheer our daughter up, nothing was right, and we knew it wouldn't change until her sister returned home.

By midday, hot and fractious, with a temperature of 38C, Rachel finally succumbed to sleep and we were able to relax for a welcome hour until the doorbell unexpectedly rang.

I answered, unaware of the shock awaiting me and the devastating news that would change my life forever — two police officers stood on my doorstep. I felt sick. They introduced themselves, showing identification which I barely registered, and asked if they could come inside. I led them in on legs that could barely hold me up, instinctively aware that their presence heralded bad news. Tom was in the lounge working on some papers, and when he saw the police officers, his face mirrored my own shocked expression. All my instincts told me that something was seriously wrong, but the officers waited until I was seated beside my husband before imparting their unwelcome news.

There'd been an accident, we were informed, on the A57 Snake Pass. James' car had veered off the road, down a steep incline. All four occupants were dead – my whole family wiped out in one moment! The young police officers offered their condolences and asked if they could contact anyone for us. I barely heard their words – inside my head, I was screaming that it wasn't true, it couldn't possibly be happening, my beautiful daughter, my sister, her husband and my niece – all dead. Surely it wasn't possible. It was cruel, abhorrent. I couldn't take it in!

11

1996

Looking back on that most harrowing of times, so much of the detail is hazy. I remember breaking down and sobbing in Tom's arms, shouting 'no' repeatedly and insisting that the police must be mistaken. Maybe it was someone else's car, someone else's family, not mine. These things happened to other people, we watched the reports on the news and shook our heads with sympathy, but it couldn't happen to us! No, never!

Tom was the one to ask for details, but the officers were unsure as to precisely what had transpired and waffled about 'blind summits' and 'sharp bends' on what we knew was a notorious stretch of road. I didn't believe them. James was a careful driver. He would never take risks, not with his wife and family on board – and my daughter, my Jenny. I didn't want to hear their words, yet perversely I needed to know. My mind was suddenly spinning with horrific images of James' car leaving the road, rolling over and over, of Jenny, Karen and Beth screaming in wild panic. It was too much. I couldn't accept it, wouldn't accept it – but the unmistakable presence of two burly police officers in my home told me that it was true. My daughter, sister and her family were all dead – I would never see them again!

When the police eventually left, we were faced with the nightmare of telling Rachel, who at nine, was old enough to understand what death meant. She would certainly realise that Jenny was never coming home, but how much can a child of that age process? Only time would tell, but I knew losing Jenny would be devastating for Rachel as it was for Tom and me.

Rachel was awake when I went into her room and looked at me with wide, knowing eyes. Whether or not she'd heard the police officers impart the news, I will never know, but her reaction was far from the one I anticipated. Her pale little face reminded me instantly of that baby who'd first come into our lives nine years earlier. She didn't cry or ask questions but simply turned her face towards the wall and lay utterly still and disconcertingly silent. When I tried to hold her, she stiffened and pulled away from me. I asked her to come downstairs, but she ignored my words.

I left her room, sobbing, and Tom took over, gently explaining to our daughter that we needed to visit her grandparents to tell them the terrible news. Rachel rose then and came downstairs, her eyes glazed and an expression on her young face which I couldn't fathom, a fusion of despair and anger – and perhaps blame too.

My parents were our next priority. They needed to hear the news from us before it reached them from another source. This unenviable task was perhaps the singular most harrowing undertaking of my life, knowing that their sense of grief would be every bit as acute as my own.

Relying heavily on Tom's strength, I somehow managed to

find the words to impart the awful news, to speak the unspeakable.

As expected, they were devastated – broken. Losing a child is not the natural order of life and in one brief morning, they were robbed of a daughter, a son-in-law and two granddaughters, undoubtedly too great a burden for anyone to bear.

The police employed specialist equipment to recover the charred car from the steep embankment down which it had fallen – a gruesome and delicate operation. My only hope was that the impact had been so sudden and severe that they all died instantly without time to consider their fate. Perhaps a naive assumption but one to which I clung, wringing out of it any possible comfort I could.

Naturally, we tried to protect Rachel from learning the distressing facts of the accident. It was enough for her to cope with the loss without adding to her worries. We, too, tried not to dwell on the detail but couldn't avoid seeing the shocking images printed in the regional paper. The headlines proclaimed 'Local GP and Family Wiped Out in Horror Crash.' I tried not to look, but the photographs of the crash site drew my eyes like a magnet, and for days afterwards, I imagined my daughter inside that twisted, unrecognisable vehicle, taking her last breath without me by her side to hold and comfort her. Guilt became my constant companion, guilt that I wasn't with her to protect her, and a deep, hollow regret that I'd allowed her out of my sight on that awful day.

As an inquest would be necessary, we feared we may not be allowed to plan a funeral for several weeks, a protracted period we dreaded. However, the coroner, satisfied that the cause of death for all four was the accident, gave permission to hold a funeral once the post mortem examinations were complete. The inquest to determine the cause of the crash would follow at a later date.

Thankfully, this decision was reached within a week and so began the horrendous task of making arrangements to say farewell to our precious, beautiful daughter, my sister and her family. Those first few days were ghastly and I think we all functioned on automatic pilot to get through each difficult day. Sleep refused to offer respite; my dreams were full of images of carnage which remained with me long after I woke.

We held one funeral service for them all, the blackest day of my life, and one I would not wish on anyone. As we walked up the church path, it seemed much longer than on my wedding day. No daffodils heralded better times ahead. They'd withered and died in the heat of summer, like the hope that once lived in my heart. The incline seemed to drag me down, my legs leaden, and tears soaked my cheeks.

In retrospect, the minutiae are blurred, but I do remember St Giles being packed. The whole of Matlock appeared to stand still that day, collectively holding their breath and silent in paying their respects. There was perhaps some slight comfort in feeling the love and warmth of the townspeople, many of whom I'd known all my life.

It was a tragedy like nothing the town had experienced before, and they came in great numbers to show their support. Afterwards, people expressed sympathy and commented on the 'appropriateness' of the service, whatever that meant. Yet to me, the singing of 'All Things Bright and Beautiful' seemed inappropriate. We were saying goodbye to four of the brightest, most beautiful people I'd ever known. I couldn't sing that day, nor could my mother, who was weeping inconsolably, or Rachel, who stood, dry-eyed and ramrod straight between Tom and me. It was the very darkest of days.

The inquest into the deaths was held three months later and

returned a verdict of accidental death on all four victims. There were no witnesses and a subsequent examination of the wreckage failed to find any mechanical fault. It was nothing short of hell having to sit through the hearing and listen to the doctor describe the injuries that killed each member of my family. My parents were too distressed to attend, for which I was grateful. Learning the details would have devastated them and I certainly wouldn't have got through it without Tom by my side.

After the summer break, Rachel became withdrawn on her return to school, and her teachers told us that she no longer interacted with the other children. Before Jenny died, she had very few friends and generally played only with her sister, but now it seemed that she wished to have no contact with the others in her class or any of Jenny's old friends. We arranged counselling sessions, but Rachel refused to engage with the counsellor and their time together was mostly spent in silence. Eventually, we decided to suspend the counselling, hoping she would choose to go back when the time was right. It appeared that whatever we tried was futile. We simply couldn't reach our daughter.

Tom and I coped by talking to each other. Our pain only fractionally eased in the process. Still, Rachel refused to talk about her sister and went about her life seemingly emotionless, a mundane existence that our love could not begin to penetrate.

We consoled ourselves with the hope that time would heal our daughter. After all, Jenny had brought her out of isolation before; perhaps something or someone else would do the same in the future. There appeared to be little else we could do other than being constant in our love and hope and pray for a miracle.

During one of the lowest points in those dark days after the accident, Tom, who tried so hard to remain strong for Rachel and me, actually verbalised something I'd often thought and for which I'd hated myself. It was early evening, Rachel was upstairs in her room as usual, and Tom and I were clearing the detritus of the evening meal when he suddenly banged his fist on the kitchen table and said, 'Why did it have to be Jenny who died? Why our own flesh and blood?' His sudden outburst shocked me as his words fell heavily into the atmosphere. He sobbed bitterly then, tears of shame and guilt – of frustration for being unable to make things right for his family. I wasn't so much surprised at the words themselves but that he would actually speak them aloud. The very same sentiment had played through my mind on so many occasions since Jenny died, compounding my feelings of inadequacy and guilt. A little voice at the back of my mind repeated frequently, 'If only it had been Rachel who died that day, and not Jenny...' but I'd never actually verbalised my unworthy, disgraceful thoughts. To allow them to come out of my mouth would prove, without a doubt, what a wicked person I was. I loathed myself for even thinking them. It appalled me! But no matter how many times I tried to banish the thought, it crept back into the secret recesses of my mind, taking advantage of my weakest moments to pop into my head and fill me with shame and disgrace. I truly was a dreadful mother!

I held my husband then, as silent tears fell from us both, we would get through this, and we would do our best for Rachel. Somehow, we would reach her.

12

Sarah was kept busy for the rest of the day, with the residents unusually demanding, and didn't see Alice until it was almost time to go home as she passed her open door. Alice called out to her, and dutifully she entered the room, smiling her usual, cheery smile.

'Sarah, what did Rachel say to you this morning?' Alice sounded anxious.

'Nothing important, I think perhaps I'd overstepped the mark by offering the use of the visitors' lounge, but it's nothing for you to worry about.'

'Did she say anything about Millie?' Alice looked close to tears. 'I only ask because she told me she didn't have a daughter, which is ridiculous. Why would she deny her own child?'

'I think you might be getting confused, Alice. I'm sure you'd love a little granddaughter, so maybe you just imagined one?' Even as she spoke, Sarah knew the words sounded feeble, patronising even, and the pained look on Alice's face saddened her. It was as if she'd betrayed her.

'Sarah, please... you're the only one here who talks to me as if I'm a human being. Everyone else is treating me like a child or a madwoman. I know I haven't imagined Millie, and I also know that my husband isn't dead! While I'm here, I have no way of proving it, and I don't know why Rachel's telling all these lies. If only I could get out of here. Will you help me, please?'

Sarah was stunned by the sudden crazy request and didn't quite know what to say. If Alice was asking for help to escape, there was no way she could do that.

'I really can't help you to get home, Alice. It's up to the doctor to decide when you can leave and he needs to be sure you'll be safe living on your own.' Sarah knew the answer was inadequate and not what Alice wanted to hear, but what more could she say?

'I know all that,' a look of desperation crossed Alice's face, 'and I wouldn't want you to do anything that would get you into trouble, but maybe you could find Tom for me?'

Sarah was in a difficult situation; should she play along with this disturbed lady or simply say no? Finally, she decided on honesty.

'Alice, I wouldn't be able to find Tom because your husband died a few years ago. I'm so sorry, but your illness is making you forget things. Try to rest now. Rachel's visit seems to have tired you out. I'll see you tomorrow.' She gently squeezed her hand. Alice said nothing more but simply turned to stare out of the window, disappointed, her eyes brimming with tears. Sarah felt utterly wretched, but Rachel was probably right and she shouldn't encourage her in these fantasies, yet not being able to ease Alice's mind was so hard.

That night Sarah dreamed that she was smuggling Alice out of The Elms, and the two of them rode off into the night, like Thelma and Louise, in an open-top sports car. When Sarah awoke, the vivid dream stayed with her and she couldn't stop thinking about it, ridiculous though it was. Jack laughed heartily when she described the dream over breakfast, but Sarah was troubled by Alice's predicament. The sensible thing to do would be to avoid conversing with her, but that wouldn't be right either, so Sarah just hoped that Alice might have forgotten their previous day's conversation and would drop the subject.

For some strange reason, Sarah felt drawn to this resident more than to any other. Perhaps it was the fact that Alice was so young to have dementia – anyone would feel compassion for a fellow human being with such a cruel disease, and we can never be sure of our own fate. But Sarah's natural empathy for Alice meant that she couldn't avoid her either. She would care for her the same as the other residents in The Elms; to continue to do her very best.

As it happened, Alice seemed very much brighter when Sarah did pop into her room that morning and nothing more was mentioned about her strange request of the previous day. It was a relief to Sarah not to have to revisit the subject. Instead, they discussed the books she'd read and Sarah was pleased to learn that Alice was managing to concentrate long enough to read and retain the storyline in her head. It was good to have a neutral topic to discuss and there seemed to be a mutual, unspoken, agreement not to bring up the subject of the 'imagined' grandchild or Rachel's visit.

While Alice showered, Sarah made up her bed and changed the water in the bedside jug. She felt that the room would benefit from a few personal items. It was a short-stay room and rather bland in its décor; magnolia walls devoid of any pictures and the pale striped curtains, sun-bleached of their original colour. Most of the residents cheered up their rooms with family photographs or cherished possessions from home displayed on the bare surfaces. Some even brought in their own bedding and curtains of their choosing or even a few pot plants. Sarah, however, wouldn't be the one to approach Rachel with this idea.

If it looked as if Alice's stay was to be extended, then she'd leave it to one of the staff to suggest such things to her daughter.

Alice was undoubtedly something of an enigma. Her behaviour didn't quite fit into the pattern exhibited by the others on her floor, many of whom developed 'magpie tendencies', regularly taking items that appealed to them. The reservations of their former selves were lost with the illness and their behaviour reverted to being childlike again. Alice, however, generally appeared to be rational, following a conversation or the plot of a book or television programme with comparative ease. At other times, she experienced difficulty with concentration but generally knew where she was and maintained her desire to go home. But her short-term memory was letting her down and Sarah was well aware that if the diagnosis proved to be vascular dementia, gradual deterioration was expected and sadly, there would be no improvement.

Remembering Jack's words of caution, Sarah mentally warned herself not to become emotionally involved where Alice was concerned.

Later that afternoon, as Sarah approached Alice's room to offer tea or coffee, Rachel's voice made Sarah pause, not wishing to see the woman again after the incident of the previous day.

'No, it's Friday today, not Thursday.' Rachel sounded weary as she corrected her mother.

'Are you sure because we usually have fish for dinner on Friday, but we didn't today?'

'Yes, I'm sure.'

Sarah hesitated, then turned back to go into another resident's room, berating herself for being a coward. But the snatch of conversation she'd overheard troubled her. There was something about Rachel Roberts which made Sarah decidedly uncomfortable.

13

'Jack, how can I find out if someone is dead or not?' Sarah's expression suggested she was serious, but Jack laughed at her question.

'Take their pulse?' he joked.

'No, not like that. I mean in the past, if they died a few years ago.'

He straightened his face to take her seriously. 'All deaths have to be registered, and I would think you could access that information online. You'll be better at that than me; you know I'm a dinosaur with technology.'

'But you must have to do these checks at work?' she persisted.

'Yes, but I delegate to someone who knows what they're doing,' Jack explained, then smiled at his wife.

'I've already looked at a few websites, but I need the date of death, which I don't know.'

'What's this all about?' Jack put down his newspaper and looked at Sarah

'You know Alice, the lady I was telling you about at The Elms? She's convinced her husband's not dead, but her daughter told us that he died nearly four years ago. His name's Tom, so I've entered Thomas Roberts, Tom, and every other permutation I can think of, but there are dozens of them, and I don't have a date of birth or death...'

'Hang on here. If the daughter says he's dead, why are you checking up on this? You're on the dementia ward, aren't you? Surely this resident only imagines her husband's still alive?'

'It's not just that. Yes, Alice is convinced that he's alive and there's something about her daughter I don't trust, so I'm inclined to believe Alice. And then yesterday, I heard Rachel telling her mother that it was Friday when it was Thursday. So I wondered if she was deliberately confusing Alice to keep her in the home.'

'That's quite a fanciful notion. Perhaps the daughter was simply mistaken about the day herself. I sometimes get confused about what day it is, particularly when I'm on a late shift. It's hardly evidence of deliberate misdirection, is it?'

'You and your evidence, Jack. Don't you sometimes have those hunches for which detectives are famous? I just have this feeling that Alice isn't as demented as we think she is and that her daughter has a hidden agenda.'

'It can be a dangerous thing to meddle in another family's affairs, you know. These patients of yours with dementia spin all sorts of yarns, don't they? Surely the old girl's just living in the past, or not wanting to face up to the fact that her husband is dead.'

'I've considered that, but I can't shake off the feeling that there's nothing much wrong with Alice and her daughter's deliberately confusing her. Sometimes the medication they're prescribed can make them even more confused, so what if she is being held against her will? And she's not an 'old girl', as you put it, she's only fifty-five.'

'It's commendable of you to care so much, but I think it's

highly improbable that she's in The Elms against her will, no matter how much you like this lady and want her to be well again. If you have genuine concerns, perhaps you should speak to your line manager and tell her all this, or does the woman have a social worker? If so, she would be the one to find out more about the family circumstances. It's not wise for you to go poking about trying to discover these things yourself. You're only a volunteer there, so leave the diagnosis to the doctors. They know best, and I'm fairly sure they wouldn't want a newcomer telling them they've got it wrong.'

Jack was right, Sarah knew it, but an uneasy feeling about the situation lingered in her mind. Perhaps she'd have a word with Lynne as he suggested. But Sarah couldn't resist going back to her internet search of registered deaths, trying a combination of different years, months and even the specific area of Matlock where Alice had lived until recently. The search remained fruitless, dare she ask Alice for her husband's date of birth, or would that disturb the poor woman even more?

When Monday morning arrived, Sarah was keen to get back to The Elms, her priority being to make an appointment with Lynne, the dementia ward sister, to discuss her concerns. They arranged to meet in the office at lunchtime when Sarah would be having her break and Lynne would have finished her shift.

'So, what can I do for you?' Lynne asked, her head tilted to one side and a smile on her lips. She was a great person to talk to, and Sarah would be happy to stay on her ward permanently.

'It's about Alice Roberts... I've got a few concerns about her.'

'Ah, yes!' Lynne gave Sarah a look which suggested that she felt Sarah was becoming too involved with this particular resident – she would get on well with Jack, Sarah thought. 'No more trouble with her daughter, I hope?'

'Well, no... except that I overheard her telling Alice it was Friday last week when it was Thursday. I know we all get mixed up with such things at times, but it seemed as if she was deliberately trying to confuse her mother.'

'Is that all? Don't you think you're reading too much into it? Just because Rachel Roberts had a go at you doesn't mean she's the Wicked Witch of the West, you know. Relatives often take their frustrations out on the staff, particularly on the dementia ward, it's a difficult time for them as well as their parent, but it's all part of the job.'

'Yes, I know all that, but most of the time, Alice appears to be quite lucid yet regresses after her daughter's visits. Maybe she does have some memory problems but is she bad enough to be kept here?'

'Wait a minute, let's have another look at her notes.' Lynne tapped on the computer keyboard and brought up Alice's details.

'It says here that Rachel is her only relative. Alice still has the DOL order in place, but she's due for assessment by a Best Interest Assessor this week.'

'What exactly will they do?' Sarah asked.

'They'll chat with Alice and ask her a few questions and then make a decision about whether she has the mental capacity to make her own decisions. The assessor will then consult with the doctor, and if they feel Alice is capable of making her own choices, they'll ask her what she wants to do.'

'I'm certain the answer to that particular question will be that Alice wants to go home. Can her daughter reverse any decisions the doctor makes?'

'If she has power of attorney, she'll have some input into the decision, but there's nothing on Alice's notes to say her daughter has POA.'

'What if Alice still maintains that her husband is alive, and now there's this imaginary granddaughter too? Will that prevent her from going home?' Sarah could see this as a possible stumbling block.

'Not necessarily. We've had patients before who think that their partner's still alive yet have been deemed safe to live alone. Very often, their delusions are a comfort to them. Being confused doesn't automatically mean that someone has to go into care, and sadly the money aspect also comes into play. More and more people need places in care homes, and there just isn't the money available to fund them, so, in reality, only the very worst cases will get a funded place. Perhaps Alice's circumstances are such that she could fund a place privately, but from what we know, that's certainly not what she wants.' Lynne looked at the concerned expression on Sarah's face.

'Look, don't get too involved in this, okay? Our residents are transient for one reason or another, and this is a tough ward to work on. You can't afford to become emotionally involved with them all. You need to be a few degrees detached for your own sanity. Believe me, I know!'

'You're right. Thank you for explaining everything, Lynne. Can I tell Alice that this assessment is coming up?

'Of course, it's not a secret, and she has a right to be informed, but choose your moment carefully, won't you?'

'You mean when her daughter's not with her?' Sarah grinned. 'Now, I'd better grab a sandwich before I get back to work. Enjoy your afternoon off.' Sarah was heartened by what she'd learned. It appeared to be a possibility that Alice could go home after all. Sarah knew that this piece of news would cheer her up immensely.

14

Sunshine streamed through the window of Alice's room, warming her cold flesh. She allowed her eyes to close, willing the time to pass swiftly, and her thoughts drifted back to long ago. Living in the present was difficult, but she'd experienced worse in the past.

Alice 1996/97

I closed Matlock Coffee & Cake immediately after the accident, unsure if I would ever be able to continue the venture without Karen. The physical act of opening the door and stepping inside the premises on that first occasion after the accident was even worse than I anticipated it would be. My sister's ever-present laughter was gone, replaced by a heavy silence, an almost viscous atmosphere that had nothing to do with the hot weather and tightly shuttered windows. Karen's apron and cap hung behind the door in the kitchen as if waiting for her to return to work and slip them on again. The sight of them stung the back of my eyes and weakened my already trembling legs.

Dust motes filled the silent void, their dance almost mocking. Every item in the room held a bitter-sweet memory. Karen's jar of wooden utensils, the huge copper pans hanging from the ceiling rack, the blue and white pottery stacked neatly on the gleaming stainless-steel shelves. Everything so carefully chosen and loved by my sister.

Being in the place of our shared dream proved to be far too painful for me – the life and laughter had been sucked out of the place, and I could barely bring myself to look for the papers I'd gone there to pick up. It took only that one visit to know that I couldn't carry on. I'd hoped that feeling Karen's presence in that special place we'd worked so hard to create would bring comfort, but it held only raw memories, ones with which I couldn't cope, and I knew it was the end of our dream.

A couple of months after the cafe closed, I received an offer to buy the business and snatched at the opportunity. My enthusiasm had waned so much and I could no longer cope with the daily reminder of my sister's absence and everything we'd lost. The decision also gave me more time to devote to Rachel and my failing parents.

Tom and I couldn't read our elder daughter at all. She hadn't shed a single tear in the weeks since the accident, at least none that we knew of, and reverted to that small, lost child she'd been before Jenny's birth. I longed to hold her close and comfort her, to stroke her hair and kiss away the hurt, but she shrugged off any physical contact we offered, resisting all attempts at consolation.

After a few weeks, we sought help from our doctor, who advised us to give Rachel more time and space, reminding us again that the counselling route was still available.

The first year is always the hardest. I heard it from so many well-wishers, and in many ways, it proved to be true. Anniversaries were to be faced, birthdays, Christmas, and so many other meaningful dates that the first year was an arduous one. Places we'd visited as a family became no-go areas; the memories they stirred too painful.

My mother's health started to deteriorate, and almost before my eyes, she turned from being a strong, independent woman into an old lady, well before her time. The loss of her daughter, son-in-law and two grandchildren was almost too much for her to bear, and she developed illnesses, which, although not definitively connected to the grief, were undoubtedly compounded by the stress she'd suffered. Doctors diagnosed angina on top of depression and my mother declined rapidly, both physically and mentally. She lost weight at an alarming rate and became reclusive, refusing to leave the house despite our efforts.

Naturally, this profoundly affected my father, who assumed he was somehow failing his wife and couldn't be persuaded otherwise. Dad took over caring for Mum, a woman who had always prided herself on being capable and in control, the one to cater for family celebrations with such ease and lightness of spirit. Tom and I could see the changes in them both but were incapable of reversing their decline, even though we tried everything which came to mind. During that first year, I pushed my grief aside to help my surviving family, but, like my father, I too felt powerless to alter the situation.

Rachel, however, remained our chief concern. While Tom found some escape at work, I stayed at home in an attempt to make a good life for my husband and daughter. I cleaned the house frantically, often unnecessarily, to fill the long empty hours and baked more cakes than we could possibly eat. We encouraged Rachel to take an interest in things outside of school, sports or dancing classes, riding lessons, perhaps? We offered her everything we could think of to enhance her life but found nothing for which she showed even the slightest enthusiasm. Of course, the one thing she wanted was to have her sister back. It was the same for us all – but it was never going to happen.

After school, Rachel would go to her room to do her homework without a word unless I addressed her directly with an open-ended question. I began to wonder if she blamed me for Jenny's death, for letting her go with Karen and James that fateful day, or was it me blaming myself? If only I'd kept her at home with Rachel. How many times had I wished that was the case?

On the positive side, Rachel excelled at school, academically at least. She proved to be a very bright, capable student, and when the time came to move on to secondary education, she was easily at the top of her class, with her teachers singing her praises at every opportunity. Our daughter's head was always in a book, whether homework or a novel, a good habit, but I often wondered if she was hiding between those pages, hiding from Tom and me, or even from herself.

A year after the first aborted attempt at counselling, we decided to pick up the sessions again for our daughter, yet once more without success. Rachel refused to engage with the counsellor and even going to the sessions became a contentious issue, so we finally abandoned it.

Was it even right to try to make Rachel talk about her feelings? Could she be dealing with the loss in her own silent way? There were so many questions and, quite simply, no answers. Yes, we still talked about Jenny, I couldn't bear to erase her from our lives as if she'd never lived, but we tried to be sensitive and not overdo it, for Rachel's sake, yet she rarely participated in any such conversations. Looking back, I can't ever remember her speaking her sister's name after the accident. She remained almost cold, aloof, and there appeared to be no way to reach her, no matter how hard we tried or how innovative the ideas we came up with.

Another problem presented itself for us as far as Rachel was concerned. We had not told our daughter that she was adopted. Somehow the time was never right, and now, when she was on the verge of going to senior school, we felt she had a right to know. But having lost her sister, we struggled to decide if this revelation would be another significant hurdle to overcome. Would it perhaps be too much for our daughter to bear, and possibly even the final straw?

Tom and I spent many evenings discussing this issue; should we, shouldn't we? It was at times like this that I missed my sister, Karen. She was so wise in such matters and would have advised me what to do. I could no longer turn to my parents for advice, as they struggled daily with their own problems, and I didn't want to add to their burdens. Eventually, we took the easiest route and procrastinated, yet again.

'We'll know when the time is right,' we kidded ourselves. 'Perhaps the opportunity will arise naturally and we'll tell her then.' Yes, it was cowardly, but our motives were pure, or at least that's what I tried to convince myself.

The transition to her new senior school, Rockcliffe Academy, went smoothly for Rachel. Our daughter looked so grown up in her new uniform. She was turning into a lovely young woman. However, Rachel flatly refused to allow me to take her photo on the first day and insisted she walk to school alone. I was more nervous than she appeared to be, and when she left the house, I followed, keeping well back and praying she wouldn't turn around and see me. The need to be sure that she arrived safely was overwhelming, even though it was only a fifteen-minute walk from our home, and several other students were heading in the same direction. My routine of following her continued each morning for a week until Tom insisted I stop.

'We have to trust her, Alice, give her some independence, and who knows, she might make friends with other students who take the same route.' He was right, I knew, but I always worried about Rachel and harboured a feeling of being a complete failure as a parent. I'd lost one daughter and couldn't reach the other at all, no matter how hard I tried.

It was during Rachel's first term that the adoption issue arose again. A homework assignment consisted of charting a family tree to reach as far back as possible. We could have ignored the fact that Rachel wasn't our biological child and just assisted her with details of our own heritage. The thought was tempting, but it appeared to be the opportunity we'd been waiting for, and so we tried, as tactfully as we could, to tell our daughter the truth about her origins.

I always felt apprehensive when a serious conversation with Rachel was necessary, and this was no exception. Tom and I chose the moment carefully and nervously sat down with our daughter, determined to be honest and answer any questions she may ask as fully as we could. I started by showing her some of the very early photographs we took when she first came to us, hoping this would lead naturally to explaining why there was none of her as a tiny baby. Then, trying to make her origins a positive issue, we told her how much we'd wanted her to come and live with us and that she was our chosen daughter, therefore very special to us.

Rachel stared into the distance, quite unemotional, as if she either already knew or didn't care. This reaction rather nonplussed us, but Rachel remained detached, her expression, as ever, betraying no emotion, and then she simply shrugged and announced, 'Miss said that if we didn't live with our real families, we should just write about the adults we do live with, so can I go upstairs now? I've lots of homework to do.'

We were stunned and somewhat wounded that we now

seemed to fall into the category of not being her 'real family'. I wondered if somehow she already knew, had my parents inadvertently let something slip, or Karen, perhaps? Tom and I talked about the issue without reaching any conclusion. Maybe something at school had made her realise. Teachers have to deal with so many variations of 'families' these days. The only positive we could take from this incident was that it appeared to Rachel not to be a big issue. Once more, our daughter surprised us, and in some ways, it was a relief to have it out in the open. Rachel certainly didn't seem upset by the truth of her parentage or curious about her birth family.

During the days to come, the revelation that Rachel was adopted appeared not to affect her at all, for good or bad, and I was glad, relieved she'd taken it so well. I was also feeling quite optimistic that Rachel seemed to be taking the transition to Rockcliffe Academy in her stride, enjoying the challenge of the academic side of school life. She developed a particular love of sciences and excelled in these subjects. After the first year, Rachel received a prize for her grades in all subjects, an accolade she accepted without fuss and one which spurred her on to study even harder.

It seemed ironic that parents of other children her age worried that their offspring weren't applying themselves to their studies, while my chief concern was that Rachel didn't take time out to have fun. I somewhat perversely envied their problems, if only our daughter would argue with us over something, anything, but it never seemed to happen. She became like a twelve-year-old version of a character in the Ira Levin novel, *The Stepford Wives*, unemotional, almost robotic at times. I longed for her to show some real feelings, some joy of living. After all, it was nearly three years since Jenny died. When I talked to Tom about my concerns, he attempted to reassure me that I was overreacting, looking for problems where none existed.

'We should be grateful that she doesn't give us any trouble, and she's never been one to show her emotions. Our Rachel's a quiet girl by nature, a bit of a loner even.' He smiled, dismissing the subject as usual. Tom was right though. We experienced very little trouble with our daughter in those days. I never so much as needed to ask her to tidy her bedroom, as she kept her own space in pristine order, so much so that it felt like walking into a stage set. Instead of pictures of current pop stars plastered on her wall, Rachel displayed posters of the periodic table of elements, a huge world map, and a mathematics flow chart that was beyond my understanding.

On her desk, pens and pencils were arranged symmetrically, and her bookshelves groaned with some weighty chemistry books (in alphabetical order, of course), which to me seemed way too dry for a girl not yet in her teens. Tom suggested her unusual interests might simply be due to her genes, we'd never really learned much about her birth family, and I couldn't argue with that. But I did continue to worry and longed for the day when Rachel would take an interest in some aspect of popular culture or argue with me about staying out late at parties, wearing too much makeup and inappropriate clothes. Maybe if that time did come, I'd regret wishing for such problems. On the other hand, perhaps Tom was right, and I was simply an overanxious mother with too much time on my hands.

Eventually life became bearable once more. Grief never leaves you, but you learn to live with it, and our family functioned in the best way we could. There would always be that aching void, the space in my heart where our beautiful daughter should be, and the misery of my sister's family so cruelly wiped out. Still, we made a determined effort to move on from those dark days of pain and loss, to rebuild a world for Rachel and ourselves. Often, the days, weeks and months stretched ahead like an endless tunnel, with shadows threatening to reach out and engulf us. But it was imperative that we attempted to move on, to make our lives count for something. Our grief couldn't define us forever.

As time passed by, I tried to look at our loss differently. I told myself that Jenny had been gifted to us for seven precious years. My sister and her family were precious gifts too in the years we'd known them. I asked myself if I would have been happier for never having had these wonderful people in my life, and the answer came easily. No, absolutely not, for their presence here on earth enriched my life as well as the countless others they touched during those years.

Yes, their lives ended far too early, we wanted them for longer, expected them for longer, but I wouldn't have missed knowing and loving them, even though their loss brings such pain. I sought to dwell on happy memories, the joy of past times spent with my family, to discipline my thoughts to the positive rather than the negative, in an effort to ease the pain. I was truly blessed to have known and loved them all.

15

Alice

I studied my daughter closely during her pre-teen years, watching for signs – but of what I was unsure; normality perhaps, or was that unkind? Her transition to Rockcliffe Academy worried me more than it did Rachel, as did her unusual behaviour. Her insular character and preference for her own company presented problems, and Rachel's attitude could often be interpreted as rude. She had little time for our friends, and if any came to the house to visit, she could barely bring herself to be polite, with her demeanour nothing short of surly. I generally passed this off as shyness, making excuses I knew were not valid. My frequent attempts to explain social niceties to Rachel went over her head, and generally, my efforts were met with a steely glare, as if she couldn't wait to be elsewhere, and I was nothing more than an unwelcome distraction.

As our concerns for Rachel remained and my anxieties for her future development increased, I persuaded Tom to accompany me to see our GP for his opinion on getting a referral for our daughter to a child psychiatrist. My husband initially resisted the idea but eventually agreed that we should at least inquire; we didn't have to take Rachel with us for a preliminary visit.

Our GP was familiar with our family, we'd been with his practice for more years than I cared to remember and Dr Simons had seen us through some challenging times. It helped that he was aware of our past concerns about Rachel and the morning's visit was made easier by his patient attentiveness to the things we were finding difficult to verbalise. Counselling had been tried and ruled out when Rachel refused to engage with the psychoanalyst, and I found it difficult to tell the doctor exactly what kind of help we were seeking. Eventually, I simply blurted out my fears that Rachel was not normal and we were at a loss to know what to do.

Dr Simons asked questions about Rachel, an easier way for him to understand our concerns and allow us to express them.

In answer to questions concerning her behaviour, we established that she didn't present violent or unruly behaviour yet was frequently withdrawn, unsociable and often moody. The doctor asked if there were changes in her behaviour, a drop in performance at school perhaps, or any paranoid ideas and unease with others. I explained that we weren't seeking help due to any changes, but rather a continuation, and possible escalation, of traits that had always been there. Rachel's preference for her own company wasn't new but not typical in a child of her age. Her apparent coolness and lack of emotion had always been evident, but again was becoming increasingly disturbing. The only thing which appeared to surprise Dr Simons was when I told him that I'd not seen our daughter cry since she was a very young baby, and only then when she'd experienced physical pain.

The doctor's question and answer approach worked well for Tom and me and prompted us to explain things that we might have forgotten to mention otherwise. Dr Simons paused, looked from Tom to me and took a deep breath.

'I think there may be value in referring Rachel to a consultant paediatric psychiatrist, but perhaps not at this particular time. Even then the initial step would be to perform a series of tests to discover if there could be a metabolic disorder causing Rachel's symptoms.'

I interrupted, alarmed at the mention of disorders. 'What would you be testing for?'

'Hypoglycaemia, Wilson's disease, meningitis and encephalitis.' He reeled off the list and I was horrified, particularly at the mention of meningitis, a word that strikes fear into the heart of every parent, a disease I knew could be fatal.

Dr Simons, sensing my panic, continued.

'This is simply the first stage of any referral process and we would not expect to find these diseases; they're simply performed to rule them out. As Rachel's problems are ongoing and have been for some time, I would be surprised to find any such issues. Before we go ahead with a referral, I'd like you to go home and think very seriously about embarking on this next step. Rachel is still young and has suffered more than her share of trauma and time is on our side. She could grow out of the unsocial behaviour she exhibits without intervention, which I'm sure you'll agree would be the best possible outcome.'

I remember leaving the surgery after this encounter, turning to Tom and asking, 'Did he just give us a verbal pat on the head?'

Tom nodded sadly and agreed that we were no further forward. It appeared that our daughter's behaviour would have to deteriorate to levels far worse before treatment was considered necessary, an unpalatable thought if ever there was one.

Tom and I discussed our visit to the doctor over the next few days. My mind dwelt on very little else. Were we making a mountain from a molehill? My husband seemed to think so.

'It could simply be in her make-up, Alice, her DNA. We'll never know what her biological parents were like. Maybe they were introverted, unsocial people?' He had a point I couldn't argue with, so I didn't. I attempted to take the doctor's advice and give the situation more time – after all, Rachel wasn't violent or destructive in any way. Perhaps I was an overanxious mother and the problem was more with me than our daughter?

And so, once again, I let the subject drop, waiting for an improvement in our mother-daughter relationship, which never came. Did I do the right thing, or should I have fought for my daughter to be assessed by professionals? I suspect this is something I will never know.

16

A lice formed a plan. Even in her often-confused state, she identified a pattern in how she felt and became convinced that the medication, administered three times a day, was only adding to her confusion rather than easing it. Sadly, Rachel's visits seemed to exacerbate the confusion too, and her daughter's insistence on being right was hard to take and continually frustrating for Alice. She almost wished that Rachel would stop visiting, a thought she wouldn't dare voice to anyone else.

Sadly, Alice was beginning to distrust her daughter. After all, wasn't she the one insisting that Tom was dead and that Millie was nothing more than a figment of her imagination?

The plan was, in part, to stop taking the medication. It wouldn't be as easy as it sounded because the carers stood over her as she took the tablets, although some were less vigilant than others. Alice would put the pills in her mouth if necessary and conceal them under her tongue until she was alone and could flush them down the toilet. But the most distasteful part of the plan was to go along with the lies that Tom was dead and that Millie didn't exist.

Even though it went against the grain, and she was usually straightforward and honest with the people in her life, Alice felt this was her only chance of getting out of The Elms, to have the opportunity to search for her missing husband and granddaughter. Surely she was not so far gone that Rachel's lies could be true? Alice had seriously considered this possibility but ruled it out, knowing with the utmost certainty that Tom hadn't died four years earlier, and as for Millie's existence, that was true as well. At times Alice could almost feel her granddaughter in her arms, her slim little body warm and comforting as she snuggled into her grandma for one of their special cuddles. She could smell the child's scent, sunshine and fresh air – yes, Millie was real, Alice was certain.

Throughout the morning, Alice vacillated between a determination to carry out the plan and fear that she was demented and Rachel and the doctors were right. It was only her sheer frustration at the situation which delivered the courage to take matters into her own hands, and so when the nurse arrived with her medication after lunch, Alice was prepared. The nurse watched Alice put the tablets in her mouth, and offered her a glass of water. Alice took barely a sip and held the tablets under her tongue. She asked the nurse to close the curtains so she could sleep, then smiled and closed her eyes. As soon as the nurse left the room, Alice went into the bathroom and spat the tablets into the toilet bowl, flushing it twice to ensure they disappeared without a trace. It was easier than she'd expected, and if she could do the same each time someone brought her medication, Alice was sure she'd feel so much better for it, more like her old self.

Sarah stuck her head around the door and was greeted by a wide smile. 'Hello! You're looking very pleased with yourself today.'

'I'm feeling it. Come in, tell me how you are.' Alice grinned. The volunteer was always a welcome visitor, Sarah made the time to chat, and Alice enjoyed their chats.

'I'm fine, thanks, and I have some news for you.' Sarah moved closer to talk without being overheard by anyone who may be passing outside the room.

'You should be having a visit from a Best Interests Assessor in the next few days.'

'What's that?' Alice had never heard the term before.

'It's someone who's qualified to assess whether or not you're capable of making your own decisions. They'll talk to you and ask what you want for your future. Afterwards, they'll consult with the doctor to decide if you're able to do what you want to do.'

'Does Rachel know about this?' Alice asked.

'I don't know, but probably not. I've only found out this morning because I was asking questions. There's no appointment scheduled. The assessor will call in when he or she gets the chance and will probably see you here in your room.'

'Good. Don't tell Rachel, will you?'

'No, I won't. I don't think your daughter likes me very much, but whether or not the doctor will tell her beforehand, I'm not sure.'

Both women were silent for a moment, Alice speaking next.

'A Best Interests Assessor, eh? I wonder whose best interest will be served?'

'Oh, Alice, yours naturally, we all want the best for you.'

'I know you do, dear, but I wonder about some of the others...'

They discussed books, and Alice began to comment on

when she was teaching but stopped abruptly. 'Sorry, you don't believe I was a teacher, do you?'

'It's not a question of what I believe. It's what we've been told. Rachel says you never taught and mostly worked in clerical jobs. I'm sorry, Alice.'

'It's okay. It's not your fault. Perhaps I'd better not say anything about teaching when the assessor visits or mention Tom or Millie.' Tears welled in her eyes.

'Don't get upset, please. The assessment will be fine, I'm sure, and even if you do get a few things muddled up, it doesn't mean they'll keep you here indefinitely.'

'Really, do you think there's a chance that I might go home?'

'I think it's a possibility, yes, they'll certainly ask what you want to do. But worrying about it isn't going to help. Simply be yourself and answer any questions as well as you can. My husband always says that if you don't know an answer, be honest and say so rather than waffle.'

'Your husband sounds like a very sensible person; I'll take his advice and keep my fingers crossed.'

'Fingers crossed about what?' Another voice chipped into the conversation and they both turned to see Rachel standing in the doorway. Sarah felt herself blush and didn't know what to say.

'Oh, just an assessment that's coming up soon.' Sarah stammered.

'And I'm keeping my fingers crossed for you, aren't I, dear?' Alice had never sounded so lucid and was satisfied her daughter assumed the assessment was connected to Sarah.

'Yes, thank you, Alice, I'll leave you alone with your visitor now.' Sarah smiled and left the room. Rachel perched on her mother's bed,

'Really, Mum, you shouldn't encourage the staff in idle chatter. She must have work to do and why do you let her call you Alice? Calling you 'Mrs Roberts' would show much more respect.'

'I think chatting to the residents is part of her job, Rachel, and I asked her to call me Alice. Sarah *is* very respectful and cares about me.' She felt somewhat bold and held her daughter's gaze, daring her to argue the point. Rachel smiled at her mother.

'I've brought you one of those custard slices you enjoy from the bakers in the High Street. You can eat it now if you like. I'll fetch a fork from the day room.' She opened a cake box and presented her offering to her mother, who looked at it rather suspiciously.

'Actually, I've only just finished dinner, so I'll have it later. Just leave it on the side there, thank you.'

The visit passed quite amicably. Rachel made an effort at conversation and told Alice about an upcoming conference she would be attending the following week.

'I'll be away from Monday to Friday, but I'll ring every day to see how you are.'

'There's no need. I'm looked after very well.'

Rachel was somewhat puzzled by her mother's mood. Alice hadn't attempted to confront her about her father or even mention 'Millie'. Perhaps she was beginning to accept that she'd be in The Elms permanently?

'Right, I have to be getting back to work now. Why don't you eat the custard slice before I go, then I can clear the box away for you?'

'No, thank you, I don't think I could manage it yet. I'll have it with my afternoon coffee, but you shouldn't keep spoiling me with all these little treats. You get back to the shop now, Rachel. I'll be fine.'

Rachel left without seeing the doctor. She didn't want him to think that she was an overanxious daughter. They would contact her if they had any concerns. However, it would have been Rachel who was concerned if she'd witnessed her mother wrapping the custard tart up in several layers of tissue and stuffing it into the bottom of the waste bin.

17

Alice felt somewhat guilty at her deceit. Not just throwing the pastry away, but pretending to Rachel – it wasn't her style, she'd always been upfront and direct. But her relationship with Rachel had always been complicated, not what she'd have liked it to be, and it caused her grief to admit it.

2001

Finding appropriate words to portray my relationship with my daughter is almost impossible. A mother-daughter relationship should, at the very least, be warm and loving, yet this was not so in the case of Rachel and me. Any words which do spring to mind are not what they should be, and as Rachel grew, she remained remote, dispassionate, wholly self-sufficient and always quiet in our company.

Although one of the brightest pupils in her year at school, the teachers described her as introverted and withdrawn. We worried about her lack of social interaction, and Rachel rarely showed enthusiasm for anything. Our daughter lived her life following her own self-imposed regime, completing necessary tasks without complaint, both at home and school.

Friends were never invited home. There was no 'best friend' to whom she regularly chatted on the telephone. In fact, Rachel didn't appear to need friends in her life at all. She wasn't one to initiate conversation and offered only a perfunctory answer if required to do so, offering as little of herself as possible. Tom and I discussed ways to help her enjoy life more but eventually decided that this was simply how Rachel was made and we were never going to change her. And why should we? If she was content in her ways, shouldn't that be enough for us? Did I wrongly want her to conform to my version of what she should be? Did my own expectations colour what I wanted and expected of my daughter? Then there was always the reminder that she was not our flesh and blood. If this were an issue for Rachel, we would never know. Perhaps she was different simply because of her genetic makeup.

As she entered her teen years, we stopped worrying so much and determined to accept our daughter for who she was. This was not an easy thing to do, mainly because I wasn't convinced that Rachel was truly happy. Our relationship was 'cordial' – what an abysmal way to describe the bond between us! I truly loved her but was never convinced that she understood or reciprocated.

During those years, the need to stretch my mind and broaden my own understanding led me to embark upon an Open University course, an English literature degree. It was Tom's suggestion, thinking I might enjoy studying and applying myself to something academic I could complete in my own timescale.

I enrolled with great enthusiasm, finding a rich and much-needed fulfilment in becoming a student once again. Had I simply found a job and gone out to work, the burden of guilt that being away from home and family brought would have dragged me down. The course offered the best of both worlds and as flexibility was still necessary for my day to day life, it was the ideal solution. As well as wanting to provide a stable home for Rachel, my mother's health had deteriorated to such a point that my father could no longer cope alone, so when Rachel was safely off to school, I would go each day to my parents' house, where I helped to care for my mother. It was a labour of love, and I certainly didn't do it begrudgingly.

My studies provided respite from the burden of care and I loved the course I'd chosen. When Tom was away working and Rachel in her room, I was able to lose myself in the assignments that regularly needed completing or the many fascinating books on my reading list. My studies delighted me and provided a much-needed focus, something to stretch my intellect, and the time spent in my books became my 'me' time which delighted me every minute.

Sadly, my mother was not to see the new millennium and died in December 1999. Mum never really recovered from losing Karen, James and her two granddaughters. Although my mother's premature death once again brought that all too familiar sadness to our family, we comforted ourselves, knowing she was at peace and reunited with her loved ones. If Mum's death affected Rachel, she didn't show it, and, like so many other events, it became just something else which she took in her stride.

During Rachel's third year in senior school, our daughter was confronted with another tragic incident. A boy in the year below her fell down the stairs at school and sadly died from a broken neck. For such a tragedy to happen on school premises affects the whole community, both pupils and staff. The young boy, Harry, had been sent on an errand for his class teacher and fallen, unnoticed, while the corridors were quiet and the other children were in lessons. Rachel had asked to be excused to visit the cloakroom and was the first to come across the boy's lifeless body.

Naturally, it was a shock, but she had the presence of mind to seek help from the teacher in the nearest classroom. By the time the teacher called us to the school to collect our daughter, she was pale and even more silent than usual when obliged to recount her experience to the headteacher and later to the police. As we sat with her throughout this ordeal in the headteacher's study, my heart ached for her. Seeing a fellow pupil dead was something I feared could have a detrimental effect on our daughter. Surely the heartbreak of losing her sister and aunt's family was enough. It seemed so unfair that Rachel had to cope with another tragedy. I observed my daughter carefully over the following months, fearing it was all too much to cope with.

As with our own family's loss, the people of Matlock came together once again to mourn the life of young Harry Chapman, and our hearts went out to his family. We gave Rachel the choice of attending the funeral. At fourteen, we thought her old enough to understand and to make her own decision. She decided to attend with us.

Naturally, memories of our own loss came flooding back as once again the parish church was filled with mourners, gathered to say goodbye to yet another of the town's children, a life ended far too early. I silently railed at the injustice of it all as I witnessed the weighty sense of loss and the pain of Harry's parents. How much grief could one community suffer?

Rachel coped remarkably well and managed to hold herself together during the service when so many of her fellow pupils were weeping. It was indeed another sad day for the town and most certainly for Harry's parents. I knew all too well how they must be feeling.

By chance, about three weeks after Harry's funeral, I met his mother, Brenda, in the High Street, and we stopped to talk. Harry had been in Jenny's class at junior school, so Brenda and I had met previously on occasions at school events, but I wouldn't say we knew each other well. Perhaps the fact that I too had lost a child led this poor woman to ask if I had time for a coffee, to which I agreed – it was the least I could do.

We found a quiet tea shop, and when, after ordering our coffee, Brenda broke down in tears, I simply held her, shielding her from the few other customers in the room and silently praying for this dear lady who was on the journey I knew so well, the long, hard road of grief.

The inevitable questions poured from her wounded heart: how could she go on living, would it get any easier, why her son?

'I don't have any answers to your questions but I can tell you how I get through each day.' This was all I could offer and it seemed so inadequate but Brenda's eager expression encouraged me to continue.

'I try to view Jenny as a gift from God, a daughter who was mine for seven short years and one who brought me such love and happiness. I would rather have had those few years than not have known Jenny at all, even though her loss still brings pain every day.' I was blinking back my own tears then.

'Does it get any better with time? I'm sick of people telling me that it will.' Brenda was hurting, angry and confused. I recognised myself in her, shades of my own anguish were shining from her eyes.

'I don't think the pain gets any less, you simply learn to live with it. I'm sorry if that's not what you want to hear but this has been my reality. On the positive side, you and I both have other children to live for, and good men to share our grief.' My words felt so deficient, hollow even, but that was all I had to offer. There are no right or wrong answers. I could only share with her those thoughts that had helped me when I was at the very lowest point.

I knew of no deep and meaningful solutions and was still very much working through my own grief, but as we bared our hearts to each other, I hope she was comforted by our time together. We exchanged phone numbers and over the following months, Brenda visited my home and me hers as we formed a bond, finding in each other someone we could be honest with about our feelings. Our friendship grew, and I was grateful for her empathy as I hoped she was for mine.

Rachel was at the age of making decisions that would affect her future. Choosing which subjects to study was the first major event and we were not surprised when she opted to concentrate on the sciences, particularly chemistry and biology. It was clear that our daughter possessed a sound mind and she'd maintained her position at the top of the class throughout those first years at secondary school.

Speaking with other parents and hearing of their difficulties in getting their children to do homework and apply themselves to lessons, I was unsure if my daughter's attitude was a blessing or not. Rachel didn't need so much as a word from us to prompt her to study, and unlike her contemporaries, a social life held no attraction, and interest in boys had not yet materialised.

Perhaps I should have been glad she wasn't easily distracted from her studies, but there were times when I wished she'd let her hair down and enjoy life a little. But it wasn't our place to encourage her to be frivolous, especially as she never gave us cause to complain. Other mothers often told me that they wished their children would apply themselves as Rachel did, while I wished she'd enjoy life and even rebel occasionally, just a little, of course.

Over the next two years, my daughter and I studied hard and both reaped the rewards of our diligence. I achieved my degree, and to our delight, Rachel attained eight GCSEs, all A or A-star grades. We couldn't have asked for more. Rachel took the results in her stride. Our daughter was by then a mature, intelligent young woman, already thinking about the next phase, her A Levels and university. So why then was there an empty feeling in the pit of my stomach? Life had returned to a semblance of normality, and although we would always grieve for Jenny, there should be at least some joy in our home. Sadly, there wasn't and I felt as if we were simply treading water, waiting for something to happen, but for what, I had no idea.

18

After only four days of not taking her medication, Alice couldn't believe how much better she felt. Tiredness remained her constant companion, but that awful feeling of heaviness, of wading through a treacly fog, had lifted. Each morning when she awoke, there was still that initial, startled sensation of not knowing where she was, but the reality was present after only a moment or two, her mind once again active and no longer letting her down.

This new-found clarity did have its downside, particularly regarding Tom. Why was he not coming to see her, to sort out this injustice of being kept against her will? Alice couldn't fathom why he was suddenly absent from her life. Silently dismissing that he was dead, as Rachel insisted, Alice's mind led her down several paths of explanation, most of which were so unpalatable that she refused to entertain them. The recollection of the red coat hanging in her kitchen became a representation of 'another woman', and Alice shrugged off such thoughts. She knew Tom better than that.

The reality of her situation was now depressing. At least when the drugs kicked in, Alice was primarily unaware of how desperate her situation was, but now, the returning lucidity was accompanied by a deep sadness, an almost physical ache in her chest, and so many unanswered questions were stacking up in her mind.

If the staff noticed a change in Alice, it was only that she was quieter and appeared more resigned to being at The Elms. There'd been no concerning incidents over the last few days and she'd become a popular resident, always polite and grateful for their care, a much easier charge than the 'wild Alice' who'd thrown things and become agitated at the slightest provocation in the days after her arrival. This new calmness was attributed to the medication, which was undoubtedly true, but not in the way they assumed, as Alice had become adept at concealing the tablets from the nurses to dispose of later.

A young woman tapped on her door one morning. 'Hello, Alice. I'm sorry to be so early. I hope you've had your breakfast.' The woman was tall and slender with a pleasant face and a gentle smile.

'Yes, I've already eaten, thank you.' Alice returned the smile, hoping that this visitor was the one for whom she'd been waiting.

'Good. My name's Fiona Williams, and I'm here to have a little chat with you today if that's okay with you?'

'Are you the Best Interests Assessor?'

'Yes, were you expecting me?'

'Not specifically this morning, but I knew you'd be here some time.' Alice peered into the woman's eyes, noting her surprise. The assessor's kind attitude was perhaps a little condescending, as if she was talking to a child. But her demeanour instantly altered to a more business-like manner, as if she'd reassessed Alice. Fiona asked permission to sit down.

'Please do, but there's only the bed unless you'd like to fetch a chair from the day room?'

'No, this is fine, thank you.' She perched on the edge of Alice's bed, took a file from her oversized, well-worn handbag, and balanced it on her knee. Smiling again, she started the assessment.

'Can you tell me your full name, Alice?'

'Alice Roberts, no middle name.'

Fiona smiled. 'And your address?'

The assessment began well, with nothing Alice couldn't handle. For the first time in weeks, personal details were clear in her mind and she felt confident in her replies. She smiled at the simple questions on politics and delighted in seeing the younger woman's evident astonishment at her answers. But then the tricky bit came.

'Alice, can you tell me how you came to be in The Elms and a little about your family?'

Remembering Sarah's husband's sage advice, Alice decided to be completely honest.

'I came here from hospital after a suspected stroke. My daughter filled me in on the details, which I don't remember, as apparently I couldn't speak at first and became very confused. I want to say that the confusion has gone entirely, but there are still some things I find hard to accept.' Alice paused, mentally practising her words so she didn't sound insane.

'I'm having difficulty remembering that my husband died several years ago... and also that I don't have a granddaughter, who seems to be so real to me. It appears I've even invented a past career for myself as a teacher, which, according to my daughter, Rachel, is pure fantasy.' There, she'd been honest enough with no accusations or denunciations of her daughter and the lies she was feeding her. Alice fought back the tears. She wanted this interview to go well, to be allowed to go home as soon as possible. Fiona Williams leaned towards Alice and squeezed her hand, her eyes full of compassion.

'So, what is it you'd like to happen now? Where would you like to be, Alice?'

'I want to go home! They've been very kind in here, but it's not where I belong, and I'm certain that I'll feel better in my own home. Please, let me go home.'

'It's not entirely up to me, but I can say that after our little chat, it appears that perhaps you are in the wrong place. Naturally, I need to speak to your doctor. I have an appointment with him later this morning and we'll certainly discuss your case. If you were to go home, Alice, how would you manage on a practical level?'

'There's nothing physically wrong with me, although I'm stiff from sitting here all day, so I'm quite capable of looking after myself and my home.'

Fiona smiled. 'Yes, Alice, I think you are.'

There was another unexpected visitor for Alice that afternoon. Dr Patel knocked on her door and introduced himself, asking permission to talk with her. Alice smiled at the opportunity to show off her new-found confidence, correctly assuming that this was the psychiatrist who would also have an input into her future.

The assessment was almost a repeat of her chat with Fiona Williams. Alice played it in precisely the same way, admitting to some confusion but ready to accept others' judgement and advice. Her answer to the question of where she would like to be was the same, at home. Alice was sure she'd convinced him when the doctor left but was still anxious, longing for some feedback.

The feedback didn't come until Sarah entered her room just before tea time.

'You're the talk of The Elms, now aren't you?' She laughed, a huge grin on her face.

'What do you mean?' Alice was impatient.

'The assessor, Fiona Williams, told the doctor and the nurses you shouldn't be in here. She thinks you're more than capable of making your own choices and has recommended that the DOL order is lifted. Whatever you said must have worked because her recommendation is to discharge you as soon as possible, and the psychiatrist agreed with her decision. Are you pleased?'

'Delighted!' Alice jumped out of her chair and hugged Sarah. 'And it's partly due to you and your husband.'

'What?' Sarah screwed up her face, but Alice was beaming and already opening her wardrobe to look for her case.

'Wait a minute, you can't just walk out, there'll be paperwork to complete and the doctor will need to see you. I think they'll want some sort of care plan in place too before you leave. But maybe that doesn't apply in your case?'

Alice tutted. 'Do I look like I need a carer? I'm not that ancient yet.'

'But what about Rachel? She'll have to come and pick you up, won't she?'

'Ah, well, that's the best bit. Rachel's away on a business trip and won't even know I'm going home until I'm there.' Alice's eyes sparkled with mischief.

'But who'll take you, see that you're okay?'

'I'll get a taxi. When can I see the doctor?'

'Probably not until his rounds in the morning. You'll be on his list for then.'

Alice sighed. 'I suppose I can bear one more night here, but I can't wait to get home.'

Sarah smiled. 'Have we been so terrible, Alice?'

'Not you, never. Here, take your books back and thank you, I've enjoyed reading them. They've helped to keep me sane.'

'Thanks, but I've read them all too, so I'll put them in the library. I'll miss you, Alice. You've made working on this ward so much better than I imagined it would be.'

'I'll miss you too, you've been so kind, but it doesn't have to be goodbye, does it? You could always come and visit. See me at home and then you might not think of me as crazy.'

'I've never thought of you as crazy, and I'd love to visit. I suppose we're both newcomers to the town.' Sarah fished a small notebook from her pocket. 'Here, write your address and telephone number down for me and I'll give you a ring to see how you're settling back in. And I'll give you my mobile number too, you can ring anytime, especially while Rachel's away if you need anything, you know? So leave the packing until the doctor's been in the morning. You don't want him to think you're too eager, do you?'

Alice spent the rest of the evening with the television on, oblivious to what the programmes were as her mind was focused on one thing only, going home. It was a bonus that Rachel was away. It couldn't have come at a better time and would be *fait accompli* before her daughter even knew and could devise some way of thwarting her plans, which Alice was sure she would try to do.

The morning couldn't come quickly enough, and Alice made mental lists of her priorities for when she was back in her own home, number one being to find out exactly where Tom was.

19

Richard Edwards was stunned by the change in his patient, the assessor was correct and Alice was undoubtedly capable of making her own decisions. There was nothing more he could do, therefore, except to discharge her immediately.

He'd last seen Alice two days previously and noticed a significant improvement even then. She hadn't insisted that her husband was alive and admitted to being confused about facts pertaining to her past, which was all very positive. This morning, Alice appeared even better, remarkably so. The only niggling concern Dr Edwards had in discharging her was that Rachel Roberts was away from home. She'd been ringing The Elms each day, and the nursing staff provided her with verbal updates on Alice's condition, but he instinctively knew she wouldn't be happy if they discharged her mother while she was away.

'Mrs Roberts, don't you think it would be prudent to wait until your daughter's return before you go home? It's only a few more days.' Dr Edwards asked the question, guessing correctly what the answer would be.

'There's no way I'm staying here another night. Besides, why should I occupy a bed which a patient with a genuine need might need? I'm not old or infirm and therefore don't need my daughter to look after me or give her permission to do anything. I have a home to go to, and I'm going today.' She was emphatic but polite and there was nothing the doctor could do to stop her. She also had a point about the bed; there was a waiting list growing by the day.

'Okay, I understand, but if you do feel at all unwell once you're home, ring your GP or dial III. It's been a difficult time for you, and you could relapse, so please be aware.'

Richard Phillip's initial diagnosis of dementia had always troubled him. The questions Alice asked during their times together demonstrated good cognitive thinking. Still, there was no doubt she was delusional in other ways, inventing a career which had never been, a grandchild who didn't exist, and insisting her husband was still alive. Yet over the last few days, Alice hadn't maintained these fantasies so vehemently, so perhaps her memory was returning to what it should be. The cause of her delusions still puzzled Dr Edwards. Something must have caused them, an infection maybe, but it was possible they might never find out. This morning, he admitted to himself, there appeared to be nothing wrong with her at all.

Alice took her suitcase from the wardrobe when the doctor left the room, threw it on the bed, and hurriedly filled it with her few possessions. Most of the clothes were not her own, but she packed them anyway. Insisting they didn't belong to her might give them grounds to rethink their decision to discharge her, the last thing she wanted. Since stopping taking the medication, Alice had been cautious with every word she'd spoken and every little action. It was heartbreaking to tell the doctor she was confused about the details of her past and especially about Tom when she knew in her heart that he was alive, but the pretence was necessary to convince them to allow her to go home. At least when she was home, she could embark on her search for Tom and Millie.

'So, you're leaving us, are you?' The gruff voice startled Alice, and she turned to find Mavis's unwelcome presence, freshly returned from her holiday.

'I am.'

'Sister asked me to give you this.' Mavis handed over an envelope. 'It's your discharge letter.' Turning to leave the room, there was no offer of help or fond farewells, Mavis's feelings for her charge clearly equalling those Alice felt for her.

Within the hour, Alice climbed eagerly into the back seat of a taxi while the receptionist at The Elms smiled and wished her well. A sense of relief washed over her at actually being on her way home, an event Alice had at times doubted would ever happen. Two full days stretched out before her until Rachel was due to return from her trip, two uninterrupted days to settle in, collect her thoughts and form some kind of plan.

The idea of being home was so very welcome, although simultaneously tinged with apprehension over what she might find out. But Alice needed to be home. It was the logical starting point for discovering precisely what was happening. Convinced there must be a rational explanation for Tom's disappearance, and without the medication and being free from those who purported to be helping her, Alice could finally think clearly. But that same clarity elicited a feeling of being very much alone, as the task before her loomed large and daunting. For all of her plans over the last twenty-four hours, it was difficult to know where to begin and the depressing thought of having no one to turn to for help was almost overwhelming.

Peering from the taxi window, Alice realised how little she knew about Penrith and the surrounding area. The five-mile drive to Melkinthorpe took longer than she'd expected, and a sudden thought about paying the taxi driver popped into her mind. Her handbag contained very little cash, Rachel had seen to it that she had little of anything, not even a door key, but Alice hadn't admitted that to the staff at The Elms. A key was hidden under a stone in the garden which she would use, and if there was insufficient money in her purse to pay the driver, she'd ask him to wait while she went inside to find more. These minor obstacles were the first of many Alice would need to overcome, but the facts were clear in her mind, Tom was missing and Rachel wasn't to be trusted. Alice was very much on her own and would need all her determination to discover precisely what was going on.

Alice's relief was almost tangible when she found the key in its hiding place, a simple matter which validated her recent actions and restored confidence that she wasn't as batty as others thought. Thankfully there was also enough money in her purse to pay the driver, with a small tip and thanks for her freedom, which he would never fully understand.

As she entered the cottage for the first time in weeks (exactly how many weeks was still a little uncertain), a strange sensation washed over her, but her doubts and uncertainties were something else to keep to herself. Alice was fighting to restore the world's perception of her and she wouldn't readily admit to any weakness or lapse in memory from now on.

Alice's initial reaction was to call out for Tom on walking through the front door, although she knew how futile that would be. It was an instinct, one of many she'd have to evaluate before acting upon. If Tom were there, he would most certainly have visited her at The Elms to bring her home.

The house felt hollow and cold, even though it was a beautiful warm summer's day. Alice moved through the empty rooms, opening windows to allow the sunshine and the fresh gentle breeze inside her home. This moment was one she'd longed for but was unsure, or perhaps even a little afraid, of where to start.

Alice carried her small case to the bedroom, opened it and tipped its contents onto the floor. There was nothing she wanted to keep; the clothes belonged to other residents, and everything was impregnated with the smell of The Elms, a place she desperately wanted to forget. Her next action was to open Tom's wardrobe. Alice stifled a sob and examined the contents which hung there in place of Tom's clothes. Her winter attire, coats neatly covered with garment bags, hung where Tom's should be and on his shelf were her woollens, gloves and scarves.

Turning to her own wardrobe, she was again disappointed. It was full of her own summer clothes. Alice's heart rate increased as disappointment flooded through her.

Scanning the room and looking for anything else out of place, or anything belonging to Tom, Alice noticed his leather cuff link box on the top of the tallboy, and a faint spark of hope blossomed from her despair. She grabbed at it greedily, longing to find something of her husband's, anything to bring comfort, but on opening the lid, instead of the assortment of cuff links it usually held, there was just one single item – Tom's wedding ring.

'No!' Alice couldn't process what this meant. Her mind didn't want to think about it. Staggering to the bed, she slumped down upon it, the ring still clasped in her hand. Examining it closely in the hope that it was just a similar ring, the engraved inscription of their wedding date and their initials on the inside confirmed what she did not want to believe. The ring *was* Tom's.

This distressing discovery only presented more questions. Tom never took the ring off, so why would he do so now? Her thoughts travelled back to that awful day when he'd gone missing – when her life turned into a complete mystification. The question she asked then popped back, unbidden into her mind, had Tom left her, perhaps even for another woman? Hot tears began to flow and Alice gave way to huge sobs of grief as she lay on the bed, alone and suddenly very afraid.

20

When the sobbing eventually subsided, Alice was momentarily confused, but the feel of the gold band in her palm confirmed her discovery with an unwelcome stab of pain. Her husband hadn't taken that ring off since the day they were married, so why would he do so now? As she dragged herself from the bed and made her way to the bathroom, Alice was sure the answers to her questions must be somewhere here, in her home.

After splashing cold water onto her face, she tentatively opened the wall cabinet where Tom stored his shaving things, only to find it empty, and a search of the other cupboards revealed her own toiletries, nothing at all of her husband's. Steeling herself for whatever else she might, or might not, find, Alice went downstairs to the lounge and gazed around. Her eyes rested on their carefully chosen furniture, the pictures on the walls and the various ornaments collected over the years of their marriage, all very familiar but also somehow different. These possessions held memories, but Alice couldn't afford to dwell on them; it was time to be dispassionate, to concentrate solely on facts, abandoning sentiment, for now at least.

The family photographs on display were familiar too, but on closer inspection, incomplete. Precious images from the past were still there, her wedding photograph, her sister's wedding and subsequent pictures of Karen, James and Beth, a family group including Rachel with Alice and Karen's parents. Tom's mother smiled widely from a silver photograph frame and there were several photographs of their beloved Jenny, their golden-haired, beautiful daughter who would always remain just seven years old.

The images brought more tears to Alice's eyes, but ignoring the ache in her heart, she concentrated only on which photographs were missing. There were no recent images of Tom; there should be a holiday photo from last summer when they'd toured Scotland with Barney. They'd asked a passer-by to take them together and it was one of the few good photos they possessed of the two of them. Surely she hadn't imagined that? And then there was Millie. Alice distinctly remembered a photograph of her granddaughter in a pretty enamelled frame – an image of the child as a toddler, grinning into the camera – a picture which Tom had taken on one of the rare occasions when Rachel allowed them to take Millie out for the day. Alice loved that photograph; it couldn't be a false memory, a figment of her imagination, it simply couldn't.

Alice ventured into the kitchen, surprised to see that it was almost 3pm. Functioning in an automatic daze, she filled the kettle and opened the cupboard for the coffee. As expected, there was no milk in the fridge and no bread either, so she took a loaf from the freezer and prised off two slices to put in the toaster. She was hungry but possessed neither the energy nor desire to consider making a meal.

In her peripheral vision, Alice caught sight of the red coat hanging on the rack by the back door and remembered seeing it on the day she took ill. Rachel claimed it was hers. She approached the coat as if it was alive and might bite her, but a necessity to inspect it closely overcame her caution. The coat was in her size, but Alice couldn't remember ever having bought or worn it. Rachel must be mistaken; it wasn't the style of coat she wore and red certainly wasn't her colour.

Turning her attention back to the coffee, Alice added two large sugars to compensate for the lack of milk and buttered the toast. The coffee still tasted bitter and the toast didn't appeal but she'd promised Sarah that she would look after herself and, feeling slightly light-headed, common sense told her to eat and drink something.

Placing her mug and plate in the dishwasher, Alice took a deep breath and went back into the lounge to continue the search. Her plan now was to go through all the family photograph albums and find the tin box where Tom kept all their important documents. What she was hoping to find was unclear in her mind, but there must be clues somewhere.

Several albums from childhood were pushed aside, as was her wedding album and a couple from before the accident. Alice searched for more recent pictures to prove that her husband was alive and perhaps some images of Millie. The most recent photos were stored in boxes. She'd long ago given up putting them in albums to save space which fortunately made it easier to go through them.

In the box marked *Holidays,* Alice dug deep, pulling out handfuls of glossy photographs and fanning them out on the floor, looking for photos of their holiday in Scotland the previous year, for proof that Tom had been alive and with her then. Nothing. There were no holiday snaps since Rachel was a teenager and then very few. Their daughter hated having her picture taken and generally frowned into the camera rather than smiling. A second search through the box confirmed the worst; the images were missing, and there were no photographs of Millie either.

Moving to the next box, marked *Family Occasions,* Alice again grabbed a handful to spread out on the floor but halted as her hands touched something larger than a photograph. It was a folded card, and on the front was a photo of Tom. She stared at it, shocked and confused. Tears blurred the words as Alice tried to read them:

Order of Service for the funeral of Tom Roberts
April 10th 1963 – December 5th 2014

A loud, wailing sound filled the room. Alice barely recognised the noise as coming from somewhere deep inside herself. When the wailing stopped, she repeated *'no, no, no',* over and over again, grasping the photograph of Tom to her chest. The pain was unbearable, she wished she were dead too, but she was alive and so utterly alone. Rachel had been telling the truth all along – Tom, her beloved Tom, was dead!

Alice was experiencing the same overwhelming grief that had been a constant in her life when Jenny, Karen and her family died. Surely, she couldn't cope with such agonising emotional torture again. It was unbearable, excruciating. Maybe this was why she'd doubted Rachel and insisted on the fantasy that Tom was still alive. Didn't they say that your subconscious blocks extreme trauma as a coping mechanism? But now Alice was forced to admit the truth – her husband was dead and her mind was playing cruel tricks on her.

I've been such a stupid, stupid fool, insisting I was right! I'm a silly woman, clinging to the past, inventing stories simply because I want a different reality. Is this what dementia looks like from the inside? I'd always thought I'd be so far gone I wouldn't be aware of what was happening to me, wouldn't care even, but this – this is pure hell on earth!

Alice sat on the floor surrounded by the photographs, the order of service and Tom's wedding ring in her lap for over an hour, unaware of time and with her mind in turmoil. Grief and pain consumed her body, so much so that she didn't even possess the energy to stand up when she heard the doorbell ringing. She tried to ignore the insistent noise but whoever was there knocked loudly until Alice pulled herself up and went to open the door.

'Sarah!' Alice almost fell into her visitor's arms.

'Alice, whatever's the matter? Are you ill? Shall I call the doctor?' There was something seriously amiss. Half carrying Alice back into the house, Sarah settled her onto the sofa, noting the mess on the floor.

'What's happened, can you tell me?' Sarah asked softly.

'Oh, Sarah, they were right and I was wrong, and it hurts so much...' The order of service for Tom's funeral was clasped to her chest and she handed it to her visitor before falling back onto the sofa, exhausted.

Sarah read the front of the card...

'I'm so sorry; this must be an awful shock for you.' There was an uneasy silence for a few moments as the women contemplated the relevancy of the find. Alice spoke first, distraught at finding out that Tom really was dead, as Rachel had maintained all along.

'I've blamed Rachel and accused her of lying, and now I feel terrible. How can I not remember, and what about all the other things? Millie, me being a teacher, even the dog. What a fool I must seem.'

'No, Alice, you're not a fool, far from it. Dementia's an illness. It's not your fault, but you can learn to live with it.'

'But won't they send me back to The Elms? I'm not sane anymore!'

'Not necessarily. They lifted the DOL order as the assessment ruled that you're able to make your own choices; this doesn't change that. Many people with dementia stay in their own homes for years. It can be managed, particularly in the early stages.' Sarah felt somewhat out of her depth, with no formal medical training, only what she'd picked up from experience, but she spoke kindly and, as far as she was aware, accurately.

'What about these delusions? Am I safe to be alone?'

'If you still want to live here, Alice, the risks can be assessed, but if you're worried about being alone and feel you'd prefer some kind of residential care, then I'm sure that's an option which will be open to you.'

'No, I'd rather be here. I just don't know if I can trust my judgement any longer.'

'That's understandable, but this is all so new and raw. You can discuss these things with Rachel when she comes home. Have you eaten since you left us this morning? You look as if you could do with a strong cup of tea.'

'Yes, I think I could, although I did have some toast and coffee a while ago. But you must have somewhere to go, Sarah, you don't want to spend your free time with me, isn't that a bit of a busman's holiday?' Alice attempted a smile.

'There's nowhere I need to be and Jack's still at work, so unless you want to be alone, I'll happily stay for a while.'

'Please, I think I could do with the company. It's all been quite a shock…'

21

It was 9pm by the time Sarah arrived home. Knowing how much Jack worried about her being out alone, she'd sent a quick text earlier to tell him where she was and that everything was okay. As she closed the door, she shouted his name.

'Hello, love, shall I put the kettle on?' Jack greeted his wife with concern.

'Not for me thanks, I've had enough tea to last me for a week.' Sarah hugged her husband and flopped, exhausted, beside him onto the sofa.

'How's Alice?' Jack asked.

'Shocked and washed out. The poor woman was certain that her husband was still alive, but now she's home, the evidence is plain to see. I must admit Alice was quite convincing at The Elms. I almost believed her myself. She was so certain of her own mind.'

'Yes, I remember. So, your detective work was all in vain?' Jack grinned, earning a playful punch in the ribs from his wife. 'Tell me, what's convinced her otherwise?'

'When I arrived, Alice had just found the order of service for her husband's funeral...'

'Goodness, what a cruel way to find out. The poor woman must have been shocked.'

'Yes, but she wasn't finding out for the first time, was she? That's the trouble with dementia. Sometimes patients have to go through the same distressing trauma over and over again. She'd also expected to find a photograph of her 'granddaughter', but sadly that seems to be another figment of her imagination.' Sarah snuggled closer into her husband's side, needing the comfort of his presence.

'Poor Alice feels so stupid now. It's almost sad she's lucid enough to know the mistakes she's making; patients who are so far gone they're not aware of anything generally tend to be happier, or at least more content.'

'Do you think she'll have to go back to The Elms?'

'No, she's still functioning reasonably well, so the assessment decision will stand, but if things get worse, the situation might change and she'll need monitoring, initially at least.'

'It just goes to show that none of us actually know what's waiting around the corner for us, do we?'

'Aw, Jack, don't get all maudlin on me. I need cheering up.' Sarah thumped him playfully on the arm.

'The poor woman must have thought that everyone was conspiring against her. What a terrible thing, not to feel you can trust your own family.'

'Conspiracy theories are common with dementia and it's why they have an open-door policy at work. The doors are only closed when a carer's delivering personal care and even then two staff members have to be in attendance. Accusations of staff stealing money and possessions are the norm, I'm afraid, but generally, the family bears the brunt of it. Residents tell anyone who'll listen that their families have locked them away and sold their homes for the money. I've heard so many variations on this theme already; it must be hard for the families who only want the best for them.'

'Sarah, you must promise me that when I get to that stage, you'll whisk me off to Switzerland, to one of those places where you can choose to slip away in peace.'

'Jack! Not everyone gets dementia, you know, and there's no way I'd do that for anyone, especially you. Now, I'm ready for bed. It's been a long day.'

'Sounds like a good idea to me!' Jack grinned and took his wife's hand, entwining his fingers with her own as he led her upstairs.

22

Rachel tapped her foot impatiently as she waited to see Dr Edwards, her eyes narrow and her lips pressed tightly together. Her arrival home late the previous evening meant that this morning was her first opportunity to check on her mother at The Elms. It was a shock to learn that they'd discharged Alice, and she now wanted to ask the doctor why.

After a few minutes, a patient came out of the doctor's office and Rachel jumped to her feet, catching the door before it had chance to close, pushing her way into the office.

Even though she was already in the room, Richard Edwards said, 'Hello, Rachel, come in, please.' This was an interview he'd been expecting, and he'd correctly anticipated Rachel's mood.

'Why wasn't I informed of the assessment on my mother? And who decided that she was fit to go home? I thought there was a Deprivation of Liberty Order on her?'

'Please, sit down and I'll explain it to you.' The doctor smiled and spoke in his reassuring, bedside voice.

Richard Edwards had plenty of practice dealing with anxious relatives over the years at The Elms. When Rachel was seated opposite him, he explained the assessment process regarding her mother's wishes.

'As you know, I've been talking with Alice regularly, but she's also seen a Best Interests Assessor and an independent psychiatrist–'

'But why wasn't I informed before these meetings? I would have been here for them.'

'Sometimes it's better if the patient is seen alone for these assessments. Having a relative present can put undue pressure on what is shared. We asked your mother if she was happy to go ahead with the meetings or if she would like to wait until you were present. Alice chose to meet both the assessor and the doctor on her own.'

'But she doesn't always know what she's saying. You know she comes out with some strange ideas and has a minimal grasp on reality.'

'At the time of the assessment, your mother presented as quite rational. She answered all the questions correctly and admitted to some confusion about her past. The assessor was in no doubt that Alice is capable of making her own decisions, and when asked what she'd like to happen in the future, she elected to go home.'

'She *would* say that, but that doesn't mean she's safe to be alone, does it? What if she becomes confused again, or could wander away, or let anyone in the house? She's vulnerable.'

'I'm sorry you don't agree with our decision, Rachel, but both the assessor and the psychiatrist agreed to lift the DOL order, and after seeing Alice for myself, I have to concur with that decision. I think you'll find that your mother's much improved since you went away.'

'But how can she be so much better in such a short time? I'm not at all happy about this.'

'Perhaps you should go to see her and then you might feel otherwise. I saw her on the day she was discharged, and she was quite well and delighted to be going home.' Dr Edwards stood to indicate the meeting was over. There was nothing else he could do for Rachel Roberts. The woman would hopefully feel differently after she met with her mother.

Rachel left The Elms and drove straight to her mother's cottage, not knowing what might greet her. It was two days since Alice's discharge; this would be her third day at home alone. Rachel rang the bell and then used her key to enter, calling out as she did so.

Alice heard her daughter from the kitchen and took a deep breath, unsure what Rachel would say or do now that she knew she was home.

There'd been plenty of thinking time for Alice over the last couple of days. Apart from a bit of food shopping, she'd done little else. The shock of finding out that Tom was dead was a heavy blow and a fact with which she still struggled. At times she'd found herself searching for clues to prove that her husband was alive, but her rational side told her this was futile. Perhaps she even owed her daughter an apology, the recent past was still somewhat hazy, but Alice knew she'd acted out of character at times, and she remembered some angry scenes from her days at The Elms.

She came out to meet her daughter with a smile fixed on her face. 'Hello, Rachel. How was your trip?'

'Fine, but I'm more concerned about you. You're not well enough to be alone, Mum. You should have waited until I came home.' Rachel looked wary of her mother as if she was sizing up her mood.

'But I'm home now, and I feel so much better for it. I'll make us a coffee, shall I, and then we can have a chat.'

Rachel followed into the kitchen, where the back door was open, allowing a pleasant breeze to waft through the warm sunny room, carrying on it the scent of freshly mown grass. Silence hung heavily in the air as both women pondered how to open the conversation.

'How did you know I was home?' Alice spoke as she went through the motions of making coffee.

'I got back late last night, so I didn't visit The Elms until this morning. It was quite a shock to discover you weren't there.'

'Did they tell you about the assessments?'

'Yes. Dr Edwards told me, but I wish you'd waited until I was back. I could have been with you.'

'I managed perfectly well on my own and there was no need to be taking up a bed that someone else needed. Anyway, I think I owe you an apology. I still find it hard to accept, and I can't say I remember much about it, but I do know now that your dad is dead...' It was so difficult to speak those words. To her chagrin, tears filled Alice's eyes.

'That's a relief to hear, but what's changed your mind?'

'I found the order of service from his funeral. It was a shock at first, and the facts are still muddled, but I'm sorry I didn't believe you; it's just so hard to accept.' Alice did break down then; hot tears had been her companion for the last few days. The heartache was, at times, almost unbearable.

'Don't cry, Mum.' Rachel made no attempt to move towards

her mother or offer a hug to comfort her, but then she rarely, if ever, displayed such emotions. 'If you still can't remember the details, can you see now why I don't think you're well enough to be on your own?' She spoke coolly, her words held no compassion. Finally, Alice stopped crying and looked at her daughter.

'I'm not going back to that place. I might have gaps in my memory, but the doctor thinks that could be down to an infection or something; I'm quite well now.' Surely Rachel wasn't going to try to make her go back to The Elms?

'And what about Barney? Do you still think you have a dog, or can you remember what happened to him?' Her daughter's voice sounded harsh, almost cruel.

Alice grudgingly conceded. 'No, I can't remember what happened to Barney, but I believe you if you say he's gone too.'

'I'm simply worried about your safety. You don't seem to realise how ill you've been. Would you like me to get some help for you? Perhaps someone could call each day to see if you're okay?'

'Rachel, I'm fifty-five, hardly an old lady, and I don't need anyone checking up on me. I've got the telephone and I can call you if I need to, but I'm home and I fully intend to carry on living my own life, even if I am alone.' Alice swallowed hard at the implication of her own words. 'I'm sure the memories will return in time, but I certainly don't want to be treated like an invalid.' She was growing increasingly angry; her daughter's concern should have been touching, but it wasn't. They'd never really been close and she rather resented Rachel wanting to make decisions for her now.

'Okay, but if you do feel ill again or confused, I want you to tell me straight away.'

'Yes, I will, but I'm sure I'll be fine.'

After politely answering one or two questions about her trip,

Rachel left to go to work and Alice was finally able to relax. Her daughter wasn't the comfort she should be and sadly not the person Alice would want beside her if she did feel ill.

The relief when Rachel left was a familiar, almost tangible, sensation. When, she wondered, had it started to be like this?

23

Alice

No one ever doubted that Rachel would attend university, it was her single aim throughout her time at Rockcliffe Academy and she worked hard to achieve it. As the time drew near for her to leave, my feelings were conflicting. Like any mother approaching the empty nest phase of life, I worried for my daughter. Would she cope, would she look after herself properly, and make the right sort of friends? The last issue was probably the most unfounded; Rachel didn't make any friends and didn't appear to need them.

As well as these expected sentiments, things which all parents concerned themselves with, there were others which I hardly dared to voice, except perhaps to Tom. Our daughter's departure was going to be a relief. It's a difficult admission to make, but Rachel's presence in the house always brought with it a tension which her departure would almost certainly alleviate. It's not that we wanted her to go. I knew we would worry about her, but Rachel was a very mature young woman and perhaps gaining her independence would be the making of us all.

Our daughter gained excellent results in her A Levels, excelling in maths, chemistry, biology and physics. Naturally, we were proud of her as she was offered a place at Aston University in Birmingham to do her Mpharm. The master's degree was a four-year course that would qualify Rachel as a pharmacist, her chosen career.

During the weeks before she was due to leave, Rachel allowed me to help her prepare, and together we shopped for the essentials she would need to live away from home, including the purchase of a new laptop as a gift. Tom also arranged for a generous monthly payment to go into her bank account. We didn't want her to have to worry about money.

When the day of departure arrived, we drove Rachel to Birmingham, a distance of only sixty miles, and helped carry her belongings into the Halls of Residence, where she would live for her first year. Tom offered to take the three of us out for a meal before we left, but Rachel declined the offer, saying she wanted to unpack and organise her room.

The final goodbye was a rather impassive event. Being wary of showing emotion, as I knew Rachel would be embarrassed by any such display, I gave my daughter only a brief hug. She'd never sought out physical contact and barely reciprocated. Tom too attempted a hug before we left rather awkwardly, reminding her to ring home when she had the chance.

I don't think either of us knew what to say on the way home. It was a watershed moment in our lives and we each cosseted our own thoughts, almost afraid to admit what we were feeling. Later, however, once back at home, we confessed to a sense of relief and spent the evening pondering what our life would be like from then onwards.

Our relationship with Rachel was never a warm one, not for

want of trying, but we agreed that we'd done our best, and all we could do now was to be there for her if she needed us. We could do nothing other than wait and see where the relationship travelled from there.

The only other person I could confide in was my friend, Brenda Chapman. We'd both known the pain of losing a child and our friendship strengthened in many ways over the years. Brenda's two other children were both at university, so she understood, to a point, what I was feeling. She was also aware of the unusual relationship Tom and I had with Rachel, and her accurate perceptions and understanding of my confused emotions were comforting.

Sometimes guilt about Rachel stifled me. It wasn't as if she'd been problematic in ways many children and adolescents are. She was just cold, unresponsive, and almost apathetic to human sentiments. In many ways, I could be proud of her; academically, she was quite brilliant and her behaviour was generally good, so why did I feel as if I didn't know my daughter? Could the problem be with me, or was it, as we'd often considered, in the genes? Yet, I shall not go there again – we'd lost Jenny, and I was grateful we still had Rachel.

Sadly, we also lost my father at this time. His death was sudden, a stroke from which he never recovered, but mercifully it was over quickly and he didn't have to endure a long and drawn-out period of illness. Our life was changing once again and I was unsure of how the future would evolve.

For the first time in our married life, Tom and I had only ourselves to think about, and with a niggling sense of guilt, we could plan things we'd never considered before. Travel was now a possibility. Rachel loathed holidays, they took her out of her comfort zone and she made it perfectly clear that she'd rather be at home, in her usual routine. Now that we were free to broaden our horizons, we would have to relearn how to enjoy ourselves, to think of our own pleasures without the sense of guilt that so often accompanied this concept for us.

During Rachel's first term at university, she rang each week dutifully, although as time went on, with diminishing frequency. Our conversations were stilted, generally consisting of a breakdown of her studies, upcoming exams, assignments, tutorials and the like. Not that I wasn't interested, I was, but I wondered about my daughter's social life or lack of it. I longed for her to tell me she'd met a boy, to hear some excitement in her voice, some anticipation of events other than papers to be handed in and forthcoming exams. I fell into the pattern of letting Rachel dictate the conversation and it was apparent that absence did not make her heart grow fonder.

At the beginning of her second year of studies, Rachel moved into a small flat on her own, which she decided to buy using the money we paid regularly into her account. Tom and I hoped she'd make friends during those early days, perhaps someone with whom she'd wish to share a flat, or a house, as many students do. But there was never any mention of friends. She remained solitary by choice.

Rachel secured a weekend job in a pharmacy, which seemed a sensible idea and was undoubtedly compatible with her studies. Yet, I couldn't help but wonder if one reason for seeking employment was to make it difficult to come home at weekends and even holidays. Our daughter did come home a few times during that first year, but visits grew less frequent. Time in the library at university always took priority over being with us. Still, I was grateful that she kept in touch and shouldn't have been surprised at all by Rachel's choices. She'd always been independent.

Tom and I were slowly accepting this new relationship with our daughter, who was an adult, making her own decisions and planning her future. We knew we would only be included in her life if, and when, she wanted us to be. And so, it was time to abandon our worries. We'd done our best for her over the years and would continue to do so as often as she would allow.

It occurred to me that when many children were striving to reach their parents' expectations and make their parents proud of them, it was the exact reverse for Tom and me. We always tried to be the kind of parents Rachel wanted, and now that she was a young woman, I was beginning to realise that we had failed miserably in our efforts. Was I beginning to fear my daughter even then, her judgement on us as parents, and her expectations that we'd so obviously not met? It became the case that I was so afraid of doing the wrong thing that, to my shame, I did nothing, allowing my relationship with Rachel to drift, to be dictated by her and entirely on her terms. Sadly, this was the way it continued ever since.

Tom remained as busy as ever with work, but I, too, felt the need to be active, both mentally and physically and so I decided that it was time to re-enter the world of work. I'd continued with my studies and now eagerly started applying for jobs.

24

During her first couple of weeks back at home, things felt strange and unfamiliar to Alice. The cottage was still new to her, it was barely a couple of months since her relocation from Matlock, so that was understandable, but her senses were telling her that life wasn't quite right, that something was off, something she couldn't put her finger on. The feeling that Tom should be there with her was a constant and his presence at times seemed almost palpable. She knew which chair he would sit in and where his possessions should be stored, which was ridiculous as he'd never lived in this house with her.

Nor had Barney, but she still expected to hear his bark on occasions or the scuffling of his paws at the back door. Naturally, Alice admitted none of these notions to Rachel, who rang each morning before she left for work, a practice which annoyed Alice rather than comforted her. It was as if her daughter was monitoring her, waiting for something to go wrong so she could lock her away again.

Sarah visited and was becoming a valued friend. It was to her that Alice confided a few of these thoughts.

'Perhaps you should revisit the doctor, your own GP. After

all, you didn't get a diagnosis of exactly what was wrong, did you?' Alice knew that Sarah was right, but she wasn't ready to see anyone from the medical profession again just yet. Her faith in the system had been somewhat battered.

'I'll give it a while and see how I go.' Alice procrastinated, and Sarah was too kind to push the suggestion.

It was midweek when the first parcel arrived. The doorbell surprised Alice, being so early in the morning, and the young man on the doorstep asked for a signature while passing over a small package. She signed without thinking, took the box inside and turned it around a few times, examining it. As it was her address, Alice opened it. Inside was a cheap trinket box, made of resin masquerading as metal, with glass beads poorly glued into the lid, the sort of item she would never buy. A packing note was inside the wrapping, dispelling her initial thought that it might be a gift from someone as incorrect. It was from a television shopping channel and the note, a receipt bearing her name and address, was for a ridiculous amount of money for such a shoddy item. Alice looked for a return address. She would wrap it up and return it to the company it had come from, yet who could have sent it puzzled her.

Later that day, the doorbell rang again and this time, a taxi driver stood on the doorstep.

'You ready?' the man asked curtly, his vehicle engine still running.

Alice shook her head. 'But... I didn't order a taxi; you must have the wrong address.'

'Nope.' He looked at the number on the doorpost. 'Fifteen it is.'

'Well, I'm sorry, but there's been a mistake, I didn't order a taxi. I have a car and can drive myself.' Alice closed the door as the taxi driver began a tirade she didn't want to hear about time-wasters. Yet, the incident unnerved her. Was it a simple mix-up or would someone order the taxi as a joke? Perhaps if it hadn't happened so close together as the unexplained parcel, she wouldn't have thought twice about it, but it did seem strange to have two such incidents on the same day.

As part of Alice's attempts to rebuild her life, she decided to contact her old friend, Brenda, and invite her to stay. Brenda had recently retired and might appreciate the time away as much as Alice would enjoy her company. She would send an email; the computer had remained idle since her return from The Elms and it was about time she reconnected with the outside world. So, with afternoon coffee beside her, Alice switched on the laptop and waited for it to spring to life. Technology wasn't her thing. Tom was always the one to be up to date with electronics, loving all the latest gadgets, but she knew the basics and even kept a Facebook account. Admittedly, she rarely used it, unable to think of the snappy, witty posts with which the younger generation seemed so adept.

Alice went into her email account when the laptop was ready and was surprised to see that the inbox was empty. After so long offline, she'd at least expected a full spam box, but no, there was nothing. Attempting to bring up her email address book, again, there was nothing, no contacts at all. Perhaps she was doing something wrong. It was a while since she'd used it. Maybe it was best to leave it for now and ask Rachel to take a look when she next visited.

After finishing her coffee, Alice went to find her address book to ring Brenda instead. It would be lovely to hear her friend's voice again. The address book was not in its usual place in the drawer and a feeling of panic swelled in Alice's chest. Things were going wrong again; was it some kind of relapse?

After searching in all the likely places that the book might be, she sat, willing herself to calm down, to breathe normally, determined that one or two minor issues were not going to unbalance her. She needed to think positively, make a plan and keep herself busy. The only other place housing Brenda's number was on Alice's mobile phone, but that too appeared to be missing since her return from The Elms.

Alice took herself off for a long walk, finishing up at the garden centre and treating herself to a pastry from their bakery for later. Arriving home, Rachel was on the doorstep.

'Hello, I was just about to use my key. I didn't know you were going out.' Her daughter greeted her.

'I just went for a walk, nowhere special, but come in. Will you stay for tea with me?' Alice wished she'd bought two pastries.

'Well, yes, that's why I'm here. You invited me for a meal, don't you remember?' Rachel was scrutinising her mother, a frown on her face making Alice feel suddenly flustered.

'Yes, of course, I remember. I just didn't think you'd be so early.' She lied, wondering what she could produce for a meal to make her daughter think the arrangement hadn't slipped her mind. 'Actually, I thought we could get some fish and chips for a change, would that be okay?' Alice thought she'd covered her mistake quite well.

'But the nearest fish and chip shop is miles away, and to be perfectly honest, I don't have a lot of time. I need to be back for...' Rachel paused mid-sentence, then reconsidered. 'How about we just have a cup of tea now and we'll do the meal another time?' The compromise suited Alice. With no recollection of inviting her daughter and after the events of earlier in the day, it was all a little disconcerting. They went inside together.

'While I make the tea, perhaps you could have a look at my

laptop for me. I wanted to send an email, but I can't seem to get into my address book.'

'Fine, no problem.' Rachel sat down and fired up the device.

When Alice came through to the lounge with the tea tray, her daughter was still frowning.

'You don't have any addresses saved on this.' She looked blankly at her mother.

'But I do! They must be somewhere else, in another folder or something?'

'No, there's nothing. You don't have any files at all. The laptop appears to be just as it came from the manufacturers. Is it a new one? Did you buy it before you left Matlock?'

'No, it's the same one I've had for ages – surely there must be something on it. What about the photographs you sent me of...' Alice stopped herself. A memory of Rachel sending Millie's photograph flashed into her mind, but then she remembered that there was no Millie. It was all in her head, a figment of her imagination. Her daughter was still frowning, looking at her with concern.

'Who did you want to send an email to?' Rachel asked.

'To Brenda, I thought I'd ask her to come and stay for a few days, but I can't find my address book either, or I'd ring her.'

'But Brenda's gone to Australia for three months to visit her daughter, don't you remember? She left about the same time you moved here. There's no chance she'll be home yet.'

'Oh, right.' Alice had no memory of this but again wasn't going to admit it to Rachel. 'Let's have this tea before it gets cold, shall we?'

When Rachel left, Alice again searched for the address book. After exhausting every place it could conceivably be, she decided it must have gone missing during the move; these things happen. As for the laptop, there was little to be done for now, although she did seem to remember once hearing that nothing is ever really lost on a computer. Perhaps one of those repair shops would look at it for her to see if they could find her missing photographs and emails. Maybe they'd been deleted by accident, but there was no hurry if Brenda was in Australia. If her relationship with Rachel was closer, she might have asked her daughter to recommend a repair shop, but Alice was only just beginning to admit to being a little afraid of her. Perhaps it had always been that way. Looking back, most of her parenting of Rachel comprised of trying to please the child, to make her happy. Surely this wasn't how it should be?

The parcels continued to arrive over the next two weeks, at least one a day, sometimes two. Alice was startled every time the doorbell rang, correctly anticipating yet another unwanted delivery. The items were mainly from television shopping channels. However, some of the larger items came from local stores and ranged from a vacuum cleaner to perfume, jewellery, and everything in between. She decided to return them immediately, driving into Penrith and using different post offices to save the embarrassment of returning parcels daily. However, the most frightening incident was when Alice's bank statement arrived and every single item received was on the list of transactions paid for with her debit card.

After the initial shock, it occurred to her that someone must have stolen her card, but a hurried search through her purse revealed that that wasn't the case. Her second, more rational thought was that if someone had stolen her card or even knew the details, why would they send the items to her? A scammer or a thief wouldn't do that.

So far, Alice had kept these deliveries a secret from Rachel, but eventually, shaken by the fact that the parcels were paid for from her account, she decided to ask for her daughter's advice.

Rachel studied her mother's bank statement. 'But why have you bought all of this?' Her voice barely hid the anger.

'That's the point. I didn't buy them and I've no idea how this is happening.' Alice felt a mixture of shame and embarrassment. If she'd expected sympathy and understanding, she was sadly disappointed. Rachel was furious.

'They've been purchased on your debit card. You must have ordered them!'

'Honestly, Rachel, I haven't!'

'I think you probably have but then forgotten about it.'

'You still think I'm mad, don't you?' Alice was close to tears.

'No, Mum, it's an illness.' She lowered her voice. 'I know you can't help it, but this is serious. You're vulnerable and can be taken advantage of here on your own. I think we should look at taking measures to protect you.'

'What kind of measures?'

'Maybe it's time to consider making a Power of Attorney order so I can help you with your finances. We could see a solicitor who'll explain it all to you.' Rachel was so calm and business-like now that her attitude provoked sudden anger in Alice, and frustrated tears spilt over.

'I don't need it explaining to me, Rachel. I know what Power of Attorney is, and I'm far from wishing to take such a step yet.' Even to herself, she sounded irrational when she intended to be firm with her daughter while matching her coolness.

'I can see you're not in the mood to talk about this now, but perhaps you should think about it and we'll discuss it another time. For now, do you want me to go to the bank and put a stop on your debit card?'

'No, I can do that for myself. I don't know what's going on

here, but I'm certain that I didn't order any of these goods and I'm quite capable of sending them back, thank you, Rachel.'

Her daughter let the matter drop and left soon afterwards. As Alice reflected on their conversation, a cold fear washed over her. *Was this what the future looked like? Was she to be forced into giving Rachel control of her life and all her decisions?*

It was a scenario that sent a chill down her spine. There was no comfort in knowing that her daughter was the only person left to care for her in the future.

As Alice battled with these thoughts, the doorbell rang. A smiling pizza delivery man greeted her, holding out a large box and expecting payment, it was all too much for her. She shouted at the man, 'I don't even like pizza!' and slammed the door in his face.

With no one else to turn to for advice, Alice rang Sarah. With a wise head on her shoulders, her new friend would understand and perhaps be able to help her decide what to do. Sarah promised to call round later that afternoon and asked if Alice needed her to bring anything, but the answer was no, just herself.

When Sarah arrived, it was to find Alice rather tense and longing to share recent events. Alice related the strange happenings of the last few days, including the mysterious parcels, the laptop problems, and the missing address book. Finally, she showed Sarah the bank statement, which seemed to 'prove' she'd ordered the goods herself. It was so much easier to talk to Sarah than it was to Rachel. She didn't judge or make her feel stupid and consequently, Alice didn't get flustered or angry, a response her daughter frequently provoked these days. Alice's problems came tumbling out, bringing a measure of relief in sharing them with someone who understood and was prepared to listen, rather than assume she was in the wrong.

'Rachel and I had quite a disagreement. She ended up suggesting that we see a solicitor and I give her Power of Attorney.'

'And is this something you'd be happy to do?'

'No, not at all. I don't think it's necessary yet, and in some ways, it would feel like admitting I was going mad. We exchanged some rather sharp words. I don't usually get angry, but Rachel is so frustrating at times. She won't even consider that I didn't order all these things.'

'I can see why she thinks you did, but someone else may be doing it as a prank. Jack's come across this sort of thing before, I'm sure. People can be vindictive for no apparent reason other than they think it's funny. Do you think that's a possibility?'

'But no one knows me here and I can't think of anyone who would be so cruel.'

'I'll have a word with Jack and see if he has any suggestions if that's okay with you?'

'Yes, thank you, Sarah, another opinion's always welcome. I haven't a clue what to do about it all.'

'Have you double-checked the card details on this bank statement with your debit card, just to make sure there's not a technical error?'

'Well, no, I checked to see if I still had my card but not that the numbers correspond. I'll just go and get it.' Alice went to find her handbag, but it wasn't in the hall cupboard where it was usually kept. A brief search of other possible places didn't reveal where the bag was, but she decided not to worry. It must be somewhere in the house. She'd check the numbers later.

Alice returned to Sarah. 'I had it this afternoon when Rachel was here, but never mind. Shall we have a cup of tea?'

'That would be great, thanks, but then I'll have to be off.

Jack's taking me out for dinner tonight. We're still enjoying discovering Penrith's culinary delights.'

'How lovely, we'll have a cuppa, then I won't keep you, but thanks for coming, I do appreciate it.'

As Alice pottered in the kitchen, she suddenly gasped. Sarah appeared in the doorway and found Alice staring at the open swing bin. Inside was her handbag, together with a pair of shoes and a new pair of gloves.

'Forget the tea. Come and sit down.' Sarah steered a trembling Alice from the kitchen, concerned at the shock on her friend's face. 'It's just a trivial thing; you'll be laughing about this tomorrow.'

'But how did they get in the bin? I must have put them there, Sarah. Perhaps I am going mad after all!'

'Don't say that, Alice, we all do silly things occasionally. Maybe it's time to talk to your GP. You never did make that appointment. Perhaps he could help to reassure you?'

'I haven't even registered with a GP here yet, but I think you're right. It's time to see someone. I don't have to tell Rachel though, do I?'

'No, Alice, you don't. What happens between you and your doctor will remain confidential. Do you know which doctor Rachel uses?'

'No, but I think she goes to Greenfield Surgery.'

'Then you might like to try Hill Street. That's where we've just registered. It's probably nearer for you too and you've no chance of bumping into your daughter there.' Sarah smiled.

'Yes, I'll do that, thank you, Sarah. Now you go and have a good night out. I'll be fine now. I've got a handbag and a pair of shoes to clean.'

~

The next time Sarah visited Alice was a week later and there'd been five more parcels.

'I appear to have ordered a matching set of underwear, not even in my size, a gadget to take the top off boiled eggs, an ugly plastic carriage clock and a set of Union Jack bedding. Then there's that.' Alice pointed to the corner of the room where a Zimmer frame stood, almost mockingly. 'That one really made my blood boil; if someone's doing this as some kind of joke, it's gone way beyond funny.'

'I spoke to Jack about it and he suggested cancelling your debit card and getting a new one as someone apparently knows your number. He says it's not uncommon for people to do this kind of thing. They call it 'pranking', but as you say, it's not funny.'

'Yes, I've meant to go to the bank to do that but to be honest, Sarah, I'm getting so that I don't want to go out – and I dread answering the door.'

Sarah looked more closely at her friend. Since leaving The Elms, Alice had certainly lost confidence and appeared to have lost weight too. She seemed to be tired and perhaps somewhat depressed, which wasn't surprising considering everything she'd experienced since coming home. Sarah didn't tell her friend that, although Jack expressed sympathy for Alice's plight, he initially thought she must have ordered the goods herself and forgotten doing so. Sarah argued her case, convinced that Alice was not so far down the road of dementia that she'd do such a thing. Still, Jack again advised caution about becoming too involved, especially knowing that Rachel Roberts didn't take too kindly to her. Sarah was sure Alice hadn't told her daughter about their continued contact, which suited her fine. It was to be hoped she'd not encounter Rachel while visiting her mother. Maybe she was overstepping the mark by visiting and advising

Alice, but there was something about Rachel Roberts that she didn't trust.

'Is there something else troubling you?' Sarah asked. 'You don't look too well today.'

'There is... it's to do with Millie and I know she's just a figment of my imagination, but I keep having dreams about her. There's been something at the back of my mind for ages, a concern for her safety. In my dreams, she's told me things that are troubling and even though I know she doesn't exist, it still worries me. Now you must think I've really lost the plot! Are they just dreams, Sarah, or are these the false memories that the doctor at The Elms used to talk about?'

'I'm honestly not sure, but I don't think you've lost the plot. Dreams can be quite vivid and you've had so much going on lately that it's not surprising the lines of fantasy and reality are a little blurred. Again, this is something you could talk about to the doctor. Did you manage to get an appointment?' Sarah felt ill-equipped to comment on Alice's mental state and this lady had become a friend, not a case study. A doctor would be the best person to advise her.

'Yes, I'm seeing a lady doctor at Hill Street surgery on Friday. I'm dreading it, really, but you're right, I need someone to talk to who can explain precisely what's happening to me.'

'I could come with you if you like? It's no problem to change my shift.'

'That's so sweet of you, Sarah, but I have to get my confidence back and start to go out more on my own. I'll be fine, but thanks for the offer.'

PART II

THE DAUGHTER

26

Rachel glanced impatiently at the little girl with the wide, moist eyes and trembling bottom lip. Why she wondered, does everyone have to ask so many questions, my mother, and now Millie? Her five-year-old daughter had just plucked up the courage to ask why she hadn't seen her grandma for such a long time.

'Perhaps Grandma doesn't want to see us.' Rachel's abrupt answer was harsh, cruel, and one she knew would upset Millie, but she had no inclination to spare the child's feelings or answer her daughter's questions.

From experience, Millie knew better than to ask a second time, so the child turned away from her mother and went to sit with her book in the corner, confused and upset. Her mother's brief answer suggested to her young mind that perhaps she'd done something wrong, something so naughty that her grandmother no longer wanted to see her. At five years old and without the understanding to process the sudden absence of her beloved grandmother, Millie was confused as to what she might have done. Being afraid to ask again, the child carried the hurt quietly in her heart, wondering whether perhaps Grandma didn't love her as much as Millie had thought she did.

By this point in time, Rachel had expected to have her mother safely and permanently ensconced in a home where she could no longer ask probing questions about her life and Millie. Alice assumed a divine right to know everything about her daughter's life, which frustrated and infuriated Rachel in equal measures.

It had always been the case that her parents wanted more of her than Rachel was prepared to give, a situation which could be reasonably well handled from a distance. But when her mother decided to move closer to Penrith, it was time for Rachel to sort out the problem once and for all.

Simply because Tom and Alice Roberts had adopted Rachel, they held expectations and an assumption that she should be grateful for the home they'd given her, or at least that's how it appeared to her. Truthfully, even from a very young age, Rachel couldn't wait to escape from their home, a desire which a place at university presented to her. The excitement of escape was considerably increased by the certainty that once the break from her parents' home was made, she would never return. Tom and Alice, however, proved not so keen to let her go, and even though Rachel maintained the occasional duty call to assure them that all was well, they wanted, and expected, more than their daughter was prepared to give.

Looking at Millie snivelling in the corner, Rachel, not for the first time, regretted ever deciding to keep the child. Following the initial shock of discovering she was pregnant, Rachel had vacillated over what to do, knowing that the period for decisions was limited. It was a situation she'd never expected to find herself in, and her first thought was to get rid of the baby and continue the life she'd so meticulously mapped out – but she didn't. Perhaps the shift in hormones played tricks on her, or more likely, it was the memory of the only other baby she'd ever known which changed her mind – Jenny.

Rachel often thought of her younger sister, the only person she'd ever felt close to and truly loved. Jenny, with her golden hair, soft pale skin and blue eyes, was such a beautiful child. Jenny, who laughed like an angel and looked up, adoringly, to her big sister. Jenny, who loved her unconditionally, and whom Rachel loved more than anyone else in the world.

Had Rachel been naive in thinking that Jenny could somehow be restored to her through this baby who'd been so thoughtlessly and unintentionally conceived? Or did she possess that primaeval need to procreate, to produce a child, to love a child?

Eventually, Rachel decided that yes, she did want the baby, but that was then, when the rosy memories of Jenny danced so often through her mind, the most delightful time of her life, a time she'd do anything to get back again. But the reality proved to be something vastly different to what she expected.

Alice and Tom were stunned when Rachel eventually told them about the baby, as Rachel knew they would be. Their relationship's rocky journey had thrown up more than a few shocks over the years, but Rachel could tell that this news completely threw them off-kilter. They assumed that their daughter must be in a relationship but had typically kept them in the dark and questions flooded their minds again. Rachel stood firm, refusing to be drawn about the father, and insisting that he would have nothing to do with the child's upbringing. Her silence paid off, and her parents backed off, left with no choice but to content themselves with the knowledge that they were to be grandparents.

It was a remarkably easy birth, but from the moment the beautiful, tiny baby girl was placed into her arms, Rachel felt nothing. No rush of emotion, no bonding or strong feelings, simply complete indifference. Other new mothers on the ward were gushing and tearful, besotted with their new offspring. Rachel felt nauseated by their visible displays of emotion.

If she'd expected to feel anything like the love she'd known for Jenny, she was sorely disappointed and bereft of any genuine sentiment. Perhaps, if the baby had resembled Jenny, it might have been different, but with her mother's red hair, a fractious temperament, and an apparent inability to do anything but cry, Rachel stared at the child as if she was an alien being. There was no notion that this tiny scrap of humanity belonged to her – no warmth in her heart and no desire to hold and comfort her tiny newborn daughter.

Rachel was instantly aware that the decision to keep this baby was a huge mistake, especially when she sensed the hope blossoming in Alice's heart and knew that her mother viewed the baby as the key to building a closer relationship between them. Both Alice and Tom made it clear that they would provide as much help and support as she wanted, a thought which appalled Rachel.

Their involvement, however, was to be denied when, only months after Millie's birth, Rachel finally attained the prize for which she'd worked so hard and became the owner of a dispensing pharmacy in Penrith.

Leaving Millie with a childminder each working day, Rachel experienced only relief at offloading the crying infant and showed very little interest in how the woman cared for her child. Work was Rachel's escape. Her enjoyment was in the mental challenge, the precision of dispensing, and the need to concentrate on avoiding mistakes. This was her domain, where she was in charge and everything was orderly. Customers were tolerated, but Rachel generally left dealing with them to the counter staff, and the financial rewards quickly increased. Rachel had achieved the goal of being her own boss, no longer answerable to anyone. She could finally be her own woman.

Millie's childminder was adequate and her fees reasonable. Rachel was satisfied with the arrangement and took up no references nor asked any pertinent questions before leaving her daughter in the care of a woman who was virtually a stranger. As time passed and Millie appeared quiet and withdrawn when her mother picked her up, Rachel hardly noticed. It suited her not to have to cope with a noisy child, and besides, she'd been the same herself at that age. Millie's introverted ways seemed perfectly normal to her mother.

To Rachel's chagrin, even after she was settled and enjoying her pharmacy's new challenge, Alice continued to ask questions and, within a few years of Rachel's move, followed her to Penrith. It was simple enough to keep her parents out of her hair when they lived at a distance, but the move made it so much more complex, so much so that Rachel felt compelled to put an end to the problem of her mother's interference. She devised a plan, one she thought to be foolproof, but now her well thought out scheme was beginning to unravel. Why was her life so complicated?

27

Rachel's years at university were relatively good ones, second only to those brief childhood years with Jenny, the only time in her life when she'd been truly happy. Getting away from home and her overbearing parents was a relief, and Rachel felt she could finally be herself without constant interference.

Four years of studies, on which she'd thrived, resulted in an excellent degree for her trouble and presented several career opportunities for the future. Initially, medical research appealed to Rachel. The continual study and academic challenge would suit her drive, but the road to the top was lengthy and tedious, and working as a team member didn't suit her personality.

Rachel's need to be in charge led to a change of her previous ambitions and the idea of owning a pharmacy became the ultimate goal. However, working with another pharmacist to learn the ropes was expected, so Rachel acted as an assistant in an established pharmacy for four years – a place from which she couldn't wait to escape. At twenty-six, Rachel was frustrated, both in her career and the relationship with her parents – her plans didn't move on as quickly as she wished.

The one thing that was not a viable option after university and Rachel determined never to do was to return to Matlock. However, the position she'd secured in Chesterfield proved, geographically, still too close to her parents for her liking. Despite the proximity, Rachel ensured there was always an excuse not to visit her parents.

After work, Rachel rarely went out on an evening, content to stay in her own space, with her books and plans for the future. Living frugally and saving every spare penny she earned brought her dream closer, and seeking a pharmacy of her own, as far away from Matlock as possible, occupied much of her spare time.

Although Rachel didn't generally enjoy the company of other human beings, even she had needs and occasionally ventured out to satisfy them. The bar in Chesterfield wasn't the usual sort of place she frequented, but her visit was for a purpose, and that was to find a man. Not for a relationship – that was always made clear – but simply to fulfil her primal need for sex.

Rachel rarely experienced trouble in picking up a man and her requirements were purely physical. If there was no relationship to follow, intelligence didn't come into the equation; a good looking, presentable man with a clean, toned body was the only stipulation.

Rachel spotted him at the bar the moment she entered. He was tall, and being tall herself this was an attribute she appreciated. Broad, muscular shoulders and a pleasing face interested her as she approached him with the confidence of a woman aware of her own physical attractions. It wouldn't take long for her to assess whether he would fit the bill. At a guess, the man was around eight or nine years older than her and it took only a few minutes for Rachel to decide that he was suitable. Strangely, his eyes drew her, steel blue with a haunted look, intriguing and mysterious. As he appeared to be the strong, silent type, all the better, Rachel turned on the charm so rarely displayed, and the evening was decided.

Reluctantly, she took him back to her flat, it was safer than going anywhere he might suggest, and she baulked at paying for a hotel room; every spare penny was reserved for her future plans.

The sex was urgent and quick. She had no desire for any foreplay or tenderness; the man was simply there to satisfy a need. Afterwards, he fell instantly asleep in her bed and Rachel left him alone while she took a shower.

When she returned to the bedroom, the still sleeping man was restless. His body was bathed in sweat, and he writhed as if in pain, wrestling with the throes of a nightmare. Rachel looked at his naked body and felt only annoyance at his presence. Suddenly wanting him gone from her flat, she woke him to discover tears in his eyes. But his apparent torment evoked nothing in her except revulsion. She despised weakness and felt not the slightest compassion or curiosity as to the reason for his distress. If Rachel had shown even the slightest degree of sympathy, the tormented man might have opened up and unburdened himself, but she cared little for other people's needs. She was driven only by her own.

He was a troubled soul. The haunted look in his eyes, which had initially attracted Rachel, now seemed disturbing. If he had the chance to confide the subject of his nightmare, Rachel would have learned of a recurring dream – of an event from his youth for which he was deeply ashamed.

During his regular bouts of fitful sleep, the man relived a time when he was behind the wheel of a van and losing control.

He was confronted time and time again by the horrific scene of a car forced over the edge of an incline – caused by his stupidity – and the unforgettable sound of the explosion a few moments afterwards.

There was no doubt in his mind that he alone was culpable for the resulting carnage, and the images, indelibly seared on his brain, served as a constant and never-ending reminder of his cowardice at fleeing the scene. He lived with the knowledge that there would never be a way to absolve himself from the guilt which haunted him each day. He was responsible for the death of four people, two of them children. The recurring dream was a regular and disturbing recollection of the lowest point of his life – his nadir – and of his deep, abiding shame.

But Rachel asked the man to leave without learning of his torment, of his bitter regrets. He'd been used simply to satisfy a need. She was without the slightest desire for the intimacy of allowing him to sleep in her bed for the night and held no wish to converse with him on any level or share personal details about their respective lives.

They were both consenting adults. He'd been a willing participant. The pair, however, were also carelessly ignorant of the new life they created that night.

By the time Rachel realised she was pregnant, the man, whose name she'd almost instantly forgotten, was long gone, and there was no question of telling him about the pregnancy. Since the night Millie was conceived, Rachel hadn't seen him, which suited her fine; there was no room or desire in her life for a permanent relationship.

28

'How did you get my phone number?' Rachel Roberts was disconcerted and more than a little angry to hear the voice of her mother's friend, Brenda Chapman, on the phone. She was a woman whom Rachel despised.

'Alice gave it to me for emergencies. She wasn't sure what the signal would be like in Melkinthorpe and thought I should have your number until the landline was connected, just in case.'

'In case of what, exactly?'

'A situation such as this, I suppose. I haven't been able to get hold of Alice and was getting worried. Is having your number really such a big deal?'

'She shouldn't have given it to you; Mum knows I value my privacy.'

'As we all do, but if you'd be kind enough to tell me why I can't reach Alice, I'll not trouble you again... and be assured that I won't pass your number on to anyone else!'

'Good. You can't reach my mother because she's in a care home. She's recently suffered a severe mental breakdown and isn't in the best of health.'

Brenda gasped, 'But what brought this on?'

'Dad suffered a stroke from which he's not expected to recover and Mum can't seem to cope.'

'No, surely! Your dad's always been so strong and active. I can't believe this has happened.'

'Well it has, so there's no point in trying to visit. The care home is adamant that Mum needs complete rest and they discourage visitors. Dad's receiving palliative care and is unconscious, in a vegetative state, so visiting him is pointless.'

'Oh, Rachel I'm so sorry but perhaps Alice will benefit from seeing an old friend. We've always been so close.'

'No, that's not possible, the care home's policy is rigid and only close family can visit.'

'But surely as there's only you...'

'No, Brenda. Why would you want to see her in that state anyway? If she was lucid, I'm sure she'd not want to be seen the way she is, to be gawped at like some kind of sideshow.'

'So, she's not aware of her situation?'

'No. Mum's lost touch with reality completely which is probably for the best as Dad won't last much longer. I really must insist that you stay away, any outside interference will not be welcomed.'

'I'm concerned, Rachel. That's hardly interference. Will you at least keep me informed on your mother's progress, and Tom's too?'

'Yes, I can do that but I'm not anticipating Mum's condition to change. The doctors expect her to be in The Elms for some considerable time, perhaps even permanently. Now I really must go, I'm very busy.' Rachel ended the call abruptly.

Brenda was decidedly uncomfortable and more than a little sad after such an awkward conversation. It appeared that tragedy had once again struck Alice and her family, and Rachel's attitude was totally indifferent, with her manner bordering on obstructive. Yet the more Brenda reflected on their conversation, the angrier she became.

Although the daughter of one of her closest friends, Brenda had never taken to Rachel. As a child, she was cold and aloof, possessing one of the most glacial stares Brenda had ever come across in one so young. Rachel was capable of looking straight through you, with utter disdain, as if you were inconsequential. Even now, speaking to her on the phone, her words came over as cool and dispassionate, as if talking about strangers rather than relating her own parents' tragic misfortunes. The girl had all but accused Brenda of having a morbid curiosity. She shuddered at the thought.

Over the years of their friendship, Alice had confided some of the child's history with Brenda. What they knew of her background was sketchy and therefore some problems were to be anticipated. However, during the years the girl lived with Tom and Alice, Brenda witnessed much love and affection lavished upon Rachel that Brenda's sympathy for the girl dwindled. In her opinion, she should be grateful for the upbringing and advantages which her adoptive parents so willingly provided, yet this was never so. Alice often confided how she struggled to maintain any kind of relationship with her daughter during those formative years, especially after Jenny died.

Brenda understood all too well how the tragedy of losing her sister would affect Rachel, but she also knew that such a loss, devastating though it may be, shouldn't be allowed to define the rest of your life. Rachel was a grown woman. It was time to let go of her pain, or at least not to allow it to colour the rest of her life.

When Brenda's son, Harry, had died, she'd thought she'd never recover, in fact, initially, she didn't want to, but for the sake of her husband and their other two children and with Alice's help, she came through that harrowing time and very slowly picked up the threads of life once more.

The mutual experience of grief formed the early basis of Alice and Brenda's friendship, each finding in the other the confidante they needed. Though they were both married to good men, Tom's work necessitated that he was away a great deal, and Ian simply wasn't one to talk about his feelings. Realising her husband wouldn't cope well with her angst as well as his own, Brenda largely remained silent about her feelings, battling against the often-overwhelming depression and only ever crying when she was alone. Therefore, friendship with Alice was a blessing and grew into a solid and lasting bond; until Alice and Tom decided to move to Penrith to be nearer to Rachel, or more accurately, nearer to Millie.

Brenda was aware of Alice's constant worry about her grandchild, her deep concern for the child's welfare, a little girl whom she didn't see nearly as much as she would have wished. Retirement for her and Tom presented the opportunity to become more proactive in Millie's care, or could do if Rachel would allow it.

Brenda remembered the time, six years earlier, when Rachel told her parents that she was pregnant. She'd asked Alice who the father was and if a wedding would be happening soon. Sadly, Alice admitted that her daughter refused to name the father. He was apparently no longer in the picture. The two friends then speculated about the pregnancy, with Brenda trying to cheer Alice, suggesting that Rachel might have used a sperm donor. After laughing at the thought, both women agreed that it could be the case. Rachel would most certainly want to be in control, to know the history, intelligence and physical appearance of any possible donor. Yes, it was feasible, but one thing they were sure about was that Rachel would probably never tell them.

Brenda held reservations about the move to Penrith, upon which her friends were determined to embark. It was a huge undertaking, especially knowing that their relationship with their daughter was anything but close. It would surprise her if Rachel would concede and allow them any kind of active role in Millie's life. Still, Alice was determined, apparently unhappy about the childcare arrangements in place for her granddaughter.

This latest news devastated Brenda, but she was also experiencing anger. Anger on Alice's behalf at the unfairness of life, surely this family had suffered enough over the years, but also anger towards Rachel. The young woman showed very little compassion for her parents' plight, and her insistence that visitors would be more of a nuisance than a welcome distraction irritated her. Surely Alice at least might benefit from some outside stimulation and a familiar face?

Over the next few days, the conversation with Rachel sat heavily on Brenda's heart and she wavered over what to do. Alice was one of the best friends she'd ever known and had been so kind to her in her time of need. If there was any way to ease the poor woman's present situation, Brenda wished to do so. Rachel's acceptance of her mother's condition as permanent was also troubling. These events had occurred so rapidly that a definitive diagnosis seemed premature. Yes, Tom's stroke would most certainly have come as a shock, but perhaps Alice's reaction was only temporary.

Sadly, Brenda was uncertain that Rachel could be trusted to act in her mother's best interests, so at the risk of being labelled 'nosey', she decided to visit Alice at The Elms without telling Rachel.

The drive to Penrith was not unpleasant, yet Brenda would

have enjoyed it much more if her mind wasn't full of concern for Alice and Tom. She intended to go directly to The Elms to assess the situation for herself and then contact Rachel to let her know that she was in Penrith and wished to visit Tom. Having travelled so far, she hoped that the care home staff would allow her to visit, at least for a short while.

Not being the most confident of drivers, Brenda was grateful for the sat nav into which she'd programmed the details of The Elms from her search on the internet. Eventually, turning into the small car park, she sighed audibly and gratefully stepped out into the warm sunshine to stretch her stiff limbs.

It appeared to be a pleasant enough place. Brenda had expected more visible security from what Rachel implied, but the front doors stood open, as if in welcome, and a keypad offered a button to press with an intercom for visitors to gain access through an inner door. The door buzzed open without Brenda needing to explain the reason for her visit, and a pleasant receptionist greeted her inside the hall, asking if she could help. Brenda smiled at the young woman.

'Hello, I'm here to visit Alice Roberts. Can you tell me which room she's in, please?'

The receptionist looked puzzled for a moment before replying, 'I'm sorry, but Mrs Roberts left us over a week ago.'

Brenda's eyes widened. 'But her daughter told me she was here. Has she gone to another facility?'

'No, Mrs Roberts went home. I saw her into the taxi myself. I'm sorry you've had a wasted journey.'

'It appears I've got the wrong message... I'll visit Alice at home. Thank you for your help.'

The receptionist buzzed a somewhat perplexed Brenda out. She returned to her car, took her address book from her bag, looked up Alice's new address and fed the information into her sat nav. It seemed the village wasn't too far away, but she was unsure if she'd find Alice at home. On impulse, she decided to ring Rachel to find out what was going on, but the number went straight to voicemail.

'Rachel, it's Brenda here. I've just been to The Elms only to be told that your mother's at home. Can you ring me back when you get this message? I'm on my way to Melkinthorpe now, but I'd like to talk to you soon.' The message was perhaps rather abrupt, but Brenda was angry. What was Rachel playing at? She certainly hadn't given the impression that Alice was well enough to go home or would be soon, so what exactly was going on?

29

The message on her phone came as a shock to Rachel, jolting her out of her reverie about the meeting she'd just attended. It landed on her phone nearly an hour earlier, so it was pointless to try to return the call and stall her mother's friend. Brenda would almost certainly be with Alice by now. With a degree of trepidation, Rachel could only imagine their conversation.

An interfering friend was the last thing she needed, or indeed anticipated, and the consequences of Brenda meeting up with Alice could, and most probably would, ruin everything. She listened again to the message, to the barely veiled anger in the woman's voice and Rachel knew she needed to act quickly. Was it all over, or could she still salvage something of her plan?

Dashing into the pharmacy, Rachel instructed her deputy, Pauline, to take charge for the rest of the day. Without allowing the woman to question the sudden change in routine, Rachel hurriedly left the shop to go to Millie's school.

In a blind panic, Rachel risked parking on double yellow lines, knowing she'd be in and out before the traffic wardens made their usual afternoon trawl of the streets surrounding the primary school. Impatiently ringing the buzzer on the intercom system, she tapped her foot, cursing herself for not foreseeing Brenda's actions and being remiss in letting slip the name of the home in which her mother had been.

When the secretary's voice came over the intercom, Rachel garbled an excuse for picking Millie up early, saying that her mother had been taken ill and they needed to travel to see her. The anxiety in her voice gained her immediate entry and the secretary led Rachel straight to Millie's classroom, oozing sympathy and attributing the young woman's detached aura to worry.

The atmosphere in her daughter's school always brought memories flooding back to Rachel's mind, memories of Jenny, and those fleeting years of happiness. Jenny had loved school with infectious enthusiasm. Her boundless energy made her a popular child with both teachers and other pupils.

But Jenny had belonged only to Rachel.

Theirs was a special relationship.

At times they needed no words to communicate. The bond between them was so strong and exclusive that even their parents could see that Jenny belonged more to Rachel than she did to them, which was why they had to pay for what they'd done, for taking Jenny away from her.

Millie looked up from her work as her teacher called her name, looking both surprised and disturbed at her mother's unexpected presence. It was even more confusing when she heard the secretary tell her mummy that she hoped her mother would soon be better.

'Are we going to see Grandma?' Millie asked, hope rising within her chest as Rachel bundled her into the car.

'No. Now don't ask questions; we need to get home quickly.'

Millie was used to not asking questions and so sat silently in the back of the car, not daring to tell her mother that in their rush, she'd forgotten her school bag.

Arriving at their home after the short, silent journey, Rachel unlocked the door and headed straight for the kitchen, her daughter trailing meekly behind.

'I need you to take some of your special medicine, Millie, and you can have extra today as Mummy has lots of things to do.' She opened the cupboard and took out the bottle of liquid that Millie so detested. It tasted awful and the child knew that it would make her feel quite sick and dizzy. She didn't understand why she was to take extra but didn't dare to ask another question.

The little girl dutifully swallowed the clear foul-tasting medicine and went to sit on the sofa as she'd been told, pleased to see her doll Dorothy was there, waiting for her. Millie grasped the doll close to her chest and tucked her knees up, careful to remove her shoes first. Her mother didn't seem to notice what she was doing; she was busy searching for something, and then disappeared upstairs.

Within an hour, Rachel managed to pack all the essentials into a large suitcase which she then dragged downstairs. With everything necessary done, she took a last long look at her home, almost certain she would never see it again. It was comfortable and quiet and her life was orderly, just how she liked it. Rachel had always been content there. The trappings of her success lay around her, comfortable furnishings, a few original pieces of artwork, bought as investments, and the expensive clothes she so enjoyed the feel of next to her skin. Now all she could take with her was the contents of one case.

Rachel glanced at her daughter, who had slipped into a deep sleep, and felt nothing. No love, compassion or even pity for the unwanted child.

Lifting the slight limp body, she carried the girl upstairs and laid her on the bed in the little back bedroom, bolting the door on the way out, from habit rather than necessity.

To Rachel's mind, it was all her parents' fault; everything wrong in her life could be traced back to them. They provoked everything she'd been forced to do over these last few weeks.

It was only fair they should suffer.

They deserved it.

It was justice for Jenny.

Yet now, things were beginning to go wrong. Rachel's well-executed plans were collapsing like a house of cards.

Rachel locked the front door and climbed back into her car, setting off in a southerly direction, as yet without a fully formed plan, other than to get as far away from Penrith as possible.

It was not the way events should have worked out and she was angry at the unexpected glitches which had occurred, angry at Brenda, her mother and herself for not anticipating this hitch, just when everything had been running so smoothly.

Rachel assumed the most challenging part of her scheme was over. All the effort, time and planning were about to pay off. But now, it looked as if it was all falling to pieces when the whole matter should have been tidily wrapped up. But she would survive. Life had taught her how. With her natural resilience, Rachel was confident she could start over again somewhere else, this time entirely unencumbered by family.

30

Melkinthorpe appeared to be more of a hamlet than a village to Brenda, but she could certainly see its attraction as she drove past pretty stone-built cottages sprawled alongside the narrow roads; it was a beautiful area. The gardens were at their brilliant best too, set off by the afternoon sunshine, and the scent of newly mown grass wafted through the open car window. Her sat nav guided Brenda to the south of the village, past a sign for Melkinthorpe Hall and a large wooded area, beyond which, her device informed her, was the river Leith. Alice's cottage was a property standing on its own, just off the main road and she pulled tentatively onto the drive, trusting she had the correct address.

The attractive double-fronted cottage reminded Brenda of Alice and Tom's home in Matlock, although much smaller and certainly in a quieter spot. The thought that perhaps subconsciously, they'd chosen a similar home as the one they'd loved and left crossed her mind as she parked her car in front of the garage. Brenda grabbed her bag from the passenger seat and threw open the door, anxious to see Alice and hopefully learn the answers to some rather troubling questions.

When she heard the sound of someone coming to answer the doorbell, Brenda almost shouted *'hallelujah'*, and as the door opened, just a crack at first, relief flooded through her as she found herself facing a startled and nervous-looking Alice. Her friend looked pale and had lost a considerable amount of weight since they'd last been together, but a smile lit up her face and tears glistened in her eyes at the sight of her friend on her doorstep.

'Brenda! What are you doing here? I thought you were in Australia?'

Brenda scowled. 'Why would I be in Australia?'

'Rachel said you were visiting Chloe for three months...' Alice looked confused but stood aside to allow her friend to enter her home. The two women hugged then stood back to look at each other properly.

'I think Rachel has a lot to answer for.' Brenda frowned. 'She told me that you were in The Elms, permanently, after a breakdown.'

'What? No, I was in there for a few weeks, but I'm home now and much better, as you can see. Come through to the kitchen and tell me when you spoke to Rachel.'

Alice led Brenda through the house to the kitchen, automatically putting the kettle on to boil. It was as if they'd never been apart and the ease of their friendship, picked up again so readily, comforted both women. Brenda took in the generously sized farmhouse style room with the window overlooking open countryside. The kitchen door stood open and the sounds of birds drifted in on the scent of roses. It could have been an idyllic setting for Alice's retirement, but things seemed to have gone badly wrong. Brenda wondered if she should ask about Tom or wait for Alice to tell her in her own time. She accepted the tea placed before her and smiled.

'So, you're feeling much better now then? Why didn't you let me know you were home? I could have come sooner.'

'I would have, but my address book seems to have got lost in the move and I couldn't remember your phone number.' Alice didn't like to admit that she'd hardly been able to remember her own name at times.

'You could have emailed?' Brenda suggested.

'Ah, that's another story. I seem to have deleted all my contacts on the laptop too. Things have been so strange lately, but I really am much better. So, did Rachel get it wrong then? Have you been to Australia?'

'No, Alice, that was never on the cards. Chloe lives in London, not Australia.' Brenda's brow furrowed again. Perhaps her friend was still confused.

'I thought so, but I'm sure that's what Rachel told me...'

'Don't worry about it, I'm here now and if it's okay with you, I can stay for a few days. I brought an overnight bag expecting to stay one night in a hotel somewhere, but now that you're home, we can spend a bit of time together. But I might need to borrow a change of clothes?'

'That would be lovely. I've missed you so much and it's quite lonely here at times.'

'Don't you see much of Rachel then?'

'She rings each morning to check up on me, but quite honestly, we've not seen eye to eye lately, ever since I went into The Elms. She wanted me to stay there, but I'm not as bad as my daughter seems to think I am.'

'What do you mean by 'bad', Alice? What exactly has been the problem?'

'At first, the doctors thought it was a stroke, but it wasn't. Then they thought dementia, which it probably is, but Sarah assures me that there are people much worse than me who can still live independently. What did Rachel tell you?'

'She did mention dementia but said you'd had a complete breakdown... who's Sarah?'

'A volunteer at The Elms, but she's become a friend since then. She's a lovely lady, a policeman's wife and so caring. I can talk to her when I can't talk to Rachel, which sadly is most of the time.' Alice looked thoughtful before asking her friend what was on her mind. 'Brenda, do you know who Millie is?'

'Of course! She's your granddaughter and the reason you and Tom moved here.' Brenda was confused now and found it difficult to assess just what her friend's state of mind really was.

'Did you say Tom?' Alice almost dropped the cup she was holding. Her face paled and tears again clouded her eyes. 'Rachel told me that Tom died four years ago – from a heart attack and that I don't have a granddaughter...'

'Alice, you're not making any sense. Rachel wouldn't say those things, surely? Tom's in hospital. He's had a stroke, don't you remember?'

Alice's hand flew to her mouth. 'And I suppose Rachel told you that!' She was suddenly furious as her mind raced and things started to fall into place.

'I'm going to ring Sarah; I want you to meet her.' Alice left a very puzzled Brenda in the kitchen and went to telephone her friend. At least Sarah would back her up as to what Rachel had, or hadn't, said.

'Here, look at this!' Alice returned from making her call and thrust a piece of paper into Brenda's hands. After reading the front page, Brenda felt quite nauseous and gasped.

'But what's this? Where did you get it?' She was shocked to read the order of service for Tom's funeral, dated four years previously.

'Can't you guess? Rachel! Tom isn't in hospital after a stroke, it appears he's missing. I don't know what my daughter's playing at, but I'm going to find out. Sarah's coming straight over, and when you've heard what she has to say, I'd like you to come with me to visit Rachel. She's certainly got some explaining to do.'

While they waited for Sarah, the two women speculated on why Rachel had been deliberately lying, but the biggest concern to Alice was where Tom and Millie were.

Since leaving The Elms, Alice hadn't visited Rachel's house. There seemed no point as she'd accepted that Millie was just a figment of her supposedly muddled mind. Now, however, all previous concerns about her granddaughter's welfare resurfaced and her head throbbed with the shocking knowledge that Rachel was deceiving and manipulating Alice. How could she be so cruel, so heartless? But what about Tom? Dare Alice hope that her husband was still alive and if so, where was he?

When Sarah arrived and quick introductions made, Alice asked Brenda to tell her new friend about Millie. Sarah's face drained of all colour as she listened to this woman confirming that Rachel Roberts actually did have a daughter called Millie. Alice wasn't confused. She was right all along – Brenda had even met the child on a couple of occasions.

'Now tell her about Tom.' Alice's voice was breaking, there was so much to process and she felt exhausted with the effort and the painful knowledge that her daughter had so callously deceived her.

'The last time I saw Tom was a week or two before they moved here from Matlock.' Brenda confirmed. 'He came round with Alice to have a meal with Ian and me. He was as fit as I'd ever seen him and looking forward to retirement.'

'But Rachel told us at The Elms that Tom died four years ago, and she certainly denied having a daughter! She almost bit my head off for believing Alice. Tell me, was Alice a teacher at Matlock Primary school?'

'Yes, and a rather brilliant one too! Look, it's quite obvious that Rachel's the one who's living in a fantasy land, not poor Alice. That girl's told lie upon lie until it's almost impossible to know the truth, but the question now is what do we do about it? I know Alice wants to go round and confront her but is that the best thing to do?' Brenda and Alice both looked to Sarah, who was still reeling with the incredible knowledge of Rachel's deceit.

'I feel out of my depth here and can't advise you but I don't think it would be wise to confront Rachel. If she's capable of such deception, who knows what else she's capable of? Alice, would you mind if I rang Jack and asked him to come and see you?'

'Not at all, it would be such a relief to hear his advice. Sarah, do you think Tom might still be alive?'

31

The wait for Jack Priestly seemed interminable. Alice grew increasingly agitated, picking up the telephone several times to ring her daughter but being persuaded by her friends to wait until Jack came. She paced the room, wringing her hands, first worrying about Tom and then about Millie. Two questions vied for their unavailable answers in her mind: why and how. Why had Rachel done this, and then how?

Alice hardly dared to hope that Tom could still be alive. She was only just getting used to the idea of his death. But if Tom was alive, where was he and why hadn't he moved heaven and earth to see her? Part of her didn't dare to hope to see her husband again, yet hope was all Alice had left. She clung to it as an anchor to ground her, to strengthen her for whatever the truth might be. Some of the strange happenings of the last few weeks suddenly began to fall into place in Alice's mind.

'Sarah, do you think Rachel could have been the one sending all those parcels?'

'Sadly, yes, I think that's quite likely. Rachel would have access to your debit card so it wouldn't have taken much effort. I did wonder about some of the other weird happenings, like your handbag and shoes in the bin? That happened just after Rachel's visit, didn't it? It seems your daughter's been on a mission to make you think that you were losing your mind. I'm so sorry; this must be very difficult for you to take in.'

Alice simply nodded, her mind spinning with questions.

Brenda, clearly horrified at the cruelties her friend had suffered at Rachel's hand asked, 'But where's Tom? I think I'm missing something here; do you think he could be in a hospital somewhere and for some reason Rachel's keeping that from you? It's all so confusing.'

'I think that's another of her lies; a story invented to keep you away.'

There was no time to discuss the possibility as they heard a car pull up outside and a measure of relief lifted the mood as Jack Priestly rang the bell. Sarah let him in, pausing in the hallway to briefly outline more of the situation before introducing him to both women. Jack shook hands with them, Alice's hand trembling in his.

Jack asked several questions designed to grasp the complete picture of what had been happening. Sarah sat, holding Alice's hand as the frightened woman recalled some harrowing incidents.

'What I want to know is if all these lies Rachel has told constitute a crime?' Brenda interrupted, angry and frustrated with the appalling facts she'd so recently learned.

'Yes, there are certainly several things we can charge her with: conspiring to have her mother held against her will, even harassment if we can prove she sent the parcels. But some of her actions are not specific crimes, like maintaining she didn't have a daughter and that her mother was never a teacher. However, my primary concern, for now, is the welfare of the child. I want to check up on Millie if you could give me an address, Alice, and we'll look into the whereabouts of your husband too. Mrs

Chapman has confirmed that he was alive and well when you left Matlock, for which we'll need a formal statement sometime soon.' Jack looked at Brenda, who nodded vigorously, clearly eager to help.

'And as far as you're aware, Alice, Tom was living here with you when you moved?' Alice nodded too and Jack continued.

'Rachel is the key to this whole mystery. I need to speak to her as soon as possible. So, if you're happy to report your husband as a missing person, I can get a warrant and visit Rachel's home in the next few hours.'

'Yes, please... Do you think Tom might be there?'

'It's too early to say as yet, but if I can question Rachel, she might tell us exactly what's going on. I'm going to make a few calls to arrange a warrant and then leave you here. I'm sure Sarah will stay as long as you want her to.' His wife smiled her agreement.

'I would ask, though, that you don't try to contact Rachel. The element of surprise will give us the advantage and it's best if she doesn't know that we're coming.'

'Oh, no!' Brenda gasped. 'I think I've probably ruined your chances of that. I rang Rachel when I was on my way here and left a rather angry message to say I was visiting Alice at home.' Brenda clearly regretted her earlier phone call, but it couldn't be undone. She'd unwittingly warned Rachel that her lies were about to be discovered.

'Don't worry about it, Mrs Chapman. If we find the property empty, we'll have good cause to enter it and search for signs of Tom and Millie. It may even be that I don't need that warrant after all.'

Jack made the calls and left. It was early evening and Brenda insisted on making something for them all to eat, even if it was only a sandwich. The three women could be in for a long night and being faint from hunger would help no one.

~

Alice made a half-hearted effort to eat, constantly listening for the telephone in case DI Priestly rang to update them.

'It won't happen quickly,' Sarah explained. 'But he'll ring as soon as there's anything to report.'

'I know and I'm sorry to have dragged your family into all this...'

'Don't be. It's Jack's job and I'm only too happy to help. But sadly, I believed Rachel's lies too, Alice when I should have accepted that you were right, and I'm sorry for that.'

'Why *wouldn't* you believe her? She even convinced me in the end. My daughter seems to be a very accomplished liar. But Tom, and that fake order of service, how could she be so cruel? Does she hate me so much?' Alice spoke with sadness more than anger and then lapsed into silence, offering a prayer for the best outcome there could be.

PART III

THE INVESTIGATION

32

DI Priestly gathered his team in record time. DC Claire Swift met him at Rachel Roberts' address, with DS Owen Hardy and two uniformed officers. The stone-built end terraced house was in an affluent area of Penrith, a large family property over three floors, which appeared to be well-maintained, as did the neighbouring properties. It seemed a large house for a single woman and a child, but Rachel was already something of an enigma to Jack. He rather relished the chance to interview her and find out exactly what made the woman tick.

Unsurprisingly, the property appeared empty but Jack, supposing there could be a child at risk, decided not to wait for a warrant and proceed inside. The team affected their entry rapidly and began a quick search of the rooms. Claire Swift and the uniformed officers took the first and second floors while Jack and Owen Hardy scanned downstairs.

The lounge was beautifully furnished, show home standard and almost unnaturally tidy. If a child did live here, there was very little evidence of her. Jack remembered when his boys were little; their home never seemed tidy, with signs of their presence in every room. This room wasn't sparse enough to be minimalist but very modern with a few tasteful and presumably expensive objects d'art. A bronze figurine caught Jack's eye; it was of two little girls, the elder one shielding her eyes whilst gazing into the distance. Her free hand held the younger child, who was looking up with an expression of adoration. Both girls' features were finely sculpted and similar enough to be sisters. It was an enchanting piece, one of many.

A doll lay on the floor beside the sofa, a single abandoned toy, the only clue that Millie had ever been there. He picked it up and turned it over in his hands. It was an old-fashioned rag doll, obviously well-loved and worn in several places. He imagined the little girl must have had it since she was a baby.

Next, Jack searched an understairs cupboard, always bracing himself for whatever he might find, while DS Hardy went through to the kitchen and utility room. It was only a few moments before an anxious shout from upstairs caused them to break into a run.

On the first floor, Jack hurried into an open bedroom to find DC Swift leaning over the motionless body of a child on the bed.

'She's alive, but her pulse is very weak,' Claire said, trying to rouse the girl. Owen Hardy was already on the phone for an ambulance, urgently barking out the address's details and the little girl's condition. The others were right behind them and Jack sent one of the officers outside to await the ambulance while he looked around the room. He'd noticed a bolt on the outside of the door, not something you'd usually expect on a five-year-old's bedroom, and, in comparison to the living room he'd just left, this room was positively spartan.

The walls were drab, with washed-out curtains hanging at the window. A narrow bed, a chest of drawers and a single wardrobe were the only furnishings, with a small pile of books on the floor in the corner. Surely, Jack thought, this couldn't be Millie's room. Again, his mind briefly drifted back to when Jake and Dan were that age, the football-themed wallpaper in their rooms, the teddies that smothered their beds, games, books, and posters everywhere. This room sent a shiver through him and he hoped they'd find another, proper little girl's bedroom when they resumed their search.

'Was this room bolted from the outside, Claire?' Jack asked.

'Yes, sir, it was...' Claire's eyes sparkled with tears as she cradled Millie in her arms, still gently trying to rouse her. Passion always crept into a case when children were involved, ensuring the team remained motivated and worked hard.

DC Swift went with Millie in the ambulance. The paramedics were reassuring as to her condition. It appeared that some kind of sedative had been administered – tests would be performed at the hospital to determine precisely what the substance was.

Jack rang Alice to tell her they'd found her granddaughter and that she was safely on her way to the hospital. Trying to be truthful without upsetting Alice, he said that the child was found unconscious, but the paramedics were hopeful. After finishing the conversation, he and his team continued searching the rest of the house.

The top floor consisted of two empty rooms, used only for storage, while the three bedrooms on the first floor were entirely different. The master bedroom was every bit as elegant as the downstairs rooms, with plush carpet, new fitted furniture and an immaculate en suite. Rachel's wardrobe was still quite full with indications of hasty packing, so it seemed that she'd not taken much with her. The second bedroom appeared not to be in use with no evidence of it being for a child, so Jack could only assume that the room they'd found Millie in was her bedroom.

The family bathroom was also pristine, probably recently refurbished. The only item of interest was an exceptionally large number of drugs in a cabinet, partly concealed behind a hefty mirror. The DI decided to have them all bagged and taken away for analysis.

Back downstairs, Owen Hardy was busy searching an office and collecting various papers which might prove helpful.

'No laptop or passport so far, boss,' he said before pulling out more drawers. Jack nodded; Rachel would probably have taken those with her. There were an address book and a mobile phone in a desk drawer, which on examination, Jack believed to belong to Alice. He decided to leave the search for the time being and get back to the station. A crime scene investigation team would perform a more detailed search the following day. With the state they'd found the girl in and the fact that Tom Roberts was still unaccounted for, Jack's priority was to find Rachel Roberts, so they sealed the house as a possible crime scene and left.

On his way back to the station, Jack took a call from Claire Swift.

'I'm at the hospital, boss and it's good news. Millie's going to be fine!' Jack could hear the relief in Claire's voice and imagined her smile. 'It seems she's ingested a large amount of a drug to make her sleep. They haven't identified exactly what yet, but with Rachel being a pharmacist and presumably knowing what she was doing, it appears her intention wasn't to kill the child. Still, she abandoned her daughter, drugged her to keep her quiet and locked her up not knowing when she'd be found. It's unbelievable! Who knows what might have happened if you hadn't decided on a search?

'Mrs Roberts and her friend are here now and intend to stay the night, even though Millie will probably sleep for some time, so I'll get off for the night. It'll be lovely for her to have her grandmother there when she wakes, if Mrs Roberts can stop crying!'

Jack thanked Claire. He assumed that Sarah would have gone home when Alice left for the hospital; he'd ring her later. Goodness only knew when he'd get home.

33

At midnight, Jack finally left the station to go home. When Sarah had alerted him to Alice's situation, he'd already finished an eight-hour shift, so was bone-tired, yet content to know that he'd done all he could for the time being. Everything possible was in place and the search for Rachel Roberts had begun in earnest.

Jack remembered his previous scepticism as to Alice's state of mind with some regret, he'd been too quick to assume Rachel was telling the truth and Alice was confused; with his experience of human nature, he should have known better and kept an open mind. He hadn't taken Sarah's concerns seriously either although he knew his wife to be an intelligent, discerning woman. Yet regrets were something Jack spent little time on worrying about. He would learn from them and move on to do his job to the best of his ability, as he always did.

Thoughts of his home and wife crept into his mind. Jack was confident that Sarah would be waiting up to find out what had transpired, and, after telling her, he could hopefully sink into bed for a few hours' sleep before the search resumed early the following day.

Sarah was in the lounge, her feet up on the sofa, dozing. The sound of her husband's key in the lock made her jump, suddenly wide awake and fully alert.

'Any news?' She wrapped her arms around Jack and leaned her head on his shoulder.

'No, it's too early, but we'll find her. How about you, are you okay?'

'A bit numb, but nothing compared to what poor Alice is feeling. It's enough to make anyone doubt what's real and what isn't. It's incredible that Rachel could do that to her mother, and as for her father...'

'I know, it's hard to believe, but everything's pure speculation at the moment. Tomorrow we'll get straight back onto the search for Tom Roberts. I've added his details to the national computer for missing persons, so the wheels are already turning. I'll need to interview Alice formally too, as soon as possible. Do you think she'll be up to it?'

'If it brings her any closer to knowing what's happened to Tom, yes, and having Brenda there will help too. Alice intended to stay at the hospital with Millie overnight if they'd let her. Do you think if Millie's well enough to be discharged, Alice will be able to take her home tomorrow?'

'We'll have to get social services involved before anyone can make that decision. It becomes a child protection issue now, but I would imagine there shouldn't be a problem because she's the girl's grandmother. Officially, Detective Superintendent Kerr will be the SIO, but he's happy to let me take charge, at least until we know what kind of case we're looking at.' Jack was keen to take this case on board and already felt a strong connection to it through Sarah.

'I learned quite a bit more about Alice's background tonight, from her and from Brenda.'

'Go on. I'm listening.' Any background information was

useful. By this time, the couple was seated on the sofa, Jack's arm around his wife, her head on his shoulder as she spoke.

'Rachel Roberts is adopted. Not because Alice and Tom couldn't have children but because they wanted to share their home and their love with a baby who needed a fresh start in life. They did have another daughter, their natural child, Jenny, who was killed in a car crash when she was seven.'

'No, that's awful... losing a child of that age is unthinkable.'

'That's only the half of it. Alice's brother-in-law drove the car, and her sister and their daughter were also in it. They'd taken Jenny on an outing with them and all four died in the accident.'

A palpable silence hung in the air as Jack and Sarah contemplated such tragedy.

'I don't know how Alice has coped – and now, for all this to happen, it's inconceivable. We're so blessed, Jack, to have each other and the boys...'

'Absolutely. And if it turns out that Tom is dead, how will the poor woman cope?'

'It seems Alice's relationship with Rachel never recovered from the loss of Jenny. The sisters were very close and Rachel would have been on the outing herself except for a nasty case of chickenpox.' Sarah continued while Jack's thoughts drifted back to the bronze statue in Rachel's home of the two young girls, sisters, and the significance it might hold for Rachel.

'Apparently,' Sarah went on, 'Alice and Brenda's friendship developed out of mutual loss. Brenda lost her son when he was twelve. He fell down the stairs at school. You can see how the bond developed between them. Such heartbreak is unimaginable, isn't it?' Sarah paused and silently noted the sadness and empathy in her husband's face.

Sarah continued, 'I'm struggling to understand Rachel. How can she hate her parents so much and why is she doing this? Do you know, at one point this evening, Alice asked Brenda if they still had Barney, their dog, when they'd moved to Penrith and Brenda said yes, they had. We were stunned at the implication – there's been no sign of the dog as well as Tom. If Rachel Roberts has got rid of her mother's pet dog, I think I can agree with Brenda's assessment of her. She described her as an evil bitch!'

These were not words or sentiments that Sarah would usually express and Jack was a little taken aback. Still, he was having difficulty subduing the strength of his feelings about this whole situation and could perfectly well understand his wife's heightened emotions.

'Tomorrow, the search for Rachel can begin in earnest. I set up an all-ports alert before I left the station, and we'll begin a CCTV search for any sightings of her car from mid to late afternoon today, starting with when she left the school with Millie. As I say, I need to speak to Alice tomorrow, but for now, it's been a long day, so I think perhaps it's time for bed.'

'I know she's got Brenda with her, but tell Alice that I'm here for her if she needs anything, will you, Jack?'

Jack kissed his wife on the forehead and pulled her up from the sofa. They were both tired and emotionally exhausted. Hopefully, a few hours' sleep would revive them for the following day's numerous, unpleasant tasks.

34

Alice sat by Millie's bed, holding her tiny limp hand. *How could I ever have doubted her very existence?* she asked herself. But she knew the answer. The blame for everything which had transpired of late lay solely at Rachel's feet.

Sarah had gone home the previous evening when the news that they'd found Millie came through. Brenda initially accompanied Alice to the hospital but was persuaded to go back to Melkinthorpe to sleep. It'd been such a trying day and the strain was beginning to show in both women. The nurse suggested that Alice might like to go home too, but having found her granddaughter, she couldn't bear to leave her again and so they brought pillows and endless cups of tea to make her comfortable.

A doctor explained that Millie would sleep through the night and probably be quite groggy the next day. They'd taken blood from the sleeping child. Further tests would establish precisely what drugs she'd been given and if there would be any long-term effects on her organs. Alice silently prayed that Millie would recover fully but was acutely aware that the psychological effects of recent events might have a more lasting impact on her granddaughter than the physical.

Would Millie be surprised to see her when she woke, she wondered. For all Alice knew, Rachel might have told the child that she was dead. She wouldn't put anything past her daughter now.

The concerns that she and Tom had felt for Millie's welfare floated into her mind and out again, the reasons they'd moved, the actions she'd been going to take – it was still a bit hazy, yet in there somewhere. And then there was Tom. Alice hardly dared to think about Tom. Where was he? Was he alive, and if so, why had he not come to her? The answer to the question in itself almost convinced her that her husband must be dead, but how and when? It was too dark and painful to contemplate.

Alice must have dozed off in the chair and awoke when a nurse came in to take Millie's blood pressure and other vital signs.

'The doctor should know the results of the blood samples we took last night when he comes round later,' the young nurse told her. 'Would you like to freshen up before your granddaughter wakes?'

Alice took the opportunity to do so, returning quickly and just in time to see the little girl begin to stir.

As Millie opened her eyes, fear and confusion crossed her pale, sad face, but on seeing her grandma, she reached up from the bed and snaked her arms around Alice's neck. Nestling into the warm thin little body, Alice found it difficult to hold herself together, but she knew that somehow, she would find the strength to do whatever was necessary to protect this child in the future. The two clung together in silence for a few moments until Millie pulled away.

'Where's Mummy?' she asked.

'She's gone away for a little while, but I'm here to look after you now.' It was the best explanation Alice could think of at the time.

Millie looked around the unfamiliar room, 'Where are we, Grandma?'

'We're in the hospital, sweetheart. You were poorly, but the doctor's made you better and he might even let us go home today.'

A look of unease flitted across Millie's eyes. 'To Mummy's house?'

'No, to my house. Would you like that?'

Millie smiled, the colour returning to her cheeks. 'Will Granddad be there, and Barney?'

Alice swallowed hard to keep her tears at bay. 'No, my love, it'll just be you and me. We can do anything you want to do, bake cakes, go to the park or read stories, anything.'

'Shall I get dressed now?' Millie attempted to get out of bed, but her grandmother patiently explained that they needed to see the doctor first. The little girl was about to ask more questions but became distracted by the breakfast trolley arriving, and she took delight in the novelty of the little cartons of orange juice and being able to choose whatever she wanted to eat.

It would, no doubt, be a long day. Alice had no idea if she'd be allowed to take Millie home after the doctor discharged her. But why not? She was the child's grandmother, and Rachel had abandoned her, hadn't she?

Alice was tired after the traumatic events of the previous day. Sleep had been fitful and peppered with dreams and scenarios, which, in the light of day, she tried hard to shake off. The realisation that her daughter was capable of attempting to have her placed in a home, inventing such horrendous lies and abandoning her own child, was too much to comprehend, and what else had Rachel done? Dispelling such unbearable thoughts, Alice turned her attention back to Millie. The child needed reassurance and love, and her grandmother determined that she would be the one to offer it.

35

DC Claire Swift spent the early part of her morning liaising with social services and replaced the phone after talking to a rather harassed social worker. The woman had visited Millie and her grandmother at the hospital. She informed Claire that they'd decided to release the little girl into her grandmother's care after an initial assessment of the situation. There was no surprise there, Claire thought, they had more cases on their hands than available staffing to cope with them, but she knew they would continue to monitor Millie's welfare and step in if necessary. Claire made her way through to the DI's office to tell him the good news.

Claire also had her hands full working on the disclosure of their suspect, digging back as far as possible in an attempt to pick up anything which could be relevant or shed light on the whereabouts of Rachel Roberts. But for now, in preparation to accompany the DI on his interview, she'd put the disclosure on hold to build up a timeline of the last few weeks' events regarding Alice and her daughter.

A hastily set up incident room in Hunter's Lane had been buzzing all morning, identifying any possible lines of enquiry.

Computers and whiteboards were brought in – it was the kind of frenzied activity Penrith station rarely saw. Paperwork, recovered from Rachel Roberts' house, provided some vital information. They now knew which bank she used and the details of her credit cards, which had been logged into the system. If she tried to make a withdrawal at any cash machine, it would be flagged up. They'd also contacted her telephone provider, and the number was being monitored. Using triangulation from masts nationwide, if Rachel used her phone, they would again be made aware of her general whereabouts.

DS Owen Hardy was tasked with searching the CCTV from around the school and Rachel's house in order to add to the timeline. Her car number plate had also been fed into the Automatic Number Plate Recognition system, and if she were driving on any major roads or motorways, ANPR would pick up the vehicle.

All this technology made life easier in many ways, but there were still many variables to consider. Rachel might decide to abandon her car and hire another. She could have an account with a building society and have had the presence of mind to take her passbook and access money without using a bank. Jack could do little more than put everything possible in place to find her and hopefully discover where Tom Roberts was. Sadly, the crime scene investigation manager had found no physical evidence of their missing person ever having been in Rachel's house, but some DNA samples were yet to be processed.

By late morning, Jack Priestly was ready to visit Alice Roberts. He'd heard from the hospital that Millie was fully recovered and had been discharged, so the pair were back home in Melkinthorpe. As he left the station with Claire Swift, she handed him a piece of paper detailing the various drugs they'd discovered in Rachel's house the previous evening. In return, he gave the keys for the pool car to his DC for her to drive while he studied the list.

Jack was familiar with a few of the names on the list. Zopiclone had been prescribed to his wife after an illness that left her unable to sleep. He remembered how drowsy it made her feel, and she quickly stopped taking them, unwilling to feel so spaced out all the time. If a small dosage could affect Sarah in such a way, what must it be doing to Millie if that was the drug Rachel had given her?

Another thought occurred to Jack and he turned to Claire. 'Did you ring the hospitals to check on any admissions that could match Tom Roberts?'

'Yes and no. There are no patients of that name and none matching his age and description either. Sorry, boss, another blank.' Claire and Jack lapsed into silence.

Their first stop was at Rachel's house and Jack used a set of keys which they'd picked up the night before to let himself in, taking only a few minutes to collect what he wanted before they were on their way again.

A somewhat frazzled-looking Brenda Chapman answered the door and led them through to the kitchen where Alice could be seen in the garden, playing with Millie, their heads close together as they studied something in the flower bed. When they saw their visitors, Alice brought her granddaughter inside. Now that Claire could see her properly, she was struck by what a pretty little girl she was, petite and waif-like, with beautiful red hair and green eyes. But she looked pale and tired, as did her grandmother. Brenda took the child's hand and suggested that they go back outside to pick some daisies. Millie dutifully turned to do as she was told, without speaking a word.

'How is she?' Claire asked when the three of them were alone in the lounge.

'Quiet and confused, but she's used to accepting things for what they are and seems quite happy to be here with me.'

'I'm sure she is.' Claire smiled and then looked to her boss to begin his interview.

'Alice,' Jack began, 'I know this is all very difficult for you and I'm sorry to have to intrude at a time like this, but I'd like you to tell me everything you remember about the last time you saw Tom. Claire will be making a few notes. Is that okay?'

'Yes, I'll try, but things are still a bit confused. Rachel's told me so much that isn't true I'm having problems sorting out the facts from her fiction. Before we start, can you tell me if you've any idea where Tom can be? Rachel did say he was in hospital, could that be true?'

'No, I'm sorry but we've checked every hospital in the area and there's no one of Tom's description there.'

Alice nodded, resigned to what she already suspected, took a deep breath and closed her eyes for a moment before opening them and beginning.

'Rachel came here for a meal, this I can be certain of as it was the evening of the seventh of June, my birthday. Not that we celebrate family birthdays, you know – since Jenny and Karen died – well, anyway, we'd invited her round particularly to discuss our concerns about Millie. She knew we were going to bring the matter up and our daughter wasn't pleased about it. You see, since we moved to Penrith, some of the things Millie's told us have been quite concerning. I think the childminder she was left with is an uncaring woman, to say the least. We also felt Rachel deliberately avoided contact between our granddaughter and us, which is certainly not what we want. I can't remember everything said during the meal, but the atmosphere was tense. Things didn't entirely develop into a full-blown row, but it came close to it because we were determined to discover what exactly was going on with Millie.

'Rachel brought wine, and although I'm not usually a big drinker, I had a couple of glasses, Dutch courage, you know? It made me feel quite ill and I remember Tom helping me to bed, telling me he'd sort things out with Rachel, and I wasn't to worry. I was so upset by then at how the conversation was going.

'The next thing I remember was waking up the following morning, with no sign of Tom in the house. At first, I assumed he'd taken Barney for his walk, but I rang Rachel when he didn't come home. She came round and insisted on calling the doctor before putting me to bed with a couple of aspirins, and I must have fallen asleep. When the doctor arrived, I felt worse, and by then, I couldn't even speak. Before long, I was in the hospital having tests and then everything seemed to be taken out of my hands, and I ended up in The Elms.' Alice looked exhausted from revisiting what was a traumatic experience, but the detectives needed to know more.

'Mrs Roberts, are you sure it was the evening of seventh June?' Claire looked up from taking her notes to ask her question.

'Yes, as I said, it was my birthday, but that was a coincidence. It certainly wasn't a celebration.'

'Thank you.' Claire smiled and looked down at her notebook again.

'You say Rachel gave you some aspirin? Can you be certain that's what they were?' Jack asked.

'Well, no. I assumed they were aspirin and took them. Rachel's a pharmacist, you see?' Alice looked at Jack, trying to read his thoughts. 'I've wondered about this since, and I think perhaps my daughter's been giving me something in an attempt to keep me pliant. The hospital tests couldn't find anything that caused my symptoms that day, and even at The Elms, I never received a proper diagnosis. It was only when I stopped taking the prescribed medication and Rachel's little 'treats' that I started to feel better. Do you think she's been drugging me, Jack?'

'I think it's something we have to consider. Rachel gave Millie medication to make her sleep, and we found an unusually large quantity of drugs at their house, so it is a strong possibility.'

'And what about Tom, did she drug him too?'

'I don't think it helps to speculate about what's happened to Tom, but we're doing everything we can to find your daughter in the hope that she'll be able to tell us where he is. What we need to do now is to build up a picture of Rachel, her life with Millie and her relationships, and what you've told me so far is pertinent. We're also going to have to talk to Millie sometime soon. There'll be a specialist safeguarding officer to do this, but perhaps you could prepare her for it if possible?' Alice nodded solemnly.

'Can you think of anywhere Rachel might go, to a friend perhaps or an old work colleague?'

'No, I'm sorry, and I know it's no help at all, but there's no one that Rachel's close to. Even at university, she never made friends, always content with her studies and her own company.'

'If you do think of anyone, or maybe a favourite place she likes to go to, please let us know. Now, could you tell me a little more about why you were concerned for Millie?'

'Rachel never visited us in Matlock and made it clear that we weren't welcome to visit her here. It didn't seem natural. On the few occasions when we insisted on coming north, it was usually easier to stay in a hotel and meet up with her and Millie for a meal somewhere. I think we only visited Rachel's house twice, and things just didn't feel right. It's hard to explain, but it didn't feel like a home. Millie didn't appear to know how to play with the toys we brought her, and she was forever looking to Rachel as if for approval. The poor child seemed afraid to do or say anything for fear it would be wrong and she'd be in trouble. The only time she became animated was when we asked about school, but she was cagey about her friends, apparently never socialising outside of school. You might think I'm paranoid, Jack, and most of this might seem trivial but I don't want Millie to become a loner like her mother. It's essential that she builds friendships.'

'I don't think you're paranoid at all, Alice and in an investigation nothing is trivial. Background information is the starting point and we need to know as much as possible about Rachel and your life with her.'

Alice attempted a smile and continued, 'On the rare occasions when I've spoken to Millie alone, she's told me about her childminder, a Mrs Palmer, a woman of whom she appears to be scared. This childminder seems to only ever feed her baked beans. Millie's not allowed to make any noise or 'mess', which is absurd. Millie's a good child and she should be allowed the freedom to play. I asked her if she'd told her mummy about Mrs Palmer and she said yes, but Mummy says she has to be a good girl for her; otherwise, she'd have no one to look after her! I know that children make up stories and exaggerate, but the thing is, Jack, I believe her. And I have my suspicions that Rachel might leave her in the house alone at times.'

Jack thought about the bolt on the outside of Millie's bedroom door. 'Have you ever been in Millie's bedroom, Alice?' he asked.

'No, we never got any further than the lounge. Sadly, I've never felt welcome or even comfortable in my daughter's home.'

The door opened at that point and Millie ran across the room to her grandmother.

Brenda was apologetic. 'I'm sorry, she was getting upset and wanted to see you.'

'That's fine.' Alice put a comforting arm around Millie's shoulders as the child clung to her legs. 'Can we finish this later, Jack?' Alice asked. He nodded. Perhaps they'd covered enough ground for the time being.

'I have something for you, Millie.' Jack hunkered down in front of the little girl and pulled out her doll from his jacket pocket. Millie's eyes widened at the sight of her beloved toy and she reached out to grasp it, a huge smile on her face.

'Dorothy!' She clutched the rag doll to her chest, clearly delighted to have it back. After relaying Sarah's message to Alice, Jack smiled and took his leave before he and Claire Swift left the house.

'What's on your mind, Claire?' Jack asked his DC when they were alone in the car. He could tell that something was troubling her.

'The date, sir, it doesn't tally. According to the hospital, Alice was admitted on the morning of the ninth of June. So if she's correct about the meal being on the evening of the seventh and she was ill the following morning, it would have been the eighth. I'll double-check with the hospital when we get back.'

'I'd also like you to look into the whereabouts of Tom Roberts' car,' Jack said.

'We've already got traffic looking for it.'

'Good, but I think they need to search here, in Melkinthorpe. If Rachel got rid of it, it can't be far away. She'd have had to walk back to the house from wherever it's hidden. Get traffic to search the woodlands around here, will you?'

'Yes, sir.' The DS started the car, and they headed back to Hunter's Lane.

36

Jack wanted to interview Alice Roberts again and soon. There was a difficult balance between moving a case on as quickly as possible and being sensitive to the victim's plight. The information-gathering stage was crucial and speed of the essence, but the fact that it was already several weeks since the last sighting of Tom Roberts added another dimension to the case. There were so many shifting issues here and Alice's memory was still not as reliable as Jack would have liked.

Before leaving Melkinthorpe, he'd asked Brenda Chapman to come to the station for an interview and to make her formal statement. Talking to her away from Alice's cottage would offer fewer distractions and Brenda was happy to comply. Perhaps she needed a break from what must be a somewhat tense situation.

Brenda arrived at Hunter's Lane mid-afternoon. Jack and Claire Swift started the interview, hoping to build up a more detailed picture of Rachel, her relationship with her mother and anything else of relevance from an independent source.

'Thank you for coming in, Mrs Chapman,' Jack began. 'DC Swift here will take your statement shortly, but first, we'd like to ask a few general questions. Is that okay?'

'Fine, anything to help catch that monster,' Brenda replied bitterly.

'How long have you known the Roberts family, Mrs Chapman?'

'About fifteen years, I think. I always knew of them, ever since Alice's family were killed in the accident. Matlock's a small community; we were all shocked by the tragedy. Our children went to the same school too, but it wasn't until after my son died that I really got to know Alice.'

Jack nodded, encouraging her to continue. Claire opened her notebook and started writing down a few details.

'It was a bond, I suppose. Both of us have lost a child. We understood how it felt and our friendship grew from there. Our husbands got along too, and we often socialised together, but generally, it was only Alice and me.'

'And what about Rachel, what was she like as a child?'

'Rather strange. To be honest, I could never take to her – she was a sullen girl and it was an effort for her to speak to anyone. It always seemed that she couldn't be bothered with me. Alice said that Rachel was shy and a bit of a loner, but that was just an excuse to my mind. Between us, I think Alice and Tom spoilt her, always trying to make up for losing Jenny, you know? In the circumstances, it was understandable and I was probably guilty of doing the same with my own kids after Harry died, but they were normal.'

'Are you suggesting that Rachel wasn't normal, Mrs Chapman?' Claire asked.

'Maybe that's a bit strong, but she was surly and unsociable to the point of rudeness. Even when Jenny was still alive, my Harry used to say none of the other children at school liked Rachel. They only put up with her for Jenny's sake – now, *she* was a popular girl – but that's another story. Harry even went so far as to say that some of the other children were frightened of

Rachel, the way she stared at them, she looked straight through you, you know?'

'Were there any specific incidents that concerned you about Rachel?' Jack was aware that this was all very vague. They were getting a picture, but not a very clear one. He preferred facts and reliable data.

Brenda looked thoughtful. 'There was the incident with the school guinea pig...'

'Go on.'

'Each holiday, a different child was allowed to take Freddie – that was the guinea pig – home to look after. At the end of one summer term, Jenny was chosen to take him home and was thrilled. But Rachel didn't want to have him. I think she was jealous of anyone, or anything, which took her sister's attention away from her. The day before school broke up, Freddie was found dead in his hutch. His neck was broken, and the staff didn't know how it could have happened. One of the children insisted they'd seen Rachel at the hutch with the door open, but naturally, she denied it, and the matter was dropped. The children whispered about Rachel having killed the poor creature, but they were so scared of her that the whispering stopped almost as soon as it started. There was probably nothing in it, it wasn't the sort of thing you could prove, but I believed it at the time.'

Claire made a few more notes in her book, writing the words 'hearsay' and 'vivid imaginations' in the margin.

'What about Alice and Tom's relationship. Would you say they were close as a couple?' Jack was keen to move on.

'Yes, very. Tom worked away quite a bit and Alice missed him terribly – they were devoted to each other and so close, not surprising really after all they'd been through.'

'So, you wouldn't think he was the sort to have an affair?'

The question needed to be asked, all avenues were to be explored, and Brenda's reaction was exactly as he'd expected.

'That's ridiculous! Tom loved Alice. It was plain for all to see. He would never look at another woman. They were both so excited to be retiring and able to spend more time together. There's absolutely no way that Tom would leave her for another woman if that's what you're thinking.'

'I'm sure you're right, but we have to consider every possibility. And can you confirm when the last time you saw Tom Roberts was?'

'It was a short time before they left Matlock; sometime in May, it would be. I can check the date and get back to you?'

'Thank you, that would be helpful.'

The interview continued in a similar vein, with the only solid evidence being a positive sighting of Tom Roberts a few weeks earlier, proving that Rachel lied about his supposed death four years before. Other than that, Brenda's statement was mainly hearsay, bordering on small-town gossip. However, a picture of Rachel was emerging, which made Jack think she was capable of far more than the lies and abandonment they'd already discovered. He would continue to probe into the family dynamics during his next visit to Alice. His determination to find Rachel was increasing with every new piece of the puzzle they uncovered.

37

'What makes you happy, Millie?' Trisha Banks, the safeguarding officer, smiled at the solemn little girl seated before her in her office. With very little background information, intentionally so, Trisha only knew that her colleagues were desperate to find the girl's mother. It was her job to draw information from Millie about her homelife without any preconceived ideas, which may inadvertently cause her to make suggestions or put words into the child's mouth.

Using careful open-ended questions, Trisha hoped to build up a picture of Millie's life with her mother, looking for anything untoward, which could range from neglect to physical, sexual, or emotional abuse.

Millie looked at the adult she'd only just met with wide eyes, unsure whether to speak or not, although her grandma had told her she could tell this lady anything she wanted to.

'I'll go first, shall I?' Trisha smiled again. 'I have a puppy called Rosie, with a very waggy tail and long soft ears. She makes me happy when she gives me doggy kisses and wants to play with me.'

'Grandma has a dog called Barney…' Millie whispered.

'Really, and when do you see Barney?'

'I don't. Grandma says he's gone now, but we might get another dog.'

'That would be lovely. Dogs make such good pets. What else makes you happy, Millie?'

'I like school... and my friend, Evie.'

'Wow, you must be a really big girl if you go to school. What's the best thing about school?'

'All the toys and books and playing with Evie.'

'And what about at home? What do you enjoy doing at home?'

The little girl answered very politely, still clearly unsure whether she should be telling this stranger details about her life.

'Reading my books and playing with Dorothy.'

'Is this Dorothy? She's very pretty.'

Millie nodded and hugged her doll even closer; as if afraid to lose her again.

'Do you like colouring? I have some pens and paper over in the play corner. We could draw some pictures if you like?'

A brief smile crossed the girl's face, and so Tricia moved to the table in the corner and began sorting the pens. Millie followed tentatively.

'My favourite colour's blue. What's yours?'

'Yellow, but Evie's favourite is pink.'

'Why don't you draw a picture of Evie so I can see what she looks like? Or maybe you'd like to draw someone else, Mummy or Grandma perhaps?'

Millie chose a yellow pen and started to draw her school friend and then her grandma. It was going to be a slow process, but Tricia was endlessly patient. From drawing people, they progressed to drawing their houses, working side by side until Millie was chatting quite readily to this lady, who quickly gained the status of a new friend.

'Who takes you to school, Millie?'

'Mummy does, and then Mrs Palmer picks me up, and I have to go to her house.'

'And is it fun at Mrs Palmer's?'

'Not really. She smells, and her house is cold and dark. She just watches things on television all the time and I have to be quiet. Dorothy and I can read books when I'm a good girl, but if I make a noise, I have to go into the yard and she takes Dorothy away... and I can't have my beans. But if it's raining, I'm allowed to go in the shed.'

Tricia swallowed hard at the mental picture of this slight little girl, who looked as though a strong wind would blow her over, put out into a yard just so her childminder could watch television.

'And does Mummy pick you up from Mrs Palmer's house to take you home for tea?'

'Yes, she picks me up, but I've usually had my beans, so we don't eat at home.'

'Does Evie ever come to your house to play?' Tricia ventured.

'No. Mummy doesn't like visitors. I went to Evie's house once... it was fun. She has lots of toys and a trampoline, and a swing in the garden. We were allowed to watch Peppa Pig on the television too. I'd never seen it before – Peppa has a little brother who's so funny – Evie says she watches it all the time, but my mummy says cartoons are bad for me. Evie's mummy laughs a lot and never gets cross, even if Evie's really naughty and makes lots of noise. Mrs Harper cooked us fish fingers and alphabet spaghetti for tea, with bananas and ice cream for afters. She reads bedtime stories too, even though Evie can read.' Millie continued her colouring, lapsing into thoughtful silence, but then picked up the narrative again.

'When Mummy came to take me home, I didn't want to go, but I didn't dare say so. Evie's mummy hugged me goodbye, and

I started to cry. Mummy was cross. She says I'm too old for hugs and to cry – now that I'm five and a big girl.'

'And do you think you'll go to Evie's house again sometime?' Tricia was blinking back the tears as Millie spoke.

'No, I'd like to go again, but Mummy said Evie's mummy spoiled me like Grandma and Granddad do, and I'm not allowed to be spoiled.'

'So, other than Mrs Palmer, does anyone else look after you, Millie?'

'No.' The child shook her head, an earnest expression on her face as she was thinking of what to say next.

'If Mummy has to go out, I have to stay in my bedroom, alone 'cause I'm a big girl now.' She continued the colouring as she spoke, her brow creased in concentration.

'It's scary on my own, even when Mummy gives me some magic medicine, which she says will make me brave. But all it does is make me sleepy. Sometimes, when I'm alone in the house for a long time, I get very hungry, and I worry that Mummy might never come back, especially when it gets dark...'

38

In the Hunter's Lane incident room, DI Priestly surveyed his team. The mood was somewhat solemn. It was the third day since Rachel Roberts' disappearance and so far, there'd been no sightings.

The room showed signs of round the clock use, waste paper bins overflowing with polystyrene cups, fast food wrappers, and half-empty water bottles on the desks. The whiteboards were filling up with information and photographs – Rachel Roberts looked down on them, her cold stare almost mocking their so-far futile efforts to find her. A second image, one of Tom Roberts, reminded the team of the urgency of their investigation.

'Does her mother have any idea where she might be?' DS Owen Hardy asked.

'No. Apparently, there are no friends that Alice Roberts knows of, and she doesn't appear to have kept in touch with anyone from her university days in Birmingham. Rachel Roberts is very much a loner.' Claire answered. 'A real ice queen, this one.'

'Claire, did you check those dates with the hospital?' the DI asked.

'Yes, and they confirmed that Mrs Roberts was admitted on the ninth of June. She must be confused about the date her daughter was with them. It would have been the eighth.'

'No, I think we'll find that Alice is correct. It was the seventh – her birthday.'

Claire tilted her head to one side. 'But she said it was the morning after their dinner when she woke to find her husband missing and rang her daughter.?'

'That's a natural assumption for both her and us to make. But it's been bugging me how Rachel could have got rid of any sign of her father and spirited him away to an unknown destination, all in the few hours between Alice feeling ill and going to bed and waking up the next morning. I think our suspect used her knowledge of drugs to keep her mother unconscious for all of the following day and a second night too. Alice went to bed on the seventh and woke on the morning of the ninth. If you'd like to check with the staff at the pharmacy, I rather think that Rachel Roberts would have taken the day off work on the eighth – she was busy setting the scene at her parents' home and somehow making her father disappear.'

There was a moment's silence in the room as Jack's theory sank in. The cold and calculating nature of this woman was quite staggering.

Owen shook his head in disbelief. 'So, what are you saying? That she worked through the night and the following day to get rid of her father, to a place as yet unknown, then removed all trace of him from the house in a bid to con her own mother into thinking she was mad and that her husband has been dead for years?'

'That's about the long and short of it, but it's all hypothetical at the moment. Claire, why don't you make that call to the pharmacy to check whether Rachel was at work on the eighth? That should help us decide if this is a feasible scenario.'

Claire headed out of the room, already tapping on her phone.

'How far have you got with the CCTV, Owen?' Jack asked.

'We picked her up leaving the school with Millie and heading in the direction of her home. A couple of hours later, her car was driving south out of town, but nothing further. If she's left the area, she managed to avoid the main roads and motorways, and ANPR hasn't picked up the car since. So either she's not travelling, or she's dumped it and is using a hire car. There's been no activity on her bank cards or any pings on the mobile phone.'

'Could she still be in the area?' DC Neil Pearson asked.

'It's possible, but it's not such a big place to hide. If Rachel means to disappear permanently, I guess she'll be out of the area by now.' The frustration was evident in Owen's voice.

Claire Swift returned to the room, a huge smile on her face.

'You were right, boss. Rachel took the day off on the eighth of June. They remember it because it's such an unusual occurrence. She's never off work but apparently needed to attend to some personal business.'

Jack nodded. It all pointed to and was evidence of a premeditated crime. When they eventually found their suspect, she could hardly claim a spur-of-the-moment action. Taking drugs to her parents' home and taking a day off work was solid proof of forward planning.

The team was shocked at this woman's callousness, and Jack paused as a hum of whispered comments rippled through the room.

'And you were right about Tom Roberts' car too. Traffic found it in the woods near Melkinthorpe. CSI is going over it now,' Claire added, her respect for Jack Priestly growing as the case progressed.

'Okay, folks, any other suggestions or ideas?' Jack brought them back to order.

'What about the little girl's father? Do we know who he is?' DC Elaine Thompson chipped in.

Jack answered. 'No. Rachel never disclosed his identity, even to her parents and he doesn't seem to have featured at all in the child's life. The pharmacy staff seem only to know the professional face of the woman, and she's far from a popular boss. So it was a surprise to them to learn that she even had a child.'

Claire whistled. 'Wow, what kind of mother doesn't talk about her child to her colleagues? It's unbelievable!'

'And this childminder we heard about, could she know something?' DC Elaine Thompson suggested.

Most of the team had watched the tape of Millie's interview and were appalled by what they'd heard. The childminder seemed to be as heartless as the mother and it was a reasonable leap to think that she might know something or even be in league with Rachel, although a motive for that certainly wasn't apparent.

'Claire's already passed the woman's name on to social services. I shouldn't think she's registered and they'll be keen to talk to her about her 'childminding' business. As soon as we have an address, that's another avenue we can pursue. Good idea, Elaine.' Jack smiled.

Elaine flushed at the hint of praise from her boss. Like the rest of the team, she'd warmed to DI Priestly. His predecessor had been a far less approachable man who was known to shout at junior officers, mistakenly assuming that a display of anger would spur them on to work harder, more efficiently. However, the opposite was true and young officers like Elaine hardly dared to voice an opinion when he was in charge. DI Priestly was proving to be much more congenial, resulting in drawing more out of his team.

'Any other thoughts?' Jack asked.

'Only that our ice queen is a real bitch!' Owen almost spat the words. 'How can anyone treat a child in such a way – her own daughter too? Okay, she might not have beaten the girl or starved her, but there's certainly a case for emotional abuse and neglect, and if the little girl's right about being left in the house alone, that's plain unthinkable.' Owen was a recently new father himself and Millie's interview tape had clearly touched him deeply.

'I'm sure we all agree, Owen, but let's keep our focus on Tom Roberts for now. Millie is safe with her grandmother, but as yet, Tom's whereabouts is still unknown, so he has to be our priority. We can throw the book at Rachel later when we find her,' Jack reminded them.

'What do you think the chances are that he's still alive, boss?' Claire asked.

'I'm sure we all have our own opinions on that one, but until we know otherwise, we're looking for a man, not a body.' Jack's expression said it all. He was unwilling to speculate, always believing that there was hope. 'How's the disclosure coming along, Claire?'

'Nothing out of the ordinary to help us, I'm afraid. I checked with the land registry to see if she owned any other properties, but nothing's shown up. I suppose it would have been too easy if she'd owned a holiday cottage and we found her there with our missing person. But then it's possible that she could own something in another name.'

Claire's comments brought to mind an abduction case Jack had worked on several years ago. The abductors took a three-year-old girl and concealed her for fourteen years, passing her off as their own daughter, a girl of the same age who'd died in infancy. They were eventually discovered hiding out at a holiday home in Northumberland, a place overlooked in the search as it was owned in the wife's maiden name.

'That's always a possibility, Claire. But, as I've said before, there are so many variables we can't discount anything.'

'With this propensity for using drugs that she has, I suppose it's a possibility that Tom Roberts could still be alive and drugged, perhaps in another property somewhere? After all, she kept her mother sedated for as long as it suited her needs,' Owen Hardy added.

'That would be an outcome I'd welcome rather than the alternative, and one of the reasons why we need to remain focused. As a pharmacist, Rachel certainly knew what she was doing. The list of drugs we found at her home is quite staggering, not at all the usual bathroom cabinet medication. For those who haven't seen the lab report, it's on the board; check it out. Our old friend Rohypnol is on the list, and I wouldn't mind betting that's what she gave her mother from time to time, even while she was in the nursing home. There's also Zopiclone, a sleeping tablet, traces of which the hospital found in Millie's blood samples. Rachel had probably used it on her daughter with some regularity and no regard for the long-term effect on the girl's health.

'A rather nasty neuromuscular blocker called Suxamethonium was also found, the sort of drug no pharmacist can justify having in their possession. It's a powerful, fast-acting, muscle relaxant found in anaesthetics. They used to use it in the States to paralyse prisoners on death row before giving lethal injections. It was banned due to disturbing side effects, which begs the question, why did Rachel Roberts have it in her home? The only reasons I can think of are nefarious – the drug is almost undetectable as the body's enzymes break it down within thirty minutes. A pathologist would have to be specifically looking for that particular drug to find it.'

As Jack's words sank in, some of the team shook their heads in disbelief. The thought of a mother feeding drugs to her child sickened them. Although it appeared that their suspect had vanished, they were determined to track her down to see justice brought to bear.

'I think we need to visit the pharmacy to ask a few more questions. Rachel might have been the only qualified pharmacist working there, but she must have used locums. Even ice queens need time off occasionally. Owen, come with me on this one. You can use your charm to get those girls talking.' A brief look passed between Elaine and Claire as they tried not to laugh at the DI's inference that Owen Hardy possessed any charm at all.

39

Rachel's shop was still open and both assistants turned towards the door as the old-fashioned bell jingled. A smile of recognition crossed their faces when they saw Owen. He'd been part of the team to search the premises previously, seeking clues as to Rachel's whereabouts, and he now introduced his DI.

'This is Val and Pauline,' he said. 'I see you're managing to keep the shop open, ladies.'

Pauline spoke for both of them. 'We don't know what else to do, but we can't go on like this indefinitely. There's no one here to fill prescriptions and that's where most of the business is, so if Ms Roberts doesn't come back soon, we'll have to close up and put a note on the door, and what about our jobs?'

'That's a decision you may need to make as I don't think Ms Roberts will be returning to work, even if we do locate her soon.' Jack was guarded in what he could say as technically Rachel was still only a suspect in her father's disappearance and Millie's neglect. 'You mentioned prescriptions, and that's what we'd like to ask you about. Was there another dispensing pharmacist who worked here as well, or perhaps a temporary locum?'

Pauline enlightened them. 'There was until a few weeks ago. Scott Lambert worked part-time, a day and a half each week and the occasional Saturday, but he stopped coming, out of the blue, like. When we asked about him, Ms Roberts just said he'd resigned. If he'd still been around, I suppose he could have filled in for her now.'

'And you were never given a reason for his sudden resignation?' Owen asked.

'No, only like, that'd he'd not be back again.'

'Do you have any contact details for Mr Lambert?' Owen continued. 'We'd like to speak to him.'

'Hang on... Val, love, can you go and get his address and number, now please, not tomorrow.' Pauline shook her head as the younger girl sauntered through to the back of the shop.

'You didn't mention this Scott when I was here the other day, Pauline. Are there are any other employees who might have left within the last few weeks or months?' Owen continued the discussion with Pauline while Jack familiarised himself with the shop.

Pauline shook her head. 'No, no one else but him.'

'Could I have a quick look around?' Jack asked.

As Val returned with the information on Scott Lambert, Pauline showed Jack around the shop. Apart from the retail space, there were four other rooms, all accessed from behind the counter. To the right were a small but adequate staff room, a bathroom next to it, and an office and large walk-in storeroom to the left. Unfortunately, the latter two were both locked, but Pauline produced keys and showed Jack inside.

'Does anyone use the office and storeroom other than Rachel?' he asked.

'Not the office, that's very much her domain, but Scott had access to the storeroom where all the meds are to fill the prescriptions. He used that little shelf to do his paperwork, and there's a ledger he filled in. Val and I never came in here. In fact, we had the devil of a job finding keys to these rooms when your lot came before, thought you were going to have to break in.'

Jack thanked the ladies for their help and then set off with Owen to visit Scott Lambert.

The address was only a couple of miles from the shop and the two detectives were optimistic of finding Scott at home as it was apparently one of the days he used to work for Rachel Roberts. The house was in a row of pre-war semi-detached properties, small but neat, with a forecourt garden and a low wrought-iron fence. A tall thin man answered the door, his face immediately taking on the expression of a startled deer, even before his visitors announced themselves.

Lambert showed Jack and Owen into the lounge, hurriedly moving piles of newspapers and magazines and removing the residue of what looked like the previous day's takeaway.

'Can I get you a coffee or something?' he asked before even establishing why he merited a visit from the police.

Jack answered for them both. 'No, thank you, we're fine. We'll try not to keep you long, Mr Lambert. We'd just like to ask you a few questions.'

'Yes, of course. What's it about then?'

'We're making enquiries as to the whereabouts of your employer, Rachel Roberts. It's imperative that we find her quickly and we wondered if you could help us in any way.'

'Rachel? But I haven't seen her for about four weeks now. I don't work for her anymore.'

'We realise that, yet any information you can give us about her whereabouts would be helpful. Perhaps you'd tell us why you left her employment?'

'It was a disagreement, a clash of personalities, you could say.' Scott lowered his eyes, as if uncomfortable with the subject. 'Is Rachel in any danger? Do you think something's happened to her?'

Jack persisted. 'We know very little at the moment, except that we need to locate her as soon as possible. So what was the disagreement about, Mr Lambert?'

'Something and nothing really, I'm sure it hasn't anything to do with her disappearance.'

'It must have been significant for you to leave your job?' Owen chipped in. 'Was it a personal matter or a professional one?'

Scott was squirming with their persistence and obviously didn't want to share the details of his falling out with Rachel. 'Is she in any kind of trouble?' he asked after a thoughtful pause.

'Will you please just answer our questions, Mr Lambert, or perhaps you'd like to come down to the station to continue this discussion there.' Jack's eyes bored into Scott, making the younger man turn away to look down at his feet. After a pause, he decided to co-operate.

'Okay, it was a thing at work. Rachel's not an easy person to work for and expects her pound of flesh – and more. She often leaves me mountains of prescriptions to check, which she knows will take far longer than the hours for which I'm contracted. Rachel also gets me to do all the MURs, that's medical use reviews, with the patients. I don't think she likes dealing with the public, but again she expects too much. Then there's the stocktaking to keep on top of too. I can tell you, I work as a locum for two other pharmacists and neither is as demanding as Rachel. Do you know, I trained for five years to qualify? Mostly locum work is great; you get to choose your own hours and days off, but the pressure and expectations are mounting, and the pay certainly isn't.'

Owen appeared bored listening to the man's grievances. 'So, was it your working conditions that caused this disagreement?'

'Not exactly. It was to do with irregularities in the stock. When Rachel was away, a rather large order for a residential care home needed filling, and while I was in the storeroom, I had a good mooch around just to see if what we had tallied with the ledger. I started by checking the top shelf, where I found several items not on the list. Most of it was stuff we don't have any call for, so I decided to ask Rachel about them when she returned.

'She called in before I left and I mentioned it to her, but as the girls were still around, Rachel seemed reluctant to discuss it. Then, out of the blue, she invited me round to dinner at her place later that night, quite a surprise and rather out of character for her. She's a good-looking woman, I wasn't going to refuse the chance to get to know her better, so I accepted.'

'And when was this exactly?' Owen asked, for clarification.

'It'll be four weeks gone Friday. I remember the date as it was my last day of employment with her.' Scott became pensive again.

Jack encouraged him to continue. 'The dinner didn't go well then?'

Scott took a huge breath, letting it out slowly as if summoning up the courage to carry on. 'No, not well at all. When I arrived, Rachel was very polite and offered me a drink. She'd made an effort with her appearance and I felt pretty buoyed. I'd never thought that a woman like her would look twice at me, but she was actually flirting.

'Neither of us seemed to want to bring up the subject of the drugs I'd found and I wasn't going to be the one to break the mood. We had a couple of drinks, well, maybe more than a couple, and then she came on to me. I couldn't believe my luck, and as we're both single, consenting adults, I let her lead me upstairs...' Scott was blushing. There must be more to the story than a pleasant roll in bed if he'd ended up losing his job and seemingly not getting any dinner.

'It seemed to be going okay until she became somewhat demanding. Rachel said she liked it rough and asked me to er, well, to smack her around a bit. I wasn't keen, but she insisted and gave as good as she got, I can tell you. It was over all too quickly then Rachel disappeared into the bathroom for a shower. My mind was whirring. I couldn't take in what had just happened, whether she liked me or not, or even if I wanted her anymore.

'She came out of the shower, fully clothed, and told me to get dressed. Rachel went downstairs and I followed her. Her face said it all. She was angry but somehow triumphant, and before I had the chance to speak, she told me that she no longer wanted me working at the pharmacy – and I wasn't to mention the irregularity with the drugs to anyone.

'I was angry myself by then and asked her what the hell she thought she was playing at. Perhaps I came over a bit heavy-handed and told her that I'd a good mind to report her to the authorities.'

'And why didn't you, Mr Lambert?' Owen asked.

'The bitch laughed in my face. She said that if I even thought about it again, she'd go to the police and tell them that I raped her! She even got her phone out and started taking selfies of the marks on her face and body. Then she said she'd keep the sheets for DNA evidence. I couldn't believe it, the gall of the woman! There was nothing I could do after that, so I left and came home.'

'With hindsight, Mr Lambert, did you not think about going to the authorities later?' Jack asked.

'With the threat of rape hanging over me, no bloody way!'

'But these were serious breaches. Did you not wonder what she was doing with the drugs?'

'I tried to put the whole debacle out of my mind. I don't know what the woman was doing with the bloody stuff, but what's it to me?' Scott's temper was rising, but so was Owen Hardy's as he countered with equal intensity.

'Were you aware that there was a child in the house while you were with Ms Roberts?'

Scott's mood was instantly deflated; he shook his head and frowned. 'There wasn't a child there, whose child do you mean?'

Owen stared the man down. 'Rachel Roberts' five-year-old daughter was in the next bedroom, probably drugged with those drugs that mean nothing to you.'

'Mr Lambert, do you have any idea at all where Rachel Roberts might be? Is there a holiday home or a favourite place she's mentioned at work, perhaps?' Jack aimed to diffuse the tension in the room and bring the interview to a close. Interesting though this may be, and it had undoubtedly shown another facet to their suspect's character, it wasn't getting them anywhere.

'No, nowhere, Rachel was never one to engage in small talk with the staff.' Scott sounded weary.

Jack stood to go. 'Thank you for your time, Mr Lambert. We'll finish this interview for now, but if you think of anything at all that could help us, please get in touch straight away.'

'Right, I will... will I er, be in any trouble over this?' Lambert asked nervously.

Owen was quick to answer. 'It's too early to say.'

'You were a bit hard on him in there.' Jack said when they were in the car heading back to Hunter's Lane.

'Nothing more than he deserves. I want the man to stew, to think over his actions and hopefully show a little more remorse. If only the bastard had come forward sooner, Tom Roberts might still be at home with his wife, and he could have prevented Millie's close call too.'

'True, but 'if only' is a hypothetical phrase and, in my opinion, one of the saddest phrases in the English language.'

'What do you mean by that?' Owen snapped.

'We all say 'if only', and usually it's with hindsight when we're all much wiser. Don't you think that if Scott Lambert knew what the immediate future was going to look like, he'd have reported his boss? And he too didn't know that Rachel had a child. None of her colleagues was aware of that little fact.'

'But he should have reported it anyway, don't they swear some kind of Hippocratic oath like doctors do?'

'No, I don't think it's mandatory for pharmacists, but according to Dan, my youngest, they're encouraged to swear a similar oath when they finish their degrees.'

'There you are then; he should be struck off or whatever they do. He's breached a moral code if nothing else, so are we going to charge him, boss?'

'Charge him with what?'

'Withholding information, failing to report drug misuse, surely there must be a list of crimes we could charge him with?'

'Let's see how things work out for now. Finding Tom Roberts has to be our priority and Scott Lambert isn't going anywhere, Owen.'

Owen wriggled back in his seat, thoughtful or sulking Jack couldn't decide. He appreciated his DS's passion for his job and justice, but he was still young. Hopefully, a few more years would mellow his attitude and he would begin to see that not all cases were black or white. *If only* it were as simple as that.

40

The seemingly endless wait was taking its toll on Alice. Sarah could see the strain in her face and the dark circles around her eyes as soon as she opened the door. The woman looked so much older than fifty-five, her skin sallow and eyes dull and red from crying.

Sarah smiled. 'Are you up for a visitor?'

'Oh, Sarah, yes, please come on in; it's so lovely to see you.' Alice led the way to the kitchen and automatically switched on the kettle. It was late morning and Sarah knew her friend would be alone now that Brenda had returned to Matlock and Millie was back at school. Sarah felt the frustration of there being no news of Rachel or Tom and could hardly imagine how Alice felt. Hopefully, some company would cheer her up.

As she waited for the kettle to boil, Alice turned to her friend, 'Your husband rang me earlier to tell me they've found Tom's car in the woods. I don't suppose that's good news, is it?'

Sarah shook her head sadly, unable to offer the comfort Alice wanted.

'I suppose there's still hope. Tom wasn't inside and until they find a body...' Alice didn't finish her sentence and turned instead to the task of making tea.

Sarah took the cup of tea Alice handed to her and they moved into the lounge. Outside, the rain poured down, a summer storm battering the gardens, the rhythm pounding on the French windows, and adding to the room's sombre mood. It was so much easier to be positive when the sun was shining, but the gardens needed rain, even if Alice didn't.

'How's Millie settling back in at school?' Talking about her granddaughter usually distracted Alice. The little girl was the one bright spot in the woman's life at the moment.

'Really well, and so much better than I expected. Her teacher says she's far more relaxed than before, as if a weight's been lifted from her little shoulders. She's entering into activities with much more enthusiasm and happy to be with her friends again, particularly Evie. I'm pleased for her, obviously, but I miss having her here with me. Selfish, I know, but I'll be glad when they break up for the summer soon.'

'Quite natural, I would say. Still, doing the school run will keep you busy and I'm sure there'll be plenty of playdates over the holidays.'

'Yes, there's that to look forward to. I'm relieved that Millie's turning out to be a more confident and sociable child. Each time she laughs, I'm almost startled – Rachel never laughed. It's a sound I could get used to.' Alice smiled. 'She's not at all like her mother. Strange, isn't it?'

'A bit of a relief, I should imagine.'

'Yes, I don't know where I went wrong with Rachel. I feel like such a failure as a mother.' Alice was verging on tears again.

'You're far from a failure! You mustn't even entertain such a thought. You've shown remarkable strength of late, Alice, and you really couldn't have done more for Rachel than you have.

But sadly, I think there's something in her make-up you were never going to change.'

'You think so?'

'Yes, I do. You've nothing to beat yourself up about; you did as much as humanly possible.'

'Still, I can't help thinking that perhaps I could have handled things differently, been a better mother, you know?'

'We all have regrets about past decisions – children don't arrive with a handbook, we simply have to muddle through. But, for what it's worth, I think you've done as much as you possibly could. You've put Rachel before yourself at every turn, and now you're doing the same for Millie. I admire you, Alice.'

'Thank you. You've been so kind, and Jack too, I don't know what I'd have done without you both. Your husband's such an understanding and wise man, isn't he? He'd make an excellent doctor or a priest, perhaps? But I suppose the police need compassionate men too.'

Sarah smiled at her friend's words. Jack would be amused to learn that she thought he'd make a good priest; she'd tell him that one later.

'Your son's a doctor, isn't he?' Alice asked.

'Our youngest, Dan, yes. He's still training, but he'll qualify in a few more years, and I think he'll be good at it. There's a lot of his father in him.' Sarah was struck by a sudden pang of guilt at the thought of her wonderful family when Alice had lost so much. Jenny, her natural daughter, had been taken from her far too soon, together with her sister's family. And now Rachel had proven to be nothing short of evil, which must be heart-breaking for her. As for Tom, this was still a mystery, which must constantly be preying on Alice's mind. Sarah knew how blessed she was to have Jack and her boys and was so very thankful.

Almost as if Alice was reading her mind, she went on to say, 'Treasure your family, Sarah. They're the most precious gift you'll ever have.' Her mood was pensive again; the words almost drowned out by the hammering rain on the windows. 'Tom's not coming back, is he? In my heart, I've begun to accept that he's dead – it's so hard, but it's the only thing that makes sense. If Rachel was so desperate to get me put into a home, she's done something to Tom too. There's no other explanation, is there?'

41

B renda Chapman returned home with mixed feelings. Undoubtedly it was good to see Ian again. She'd missed her husband, even though they'd spoken every day on the telephone. Yet, she remained worried about her friend and intended to go back to Melkinthorpe very soon. Ian would understand that Alice needed her support, although the detective's wife had proved to be a good friend.

It was nearly two weeks since Rachel Roberts disappeared and although the police continued to work tirelessly, there appeared to be no new leads.

Brenda found comfort in talking to Ian and thought he must be heartily sick of listening to her voice by now. On her first night home, they lay curled together in bed, talking into the early hours of the morning, or at least Brenda talked while Ian listened. She described Alice's new home in Melkinthorpe and how perfect it would be if only Tom were there. She vilified Rachel Roberts in just about every sentence, still unable to believe that any human being could treat another so wickedly, especially a member of her own family.

'Did I tell you how she convinced Alice that Tom was dead?

She'd actually gone to the trouble of printing an order of service for his 'funeral'. Can you believe it? The woman drugged her mother, cleared out all of Tom's things from the house and left this cruel, disgusting order of service where she knew Alice would find it. How low can a person stoop and after all her parents have done for her over the years?' Brenda's ranting was heavily punctuated with tears, both of anger and sorrow.

Ian listened patiently, holding his wife when she needed his comfort and utterly amazed at the unbelievable callousness of their friend's daughter. Most of the facts she related, she'd told him previously during their phone calls. Still, Brenda needed to talk to get the whole unpleasant incident off her mind, to find release through sharing, although they both knew that this sorry affair was far from over. There was almost certainly more heartache to come.

Brenda was in the habit of visiting their son's grave at least every two weeks, and as they lived only a few minutes' walk from Matlock cemetery, she made the short journey on foot, taking fresh flowers whenever they were in season. On the Saturday morning after arriving home from Melkinthorpe, Brenda set off on her pilgrimage, a bunch of purple and white lisianthus clasped in her hand.

The cemetery was a peaceful place, shady in the heat of summer, with the cool greens of the trees casting dimpled shadows across the paths. Brenda found great solace from her visits here. After the disturbing events of the last couple of weeks, the familiar tranquillity was more than welcome, and the peacefulness washed over her.

It was rare to meet any other visitors, especially in the quiet of the early morning, her preferred time of day. Ian never accompanied his wife and chose to remember their son as he'd been in life, happy and vital, not lying in the earth, cold and still. But that was fine, Brenda understood and enjoyed the time alone, and as it was her practice to talk to Harry, she didn't feel self-conscious.

Turning onto the path from the main cemetery drive, Brenda was surprised to see a figure up ahead, a woman not far from Harry's resting place. Not wishing to meet anyone or intrude on another mourner's grief, Brenda instinctively slowed her pace, as yet unseen by the other early morning visitor. She halted to better study the woman, beginning to think there was something familiar about her. The woman's red hair was lifted by the gentle breeze and Brenda squinted into the distance, shielding her eyes from the sun to get a better look. A sudden chill ran through Brenda's body as she recognised the woman ahead as Rachel Roberts.

Stepping quickly behind a tree, Brenda leaned against the trunk for support, fearing her legs would crumple beneath her. Brenda's heart was beating so rapidly that she felt sure it could be heard outside of her body. The flowers were dropped, forgotten, as she pulled her phone from her pocket and tapped in her husband's number with trembling fingers.

'Ian – Rachel's here in the cemetery!' Her mind wasn't functioning correctly. Perhaps she should have rung the police, not her husband.

'Are you sure it's her?' he asked.

'Yes, I'm bloody sure! Ring the police, I'm going to watch her and follow if she tries to leave – and Ian, hurry, I don't want her to get away.'

'No, don't, she's dangerous, wait for–' Ian's fear for his wife was evident in his voice, but without letting him finish, Brenda ended the call and looked again at the woman up ahead. Yes, there was no doubt in her mind who it was. Her legs still felt like jelly. If Rachel decided to move, what would she do? Following her could be risky; the woman was a psychopath who'd probably murdered her own father. But why was she here in the cemetery?

Staying hidden behind the tree and pressed against the rough bark of the trunk, Brenda allowed herself to sneak regular looks ahead and watched as Rachel appeared to be walking around in circles. Of course! It suddenly dawned on her; Jenny's grave was there too, not far from Harry's. She'd come here once with Alice and they'd visited both sites, their shared grief bringing them closer together, two bereaved mothers.

Glancing at her watch, Brenda wondered how long it would take the police to get there. She should have told Ian to tell them to hurry, that Penrith police wanted Rachel in connection with a disappearance. Would he think to tell them how urgent it was, or should she ring them herself? As she deliberated, Rachel moved.

Brenda's heart felt as if it would burst, but rising anger and a desperate longing for justice supplanted her fear – there was no way she was letting her get away. The woman had much explaining to do. Fortunately, Rachel walked further into the cemetery rather than back towards the entrance, so following at a distance was still possible. Brenda dashed from one tree to the next on shaking legs, keeping her quarry in sight and willing the police to arrive quickly.

Rachel paused to look down, causing Brenda to almost burst with indignation. The woman was standing by Harry's grave! What was she doing there? Without thinking, Brenda allowed her anger to propel her out from behind the tree towards the younger woman who was running her hand across the top of Harry's gravestone.

'How dare you go near my son!' The angry shout shattered the morning silence, and a small cloud of blackbirds rose squawking from the trees. Rachel looked up, momentarily startled.

'Get away from there. You're not fit to be on hallowed ground!' All fear dissipated, and Brenda was emboldened by her sense of outrage, not thinking of her safety or that her outburst could prompt Rachel's escape. The latter watched Brenda's approach and a smile crossed her face as she tilted her head upwards, adopting an arrogant stance. When the women were close enough to touch, one was filled with anger and the other simply laughed in her face.

'You're wrong. I have every right to be here – after all, I put him there.' Rachel spoke the words calmly, the sardonic smile still in place.

Brenda suddenly paled, anger turning to shock and her legs almost buckled beneath her as she processed the words.

Rachel continued, her smile still in place. 'Yes, you heard me correctly. I pushed your precious son down those stairs. He was a bully; he hurt my Jenny and had to pay for it. I only needed to wait for the right time...'

Brenda suddenly lunged forward and grabbed at Rachel, tears streaming down her face and her mind in turmoil. She wanted to tear the woman's hair out, to scratch at her face and hurt her physically, as *she* was hurting. But Rachel was taller and stronger. She pushed at her adversary, knocking her to the ground with ease, then ran towards the cemetery entrance. Brenda struggled to her feet, still intent on catching this mad woman who had killed her son, but a sudden pain shot through her ankle and she stumbled. Looking up from the ground, she saw Ian approaching, heading towards them.

'Stop her, Ian. She killed Harry!'

Ian reacted quickly. A big man and still fit for his age, he blocked Rachel's path, and when she tried to push past him, he grabbed her arms, pinning them to the side of her body. Then, as she continued to struggle, with surprisingly more strength than he expected, he pushed her to the ground, falling on top of her with his considerable weight making escape impossible. With the sound of police sirens quickly approaching, Ian held fast, hoping his vice-like grip was hurting this evil woman who persisted in fighting for her freedom.

The police quickly took charge of the situation, and Ian helped his wife limp towards a waiting police car.

Statements would need to be taken, not only about the morning's events but about the shocking confession Brenda had been confronted with, one which stunned her to the core and which she did not want to believe was true. Knowing Rachel, however, in her heart, Brenda didn't doubt her.

On the way to the police station, Brenda wept quietly into her husband's shoulder while he remained silent, shocked at this appalling development.

Over the years, they'd wrestled to come to terms with Harry's death, struggling to live with the pain and the loss. But things had changed, and the knowledge that it hadn't been an accident hit them like a physical blow. Instead, their beloved son's death was needless, violent and vindictive, and they desperately wanted this woman to pay for her crimes.

42

J ack and Sarah were enjoying a quiet Saturday morning at
home. Earlier in the week, a successful visit to the garden
centre resulted in several trays of new plants waiting for
their garden. But before the task, they were indulging in a
leisurely breakfast. It was the first day Jack hadn't been into the
station since Rachel Roberts disappeared, which was almost two
weeks earlier.

The investigation had slowed considerably and was simply a
waiting game. Jack's best guess was that Rachel was laid low
somewhere, making plans and waiting for the right moment to
execute them. She would have to break cover sometime,
possibly in an attempt to leave the country, but it was pure
speculation, as was Tom Roberts' fate. There was a slim
possibility that the man could still be alive and that his daughter
could be holding him somewhere, but then what was her long-
term objective?

'It's nice to have a weekend together, but I get the feeling that
you're not really with me.' Sarah teased her husband.

Jack smiled; Sarah could always read his thoughts but he
knew she was as anxious as he was for this case to be resolved.

'You're right, love, sorry. It's just that I'm not much good at waiting. Another cup of coffee and we'll get out in the garden, eh?'

But before Jack got the chance to drink his second coffee, the phone interrupted them. He answered and his expression told Sarah that she'd probably be gardening alone. Jack put his phone away and hugged his wife.

'Sorry, love, but I'm going to Matlock. The Derbyshire police have arrested Rachel Roberts!'

'Matlock, why would she be there? Are they sure it's the right woman?'

'Absolutely. They received a tip-off and found her in the cemetery held by a couple who claimed she murdered their son. I need to get down there.' Jack was already tapping in the number for DS Owen Hardy, knowing this news would interrupt his weekend too, yet certainly not spoil it.

'Who's she supposed to have murdered? I'm lost here, Jack.'

'It's just a hunch, but I wouldn't be surprised if the couple is Brenda Chapman and her husband.'

Within five minutes, Jack was out of the house and on his way to pick up his sergeant, leaving Sarah with her mouth open in astonishment.

Owen jumped into the car, eager for news. 'So, what's happening, boss, what's this new development?'

'It seems that Matlock police have found Rachel Roberts. She was recognised in a cemetery. A couple rang them and they arrived to find a bloke almost sitting on top of her, holding her down. They were insistent that she'd murdered their son too. I haven't quite figured it all out, but I suspect the couple is Brenda Chapman and her husband.'

'Did you know their son was murdered?'

'No. Alice told Sarah that their friendship was formed after Brenda's son died in an accident at school. It wasn't investigated as a suspicious death, but it seems there's cause to wonder.'

'Bloody hell! What's happened to make them think Roberts killed him?'

Jack entered the motorway and put his foot down on the accelerator. 'That's what we're on our way to find out.'

After nearly three hours of driving, they pulled up at the police station in Bank Road. It was approaching 1pm. Their suspect's arrest must have happened very early in the morning, for which Jack was grateful.

In the heart of Matlock, the station looked to be of the same era as their own in Penrith, and the two men entered with hungry anticipation and a degree of excitement as to what they might learn now that they were finally going to meet Rachel Roberts.

The detectives refused the offer of sandwiches from the sergeant on duty, settling for coffee and a brief update on the morning's events. The couple who reported Roberts' whereabouts were indeed Brenda and Ian Chapman, who were still at the station, refusing to leave until they'd spoken to Jack. The decision was easy, they would interview the Chapmans first, and their suspect would have to wait.

Brenda was still in a state of distress, even though several hours had passed since their initial encounter with Rachel. Introductions were made and Ian, protective of his wife, related what had occurred.

'Brenda always visits the cemetery in the early morning during the summer months, it's more peaceful and she can be alone with our boy. She'd only been gone twenty minutes when I got a call to say Rachel was there and for me to ring the police.

I told her to wait for them, but she's so impatient, she approached the wo–'

'Only because she was touching Harry's grave!' Brenda interrupted.

'You still should have waited. It was reckless to approach her, you could have been seriously hurt. Anyway, I rang the police and dashed off to the cemetery. Rachel had assaulted her by then and was getting away, so I tackled her and sat on her until the police arrived.'

Owen suppressed a smile.

Ian looked at his wife to continue the story and took hold of her hand. 'You'd better tell them what she told you, love.'

'I told Rachel that she'd no right to be at Harry's grave, but she said she did... because it was her who'd put him there!' Brenda was overcome with emotion and the tears started to fall. This revelation had been a considerable shock to the couple.

'Can you remember her exact words, Brenda?' Jack asked quietly.

Brenda wiped her face. 'Yes, I'll never forget them. First, Rachel told me she had every right to be there because she put him in his grave. Then, she said that she'd pushed Harry down the stairs at school, that he was a bully – he'd hurt Jenny and had to pay for it. Then she said that she'd only been waiting for the right time.' The tears continued to flow as Ian Chapman held his wife to his chest.

'You've done well, Brenda, and you too, Mr Chapman, thank you, both. It must be such a shock and I'm sorry you've had to go through this. At some time soon, we'll need to take a formal statement. DS Hardy has been taking notes, but now I think you need to go home, have something to eat, and rest. Please don't get in touch with Mrs Roberts. I want to interview her daughter before I let her know we've got her in custody. Perhaps we might discover news of her husband.'

'Yes, I understand.' Brenda sniffed. 'And thank you for coming. It's such a relief to see you.' She clasped Jack's hand and squeezed it.

The couple left. Owen and Jack decided to have that sandwich before interviewing Rachel Roberts.

43

Despite looking somewhat dishevelled, Rachel Roberts maintained a cool, composed, air. Neither detective had met the woman in person yet, but she was easily recognisable from the photographs they'd seen. A bruise was forming on her cheek, no doubt inflicted by Ian Chapman, and a bloodied graze was on the heel of her hand from her fall on the cemetery path. After introducing himself and his colleague, Jack asked if she wished to see a doctor.

'No, I've already been asked.' Rachel was brusque, indignant almost, with an impatient air, as if she had somewhere to go. 'And I don't want a solicitor either.'

Jack gave a slight nod of acknowledgement and started the interview. Owen had already switched on the tape recorder after they'd entered the room and now named the people present.

Jack commenced with the most crucial question. 'I'd like to ask you first about the whereabouts of your father, Tom Roberts. Can you tell me where he is?'

'No.' Rachel kept her eyes focused on a spot on the wall somewhere behind Jack's head, not meeting his eyes.

'Is that because you don't know, or just that you don't wish to tell me?' He needed clarification for the tape.

'I don't know where he is. Why don't you ask my mother, his wife?'

'Alice thinks you were the last person to see him, which would be after you drugged her and tried to have her locked away as demented.'

'She is demented. You can't believe anything she says.' The look in Rachel's eyes suggested that she was toying with Jack.

'Then why don't you tell me instead?' Jack's voice was even and calm. He'd interviewed many offenders throughout his career and learned to control his emotions, whatever the provocation.

She folded her arms and sighed as if bored with the interview. 'I've nothing to tell about my father.'

'Your father is missing and you're refusing to help us find him?' Jack asked.

'I don't know where he is.'

'And I don't believe you. So why did you leave Penrith and abandon your daughter?'

Rachel looked briefly into Jack's eyes but said nothing.

'Why do you think you're here, Rachel?' he asked next.

'Because those stupid people attacked me in the cemetery. I had just as much right to be there as they did.' She subconsciously rubbed her hand.

'Whose grave were you visiting, Rachel?'

'Jenny's, of course, and I thought I'd pay my respects to Harry Chapman too.' A sly smile crossed her face. She *was* toying with them.

'And can you explain what you said to the Chapmans to make them believe you killed their son?'

'Is that what they're saying? Well then, maybe I did?' She was meeting Jack's eyes, playing games with him and looking as if she was enjoying it.

'No, I don't believe you pushed Harry Chapman down the stairs. I think it was just an accident which you're using to torment his parents. You seem to take pleasure in hurting others and I rather think you said that simply to punish them.'

Rachel looked surprised by this. A look of confusion crossed Owen's face and he glanced at his boss.

'That's your prerogative; you can think what you like, DI Priestly. Perhaps I did push him, or perhaps not. Who's going to know for sure now, after all these years?' The smile was back, baiting the detectives.

Jack returned to his priority. 'I don't want to talk about Harry. I want to talk about Tom. When did you last see him, Rachel?'

'I told you I couldn't remember. I'm not exactly close to my parents, but that's not a crime, is it?'

'Why did you abandon Millie?'

'Ah, so you've finally found something to pin on me now, have you? Let's see – I was having a breakdown and simply didn't know what I was doing. Life as a single mother hasn't been easy for me, you know.' Her eyes were mocking, the subtext telling Jack that she could plead diminished responsibility. The woman was an accomplished liar and a practised manipulator.

'We found a rather large number of drugs at your house, Rachel. Why were they there?'

'I'm a pharmacist. I take work home with me sometimes.'

'Even Suxamethonium? What would a pharmacist need that for, or are you an anaesthetist too?'

'I supply to the medical profession, on occasions.'

'Okay, but we'll need proof of that. For the last week, my team has been searching through the paperwork from your pharmacy and so far found nothing relating to Suxamethonium.

In fact, there seem to be several drugs for which the paperwork is missing. Amphetamines mostly – recreational drugs. Who do you supply with those, Rachel? What kind of business do you run exactly?' Jack was pushing, angling for a reaction.

'I'm a damn good pharmacist, it's my art, and you'll find nothing amiss with my bookkeeping.' Rachel, although still cool, almost spat the words at him. Jack noticed her use of the word 'art'. It brought to his mind the 'dark arts' and how something with such potential for good, something used to heal and relieve pain, could also be used for evil.

'We'll take a break now. I'll have some coffee sent in and we'll continue shortly.' Jack stood to go and Owen switched off the tape recorder and followed.

'I think it's time to let Alice know that we've found her daughter, but I want someone with her first,' Jack told his sergeant when they'd left the interview room. 'I'm going to ring my wife and ask her to go to Melkinthorpe and I'll break the news once Sarah's there. Alice shouldn't be alone. It seems unlikely that we're going to find out much about Tom's plight today. Rachel seems intent on being evasive.'

After Jack rang Sarah, the two men went in search of coffee and Owen took the opportunity to ask his boss a question.

'I was a bit surprised by what you said in there about Harry Chapman's death. Do you really think she had nothing to do with it?'

'Actually, I think it's more than likely that she did kill him. Rachel Roberts is a psychopath, and a psychopath generally wants you to know all the details. It's a matter of pride, a way of boasting and letting you know how clever they are. I'm working on the theory that if she thinks we're inept, she'll not be able to resist putting us right. My plan is not to ask the questions she wants us to ask.' Jack smiled at the DS. 'So, would you like to take over for the next session and play the dumb cop?'

44

I t was the first time Millie had laughed out loud since Alice brought her home from the hospital. The two returned from a shopping trip with bags full of new clothes for the little girl. DI Priestly had initially offered to take them to Rachel's house to pick up some of Millie's clothes, but Alice didn't ever want to set foot in there again. She'd prefer to buy everything new. She also insisted on buying almost every toy her granddaughter showed an interest in at the department store, and now they were home, sorting out where to put their purchases.

The little girl's eyes sparkled as she kissed each teddy and doll in turn before laying them gently on her bed, unable to believe that all those toys were for her.

It wasn't their first shopping trip. The pair had visited town while Brenda was still with them and chose new bedding and curtains for the little bedroom, all in pink. Millie thought it was like her very own palace, with fluffy cushions and fairy lights around the window. When her grandma suggested that she might like to invite Evie over for tea one night, the child laughed with such pleasure that Alice mentally scolded herself for not stepping into this situation before it had grown to such dire proportions.

School was Millie's safe place, where only positive things happened, and she'd looked forward to going back. She quickly settled in. Seeing Evie had helped the process enormously, and Alice made a point of seeking out Evie's mother to introduce herself. Naturally, Alice was reluctant to let Millie out of her sight, her chief worry being that Rachel could have a change of heart and return to take her daughter away. Her friends and Millie's teacher assured her that this was highly unlikely and the child was in a safe environment. In her heart, Alice knew that Millie needed the normality of school. She was just a child and longed for the company of other children. But the little girl was the only thing keeping Alice sane – concentrating on her granddaughter's needs eased the pain of missing Tom.

As Alice was helping Millie erect a new playhouse in the corner of the lounge, the doorbell rang.

'Come in and see what we're up to.' Alice smiled, delighted to see her visitor. Sarah was becoming a familiar figure to the little girl, which could only be a good thing. Sarah took a few minutes to admire Millie's new toys, delighted at how the child was coming out of her shell. It would take time for them to heal and this ordeal wasn't over yet, especially for Alice. Would Jack's news be good or bad for her?

'Alice, Jack asked me to come around.' Sarah was quickly scrolling through her contacts to find her husband's number as she spoke.

'Have they found Tom?'

'Let Jack tell you himself.' Sarah passed the phone to Alice and moved away to distract Millie as her grandma listened. She would stay as long as her friend needed her to.

'We've found Rachel, but not Tom as yet, I'm afraid...' Jack began.

'But has she said where he is, she must know?'

'As yet, Rachel's not saying much at all, but we'll be bringing her back to Penrith tonight, and we'll continue to question her until she tells us everything she knows.'

'Where are you then? Who found her?' Alice's mind was racing with questions.

'She's in Matlock. It was your friend, Brenda, who found her and rang the police. Rachel was at the cemetery when Brenda was making her regular visit.'

'Oh, no... Jenny, she'd be going to Jenny's grave – I should have thought of that! Can I talk to her when she gets back? Perhaps she'll tell me where Tom is.'

'We'll have to see about that. It would be highly unusual and could prejudice the case...'

'I understand. Whatever you say, Jack is okay with me and thank you so much. I appreciate all you've done to find her. Let's hope you'll find Tom too.'

Alice left the room after the call to compose herself so Millie didn't see her tears. When she returned to the lounge with a tray of lemonade and homemade biscuits, Sarah and her granddaughter were both inside the playhouse, squeezed together and giggling as Alice joined in the game and pretended not to know where they were.

'Boo!' Millie shouted as she jumped out. Her grandma feigned shock and swept the little girl into her arms. She hugged her granddaughter tightly for a few moments. *It will be all right – I'll make it all right – for Millie,* she silently promised.

45

Owen led the second half of the interview with their suspect without the same kind of responses his boss received, even though the younger detective attempted to emulate Jack's questioning by switching to different topics to confuse her. Rachel appeared only to want to speak to the man in charge; that was often the case. Ms Roberts was determined to make life difficult for the detectives.

The journey back to Penrith mainly passed in silence. An awkward trio, forced to spend time together, confined in a car, for almost three hours. Rachel sat in the back seat, her hands cuffed and her eyes closed for most of the journey. Jack drove and Owen sat beside him, apparently lost in thought, and as any conversation between the detectives during the journey would need to be guarded, silence was the order of the day.

It was a relief to arrive at Hunter's Lane and to book their prisoner in for the night, after which a weary Jack told his DS to go home and get some rest, advice he intended to take himself. The interview with Rachel would resume in earnest the following day, even though it was Sunday.

'And I thought weekend working was a thing of the past.' Sarah joked when her husband arrived home. Jack was ravenous and grateful for the meal waiting for him. He'd only eaten a rather stale sandwich since breakfast. While he ate, his wife brought him up to date on Alice and Millie.

Unsurprisingly, the news of Rachel's whereabouts had come as a shock, with the poor woman berating herself for not having guessed where her daughter might have been. But worse than that, the gossamer thread of hope that Tom would also be found was severed. Alice hadn't needed to tell her friend that she was expecting the worst; the pain was etched clearly on her face.

Sarah was able to impart some positive news to her husband as she described Millie's progress. The little girl was the one bright spot in Alice's life.

Jack managed only a few hours of sleep, his mind refusing to switch off and was up and dressed before seven the following day. After a breakfast, which Sarah insisted he eat, the DI left for the police station, eagerly anticipating the day ahead.

DS Owen Hardy didn't sleep much either, although he was less confident about prising information from Roberts than his boss was. When Jack arrived, Owen was in the incident room, updating DCs Claire Swift and Elaine Thompson, both of whom had come into work even though they were not officially on duty.

Jack smiled at the eager core of his team, grateful for their presence. 'News travels fast.'

'Owen rang me last night, sir. Good news in some respect, but not the best...' Claire replied.

'No. I honestly don't know what Rachel thinks she's achieving by not telling us her father's whereabouts. Perhaps it's a control thing. She seems to like to play games, doesn't she, Owen?' Jack grinned at the DS.

'Aye, she does that. I've never claimed to understand women, but this one's in a different league completely.'

Elaine chipped in. 'We do have good news from Matlock, sir. They found Ms Roberts' car overnight, and they'll be towing it up first thing tomorrow.'

'Can't someone from their CSI team look at it today? If there's any evidence of Tom Roberts being in that vehicle we need to know now. Would you get onto that please, Elaine, try a bit of sweet-talking?' Jack didn't want to waste any time, Sunday or not.

'Yes, sir.' The young officer moved towards a desk.

'And Elaine, thanks for coming in. You too, Claire. I know how precious weekends off are.' Both women nodded, appreciating their boss's words.

'So, Owen, shall we see if our guest has had a comfortable night?'

'Good morning, Rachel. Can we get you a coffee?' Jack spoke pleasantly, noting the tiredness in their suspect's face.

'No, thank you.'

Owen did the honours with the tape recorder and the men sat opposite Rachel Roberts. The interview room they occupied was even smaller than the one at Matlock and windowless. The hum of a faulty fluorescent tube filled the initial silence and the air already felt stale, even so early in the day. Jack had requested this room specifically.

Jack jumped straight to the point. 'Did you kill your father?'

'No.' Rachel sighed, apparently bored already.

'Did you regularly drug your daughter to keep her biddable?'

Rachel smiled. 'You can't prove that.'

'The hospital found traces of Zopiclone in her blood.' Jack turned to Owen. 'DS Hardy, remind me to add assault by administering a drug to a minor to the charges against Ms Roberts.'

Rachel sighed again; her demeanour unchanged.

'What did you do on the day of the eighth of June?'

'You tell me,' she challenged.

'I think you spent the day setting the scene for your plan. You drugged your mother the evening before and probably administered more medication to keep her under for the following day and night. You also drugged your father and somehow got him into your car. Did you kill him with the Suxamethonium or just keep him under sufficiently to let him suffer? Perhaps you'll fill in the timeline for me later, Rachel, but we know you got rid of Tom Roberts at some point.' The rest of the day was spent setting the scene.

'First, you removed all signs of your father as if he'd never lived in that house. Not too arduous a task, considering your parents had only recently moved in. You even deleted all evidence of your daughter, who never existed in your little plan. Then you planted a few choice items. If I remember, there was a red coat and the order of service for your father's funeral – quite inventive. You must have been planning this for a long time, Rachel. Undoubtedly a premeditated crime. And then there was Barney, poor innocent Barney. Did you poison him with your drugs too?'

As Jack spoke, Rachel stared at him with her cold grey-green eyes; one eyebrow arched as if amused.

'What a delightful, whimsical tale, DI Priestly, but I'm rather disappointed in you. I expected so much more.' She spoke slowly, smiling at him, mocking. 'So, what if I did spirit my father away? Where is he? If I've got him locked away somewhere, he could be dying while you're keeping me here, wasting precious time...'

'Why the coat, Rachel? Just to mess with your mother's mind?' Jack was going to lead the interview. He wasn't going to answer her questions.

'A charity shop find, in just the right size. I couldn't resist, knowing how much my mother dislikes red.'

Owen Hardy shuffled in his chair as Jack coolly continued.

'And the order of service, did you have to be so cruel?'

'A stroke of genius, don't you think, Detective Inspector?' She couldn't resist gloating.

'Where's your father, Rachel?' Jack sounded slightly weary.

'Oh, DI Priestly, what would be the fun in telling you that? Can't you work it out for yourself? You're the detective. Okay, I'll help you out a little here, just a tiny clue. Tom Roberts is exactly where he deserves to be.' Rachel, who'd been leaning forward with her hands on the table, sat back and folded her arms – she was finished talking.

Jack decided not to push for more and stood to leave the room without another word. Owen switched off the tape and followed, somewhat perplexed and wondering if he'd missed something.

'What kind of clue was that supposed to be?' he asked, catching Jack up.

'Probably the only one we're likely to get.'

'Bloody hell, she's an evil one all right, the hairs on the back of my neck were tingling in there. I thought she was about to confess!'

Jack shook his head, 'Rachel's finished, for now, and feeling smug with herself, so I think the best thing we can do is to let her sweat it out for the rest of the day. Get someone to take her back to the cells, keep her guessing. We've got enough to hold her, so we'll use the time to brainstorm what she's told us so far.'

46

The four detectives listened again to the tape of the morning's interview, analysing every word and making notes of anything which stood out.

Claire spoke her mind. 'I can't believe this woman. She's the personification of evil, a real bitch! Can anyone work out what this 'clue' is supposed to be?'

'Try to put yourself in her shoes,' Jack suggested.

'I'd rather not!'

'Metaphorically speaking.' He smiled. 'If you hated your father so much, what would you think a suitable punishment would be?'

'That depends on what she thinks he's done.' Owen scratched his head. 'As far as we know, he didn't abuse her in any way. On the contrary, she appears to have had all the advantages of a good upbringing, university, financial help from her parents. So what the hell did the man do to make her hate him so much?'

Elaine's small voice broke into the conversation. 'I think it all goes back to Jenny.'

'In what way?' Claire asked.

'From everything Mrs Roberts has told us, Rachel idolised

Jenny. Yes, there were problems with Rachel before her sister died, but things seemed to escalate after that. I think she blames her parents for Jenny's death.' Elaine offered her opinion.

'I agree. Even Alice has hinted at this, although it's a bitter pill for her to swallow. But why wait until now to get revenge?' Jack asked.

'Could it be the Roberts' move to Penrith? Rachel probably thought she'd got them out of her life and then they turn up on her doorstep, wanting to see Millie,' Elaine asked.

'Yes, all this is valid, but it still doesn't tell us where Tom Roberts is. Where would you hide a body, Owen?'

'Are we looking for a body now, sir?'

'Sadly, I think we are. What did Rachel mean by 'where he deserves to be'?'

'Back in Matlock? What about the cemetery, boss? Maybe she was visiting more than those two children, what better place to hide a body than in a cemetery?' Owen sounded quite animated by his idea.

'That's a good shout Owen, but I can't see the immaculate Rachel Roberts with a shovel in the dead of night. I know I wouldn't be up to it,' Claire added.

As they pondered the options, Jack left the room saying he needed to ring Detective Superintendent Kerr, not something to be done lightly on Sunday lunchtime. But before making the call, Jack paid another brief visit to Rachel Roberts in the cells. She seemed surprised to see him so soon.

'I didn't know you made house calls, DI Priestly.' The sly smile mocked him again.

'I just wanted to thank you for your help and to let you know that we'll be searching the site of your sister's accident at Snake Pass tomorrow.'

Rachel's smile vanished and her eyes flashed with impotent anger. She remained silent – no sardonic quip to taunt him now. Her reaction confirmed to Jack that his guess was probably correct. He left the cells to make his call.

'This better be good, Jack. I haven't had a Sunday off in weeks, which is why you've been in charge of this case. I'm at the second hole. Am I going to be able to get to the third?'

Jack knew that George Kerr had been heavily involved in some serious restructuring of the force and bogged down with budget cuts. Jack's guilt at disturbing the superintendent was assuaged only by the urgency of his request.

'I need authorisation for a helicopter, sir.' Jack then explained why such a request should be granted and was surprised at his boss's minimal argument.

He finished the call with a smile and returned to his team, ready to outline what would happen the following day. Then they could all go home to enjoy the remainder of their weekend.

47

The investigation into Tom Roberts' disappearance had taken an unexpected turn, as it now seemed highly likely they were searching for a body rather than a missing person. It became a joint venture with Derbyshire Constabulary as the search relocated from Cumbria to Derbyshire. George Kerr would need to liaise with them to work out the finer details of costs. Naturally, he'd want them to pay the lion's share for such a large operation. Jack would love to be a fly on the wall to hear that conversation.

Priestly travelled with his DS, Owen Hardy, who was delegated as the driver on a bright sunny Monday morning while Jack spent much of the journey on his phone, co-ordinating the search.

Heading to such a beautiful part of the country in a designated National Park, both men could have wished for a less gruesome reason to visit the area. Claire Swift had worked her magic in researching the original accident in which Jenny and Alice's sister's family had perished, finding an approximate location to give them a starting point.

After an early start, the detectives were on course to meet with a team from Derbyshire Constabulary at 10.30am.

Jack's phone rang for about the fourth time. He listened silently and then offered his thanks to the caller.

'What's up, boss?' Owen's expression was one of eager, puppy-dog curiosity.

'The helicopter's identified what could be our body.'

'Already?' Owen's demeanour became solemn. A respectful silence gave the men time to let the news sink in. The helicopter had started the gruesome search early; conditions had been perfect, with no visibility problems and the crew member Jack had spoken to sounded confident of his find.

'It could be that our search is drawing to its conclusion, Owen.' There was a note of weary disappointment in Jack's voice as they were confronted with the likelihood that finding Tom Roberts alive was now virtually non-existent.

The helicopter was stood down, their work complete. The discovery was within half a mile of the original accident site. Claire's research had saved valuable time and resources.

It was unusual for Snake Pass to be closed in summer. Winter was a different matter altogether; the snow and ice made driving treacherous, closure was frequent and expected. The road was also prone to subsidence following heavy rain, again resulting in closures, but the reason that Monday morning was for something else entirely.

Owen parked as close to the barriers as he could get, and he and Jack exited the car with heavy hearts. A group of officers was already assembled, waiting for Jack's okay to begin, and introductions were made.

A couple of volunteers from the local mountain rescue team were ready to make the descent from the road to the sighting location. One of them was an off-duty PC, the other a medic. Also waiting to make the climb down was a crime scene manager from Matlock, who identified himself as Rob Britton. If this did prove to be a body, the CSI manager would make an initial examination of both the body and the crime scene before they could move anything. If physical conditions prevented this, photographs would have to suffice.

Owen Hardy took a brief glance over the side of the barrier then stepped back sharply. 'Thank God I don't have to go down there,' he whispered to Jack. In most investigations, the SIO and the DS would view the scene before anything was moved. Unfortunately, today this was not possible as neither were experienced enough in such terrain.

Jack, impressed with the equipment already in place, was grateful for the co-operation of those at the scene. Nothing was visible from the roadside, but the helicopter crew's report suggested that what they were looking for was about seventy feet below the edge, caught in some shrubs. Of course, it could have been worse. The CSI manager and the PC, both dressed to make the descent, seemed to think nothing of it. Jack felt like a spare part as he watched them prepare, checking safety equipment and clipping on harnesses.

A hydraulic winch, still loaded on the back of a lorry, was parked at the roadside, the operator waiting patiently to play his part in the recovery. It all seemed surreal to the Penrith officers, but the Derbyshire team knew their stuff and worked efficiently.

As the two men embarked on their descent, the team fell silent, listening to the men's breathing, the only sound so far through their radio mikes.

Rob Britton's voice came through the speaker. 'I can see something now. It's too small to be a body; hang on, I'll get a bit closer.' A few minutes of silence followed when all they could hear was the men's movements and a few grunts. 'It's in a black plastic sack, too small for a man's body... unless it's dismembered.'

Jack felt suddenly nauseous, wondering to what awful depths Rachel Roberts had plummeted. 'Can you see anything else?' He asked.

'Yes.' The PC, whose name was Andy Grice, answered. 'There's something about six feet below me, larger than the bag, caught up in some shrubs. Could be what we're looking for.'

'Rob, how are you fixed for a preliminary examination of both items?' Jack asked.

'Not good. I've got a foothold, but it's precarious. I think photographs will have to suffice in this case, Jack.'

'Agreed, don't take any unnecessary risks. Good job, both of you.'

The winch was manoeuvred to the side of the road, and a stretcher sent down to the two men below. It was a slow process, the grinding noise adding to the horror of the task they were undertaking, but eventually, they managed to secure their first discovery, which was winched safely back up to the top.

The smell was the first thing that struck those gathered around on the roadside; a rancid stench made worse by the heat of the recent summer weather. Owen pulled on gloves and rolled the bundle off the stretcher.

'Bloody hell, it's a dog!' He turned away, clearly disgusted as the plastic covering was pulled away to reveal the decomposing body.

'Barney,' Jack whispered gloomily. It was tangible proof of Rachel's depravity.

Again the stretcher was lowered over the edge, with Jack and Owen sadly aware of what this second discovery would be. The wait was longer this time, made more unbearable by the heat of the sun, now at its peak. Jack imagined the original accident would have been on such a day as this.

Eventually, the second, heavier, bundle was winched to the

top, followed closely by Rob Britton and PC Andy Grice. The body was partly covered by what could be a blanket.

'Good work, guys, thank you.' Jack helped the CSI manager to his feet.

'It's certainly a body, the clothing suggests an adult male, but I need to get him to the morgue for the pathologist to begin the identification process. It won't be a pretty sight, Jack,' Rob warned him. 'Decomposition in this weather will have been rapid, and the wildlife will have contributed as well.'

Jack nodded. He had no reason, or desire, to view what they now knew to be a body. Identification and cause of death would take time, although the Derbyshire pathologist had assured them he would fast-track this one.

There was little more for Jack and Owen to do. With the benefit of technology, the necessary paperwork could be completed back in Penrith and shared via email with their colleagues in Derbyshire.

Having no appetite, even though they hadn't eaten since early morning, the two men set off on the long drive home, Jack again on the phone to update his superintendent and the team at Hunter's Lane.

During a silent, reflective, moment, Owen wondered aloud, 'What I don't understand is why she was so cruel to her daughter. I can understand her hating her parents, but what had the child done to be treated in such a way?'

'I'm no psychologist, Owen, but I've wondered about that too. For what it's worth, my opinion is that Rachel was subconsciously punishing Millie for not being Jenny, her sister. Perhaps the thought of a baby elicited hopes of reliving her years with Jenny. But when Millie turned out to be nothing like her, and Rachel didn't feel the emotions she was expecting, she was angry and took it out on her daughter over the years.

'It sounds weird, but I can see what you mean. Nothing

would surprise me about Rachel Roberts, and I'll be glad to see her behind bars where she can't ruin any more lives.'

It had been a difficult day, but worse was to come. Alice Roberts needed to learn of their discovery, a find which would terminate her hopes. Even though it was impossible to identify Tom's body yet, there was little doubt, and the woman had a right to know of their findings. Not for the first time, Jack wondered how much heartache one woman could endure.

48

J ack asked Owen Hardy to drop him at home and tasked his DS with going to Hunter's Lane and relating the day's events to the rest of the team, who would be keen to hear the details. The day stirred mixed emotions for Jack, and he had no heart for the celebration which the wrapping up of a case generally brought, no matter how subdued they would be. Was it too soon to celebrate? No, Jack thought not and knew that the team needed to acknowledge the successful conclusion of their investigation to maintain their sanity.

There was still so much evidence to gather in order to build a case against Rachel Roberts, and even though she might be evasive and enjoy playing her little games, she would be convicted. Jack did not doubt that.

Sarah was at home waiting to greet him, enveloping his stiff aching body and drawing him into her embrace.

'Come and sit down.' She released him from her arms and they sank gratefully into the sofa. 'Do you want to talk about it?'

'Not just now, perhaps later.' Jack would share his thoughts when he'd processed them and was ready, not before.

'Will you come with me to see Alice?'

Sarah nodded, she was ready to go... Jack went upstairs to freshen up and then rang Hunter's Lane to ask Claire Swift to meet him at Melkinthorpe. The presence of both women would hopefully make things easier for Alice.

Jack filled Sarah in on some of the day's events as they drove the few miles to impart their news. Sparing the unsavoury details, he related what he felt was appropriate, the excellent help from the Derbyshire personnel and the efficiency of the operation, but they were both aware of the devastation their news would bring to Alice.

'I suppose they're used to accidents on that road; it's quite notorious,' Sarah remarked. She was distressed to learn that they'd also recovered the body of the Roberts' pet dog, further proof of what a despicably cold, unfeeling woman Rachel Roberts was.

Claire was waiting for her boss. 'Good work today, sir,' She greeted him..

Jack smiled briefly.

Claire continued. 'Owen's given us all a full update and, by all accounts, the super's cock- a-hoop.'

'Yes, well, let's get this done now, shall we? It's been a long day.'

Alice opened the door to the little delegation on her step. Although they were not unexpected, her face registered fear as she allowed her visitors inside.

'Is Millie around? Shall I go and occupy her for a few minutes while Jack has a word?' Sarah asked.

'She's upstairs in her bedroom.' Alice's face was grim, resigned, and devoid of all hope as she led the others to the lounge.

Sarah went upstairs, calling the little girl's name.

'Auntie Sarah, come and see my new princess dress!' Millie was delighted to see her new friend and was soon showing off her latest treasures, a full tulle dress and all the accessories to turn her into a 'real princess'.

Sarah found it difficult to give the excited little girl her full attention when a huge part of her mind wondered how Alice was coping with the news. She longed to hug her friend, to tell her that it would all be all right in the end. But could she make that promise when Alice had lost her beloved husband and at the hands of their daughter too? How can anyone come to terms with such an atrocity?

'Do you like my tiara?' Millie was asking.

'Yes, sweetheart, it's beautiful!'

At least Millie seemed to be recovering well, and she would be Alice's saviour. The bond between the two was strong. Healing would come in time, but there was so much grief to grapple with before then.

Downstairs, Alice dabbed at her eyes with a tissue and blew her nose. She sobbed quietly when Jack told her the news and then pulled herself together to ask some questions.

'Are you sure it's Tom?'

'A positive ID won't be possible until after the autopsy, but I wouldn't be telling you this much if I didn't think it was likely to be Tom.'

'Did Rachel tell you where to find him?'

'Not in so many words, but she did drop hints which led us to the site of the accident.' Jack loathed these moments. Dealing with other people's grief was always difficult, and over the years, he'd found the best way forward was to be as honest and open as possible. As much as he longed to go home, he would stay as long as Alice needed him to.

'Can I make you a cup of tea, Mrs Roberts?' Claire offered.

'That would be nice, thank you.'

Claire went off to familiarise herself with the kitchen.

'I think I knew all along that Tom was dead. We were never going to find him alive, were we? Where did I go wrong, Jack?' she asked wearily.

'You didn't go wrong. None of this is your fault, Alice. You and Tom did all you could for Rachel. She was given every possible advantage. I'm sorry you have to go through this, but you do have Millie to consider. From what I've seen, she's a delightful little girl and she'll be a great comfort to you.'

'Yes, you're right. There's always a silver lining, and Millie is mine. Thank you for coming this evening, Jack. I know it's been a long and trying day for you.'

'You're very welcome and you know that if Sarah or I can do anything for you, you only have to ask.'

'I do and I'm grateful for such good friends. Now, let's call Sarah and Millie down, shall we, and have that tea.'

49

J ack went into work late the following day. He figured he'd earned a lie-in and had surprisingly slept better than he had in weeks. Over the second cup of coffee with Sarah, they talked about Alice and marvelled at her strength.

'She'd accepted that Tom was dead before you found the body, but I suppose there's always that grain of hope, that irrepressible belief that things might work out well in the end.' Sarah said.

'That's what makes us human. But now I must get off. The boss will be waiting for all the details and he's not a patient man. I'm only glad we had the right location. I'd never have heard the last of it if the helicopter sighting hadn't paid off.'

Half an hour later, Jack entered the incident room to a round of applause. He raised his hand to quieten the noise and nodded his thanks to his team.

'It was a joint effort, you've all played your part well and I'm grateful. Now, Sarah's sent this cake to celebrate.' He placed a large chocolate cake on the nearest desk, a little reward, although he knew he owed a round of drinks at some point.

There were a few questions from his team and Jack noted the various responses with interest. Elaine Thompson couldn't get over the fact that Rachel had killed the dog, which was unforgivable in her eyes.

'I still don't understand why she didn't just kill both her parents outright.' Owen struggled to piece together the 'whys' of the case. 'She seems to have gone to a lot of trouble to do it this way. All that effort to try to convince everyone that her mother had dementia.'

'Actually, I think that was her master stroke,' Jack said. 'If she'd killed both of her parents outright, there would be awkward questions to answer, funerals to arrange and inquests into their deaths. Friends might become suspicious, like Brenda Chapman, for instance, and two sudden deaths would be difficult to explain. Her parents' move to a new location allowed Rachel to get rid of both of them. By killing her father and claiming he died years ago, no one in Penrith would look into his death, and with her mother locked away in an institution, Rachel could take over her affairs, sell the house, or whatever she intended to do, with no questions asked.' Jack spoke sadly. They might guess at why Rachel Roberts had done things in this way, but they would probably never know why she wanted to kill her parents in the first place.

Jack left a rather pensive team in the incident room and went upstairs to see his boss.

'Well done, Jack.' Detective Superintendent George Kerr beamed at his DI. 'We were never going to find the poor sod alive, but you've wrapped the case up well. It's the best possible outcome.'

'Thank you, sir. Now we've got a body, I'm going to formally charge Rachel Roberts with murder so we can continue to hold her.'

'Good, you're an asset to us here at Penrith, Jack, a good result all round.'

Jack left the room and asked Claire to have Rachel Roberts sent up to the interview room.

∼

Twenty minutes later, Jack and Owen Hardy entered the room and switched on the tape.

'Did you enjoy your day trip yesterday?' Rachel appeared almost cheery.

'It was productive, if not enjoyable.'

Rachel nodded, the playfulness leaving her eyes as she waited for Jack to continue.

'Ms Roberts, today we're going to formally charge you with the murder of Tom Roberts. I would strongly advise you to have a solicitor present, as is your right. If you don't have one, we can arrange for a duty solicitor to be present during this interview.' Jack didn't want any technicalities to ruin the case. There was little doubt that the CPS would have sufficient evidence to build a strong case against this woman, but he was playing it safe.

'I don't want a solicitor. I killed my father. He deserved it.'

Taken by surprise, Jack looked to his DS and Owen immediately cautioned Rachel Roberts and then asked her if she understood her rights.

'Yes, I do.' She seemed impatient to move things along.

'Could you repeat what you said before the sergeant cautioned you?' Jack asked.

'I said that I killed him – my father – I killed him. Do you want to know how or not?'

~

For the next ninety minutes, Rachel Roberts described, in detail, precisely what she had done on the night of the seventh of June. Much of it was as the team suspected. She admitted to drugging both parents with Suxamethonium in the wine she'd brought that evening and to 'topping her mother up' with the drug throughout the next day. Tom took longer to succumb to the effects than Alice. While he was still semi-conscious, Rachel took him out to her car and drove in the cover of darkness to the place where her sister had died. It took very little effort to push her father out of the car and over the edge of the steep incline to his certain death. She seemed to think that poisoning the dog and disposing of his body with her father was fitting, a somewhat warped version of poetic justice.

Jack and Owen did not interrupt Rachel's monologue. Everything was recorded. They would ask any questions which arose after she finished her confession. She covered virtually everything. Having disposed of her father, Rachel drove straight home where she'd left Millie alone, woke the child and calmly took her to school. Rachel had spent the rest of the day at her mother's house, making sure that Alice didn't come round while she set the scene. Rachel related the facts accurately, with a sense of pride in her words. The woman wanted them to know how resourceful she'd been – that she had almost pulled off the perfect crime – and almost got away with it.

By the end of the interview, the detectives were disgusted rather than impressed.

When Rachel finished her confession, neither man asked questions. They had heard enough. They formally ended the interview and their prisoner was taken back to the cells. Rachel Roberts would not see much of the outside world for several years to come, a thought Jack found comforting.

EPILOGUE

It was nearly nine months until Rachel Roberts' court appearance for sentencing. The usual reports were compiled from various professionals during those months, reports to determine her state of mind when committing the crimes. Rachel engaged with some of the individuals appointed to assess her; with others, she did not, as the mood took her. But they were all in agreement. Rachel Roberts was in her right mind when she murdered her father and began the campaign of drugging her mother. The accused understood precisely what she was doing and was therefore declared fit to stand trial for murder. Rachel offered no argument to this decision and continued to refuse representation for the hearing.

Alice was determined to be in court to face her daughter for one last time. To look her in the eyes and search for a glimmer of remorse. She was to be disappointed on the latter issue. Sarah Priestly, Brenda and Ian Chapman accompanied her.

Rachel was led into court wearing a smart grey business suit and looked neither to her right nor left. She'd visibly lost weight which mainly showed in her face, but she walked proudly, tall and erect, taking her place as if a court appearance was an everyday occurrence. The proceedings were short. Rachel had pleaded guilty at an earlier hearing, a blessing in that a full trial was therefore not necessary, and there was now only the sentence to be determined. The charges included one count of first-degree murder, kidnapping, assault by unlawfully administering drugs, and child neglect. The CPS had undoubtedly been kept busy with this case.

Jack Priestly, Owen Hardy and Claire Swift were also in court to hear sentencing, each with their thoughts about what kind of justice Rachel Roberts deserved.

It was as expected. Fifteen years for murder, plus four years for kidnapping – two for the charge of abuse and another twelve months for neglect – all to run concurrently. Rachel would be in prison for a very long time, but for many of the people in that room witnessing justice, it was simply not enough. They too were serving a life sentence from which they would never be released.

Rachel stubbornly refused to plead either way to the charge of the murder of Harry Chapman, prolonging his parents' agony with another of her little games. She denied that particular conversation in the cemetery with Brenda and would admit nothing to the police. It was perhaps the last time she would feel in control of anything. But, in her twisted mind, this was reason enough to remain silent.

The Derbyshire police reopened the investigation into Harry's death but the lapse of time hampered the discovery of any new evidence, making a conclusion improbable. It wasn't a satisfactory result for the Chapmans, but they continued to hope that Rachel would, at some point, feel enough remorse to tell the truth. Until then, they could only be patient.

Immediately after sentencing, Rachel was asked if there was anything she wished to say. As cool as ever, she turned to face Alice and spoke clearly, her words heavy with venom.

'I heard him. I heard my father ask you, *Why did it have to be Jenny, our own flesh and blood?* I knew then that I was never truly yours, that you wished it was me who'd been in that car.'

Alice paled. The words hit her as hard as any physical blow. Sarah put a supportive hand on her friend's arm and squeezed gently. Rachel was silent once more and led away to begin her sentence.

It took several minutes before Alice was able to leave the room. Her legs trembled and her whole body shook from the shock of her daughter's words. Sarah insisted they all get a coffee before Alice even considered driving home.

Finding a quiet coffee shop close to the court, Alice, Sarah and the Chapmans sat with their hands wrapped around steaming cups. The mood was sombre and very little was said. Brenda and Ian Chapman were unusually silent, nursing their thoughts and bitter disappointment. They left the coffee shop after only a few minutes to begin the long drive home, exchanging tearful hugs and promises to be in touch soon.

When Alice and Sarah were alone, Alice tried to explain Rachel's spiteful outburst.

'Tom did say those words, Sarah, but he loved Rachel, really he did.' Alice's desire to protect her husband's memory was strong. It was important to her that Sarah, who'd never known what a good man Tom was, didn't view him as some kind of monster.

'You don't need to explain anything to me. I never knew Tom, but I know you, and I think I have a good idea of how difficult your life with Rachel has been. So whatever Tom said in his grief is understandable. I'm certain I'd have been thinking the same thing. Now, do you feel up to driving, or shall I take you home?'

Alice declined the offer, determined to be strong. That day was not only a conclusion but the beginning of her new life.

Millie was waiting to be picked up and taken home. Her granddaughter would be a balm for her soul.

Sarah wisely didn't attempt to draw her friend anymore on the events of the day. Alice would need time to process her daughter's outburst if she was ever able to do so. The important thing now was that the ordeal was over and Rachel was locked away, unable to hurt her mother, or her daughter, again.

Millie, blissfully unaware of the drama of the day, was in the care of Lucy and Mike Harper for the duration of the hearing, happily playing with her best friend, Evie. The Harpers had proved to be very supportive and more than willing to help with Millie on any occasion when they were needed. The two girls were close and wanted to do everything together.

As Lucy led Alice through to the lounge, they paused for a moment to watch the children at play. Their heads were together, giggling over a shared nonsensical joke. Millie was such a different little girl, gregarious and loving life with her grandmother. She looked happier and healthier than she'd appeared for months and was becoming quite the little chatterbox, thankfully nothing at all like her mother.

Millie rarely asked about Rachel, and when she did, it seemed as if she simply needed reassurance that her mother would not be in her life again – it appeared that she did not miss her. The child was happy living with her grandmother and had blossomed in her care. All she wanted from life was to stay with Alice and Sammy their new six-month-old puppy.

When the little girl saw her grandmother watching her, she squealed with delight and ran into her arms. Alice picked her up and swung her around.

'I love you so much, Millie Roberts!' she said.

'And I love you too, Grandma. Can we go home to see Sammy now?'

Millie's heartfelt words were precisely what Alice needed to hear. Suddenly, she felt an overwhelming rush of love for this little girl. Finally, after the long months of anguish and uncertainty, there was a worthwhile future ahead.

THE END

NOTE FROM THE AUTHOR

Thank you for reading The Pharmacist. I do hope you enjoyed it.

The story, although not the crime, was partly inspired by my mother, Enid Shaw. In her later years, she suffered from dementia, a cruel disease which I'm sure there is no need to describe in any detail here.

Shortly before her death, while Mum was in care, she told some tall tales to the staff, but not so tall that they were dismissed as a fabrication, and the staff assumed that she was relating her past. According to Mum, she'd been married three times, been a teacher in a local village school and eventually promoted to head teacher. In reality, Mum was married twice and had been a wages clerk all her working life.

The care home staff and Mum's new social worker believed her. Why wouldn't they? It all sounded utterly plausible. When we eventually compared notes, we laughed, the alternative being to cry.

One day, the ward sister told me, smiling at the unlikelihood, that Mum had even claimed that her daughter was a best-selling author. *'Well, actually...'*

However, Mum appeared happy living with these false memories, and generally, we played along rather than reminding her of painful events from her past.

Walking home from visiting Mum one day, my writer's mind wondered about the fact that the staff naturally accepted that I was the one telling the truth. But, in reality, I could have told them anything, and they would have believed me, not Mum. It was at this moment that 'The Pharmacist' began to take shape.

We enjoyed many lucid moments with Mum, but at times she came out with some hilarious anecdotes. According to her, her mother lived with her and also two of her grandchildren, a seven-year-old and a three-year-old. On one occasion, Mum refused to go to bed until the boys were in and would only co-operate after the carer phoned us, and we assured her they were safe with family. This incident resulted in a severe ticking off for us not letting her know sooner!

Other incidents appear in the book. Mum inspired the items in the bin – she lost her slippers which we eventually found, with her coat and gloves, in the kitchen bin. She constantly mislaid things, frequently tried to use the remote control to make phone calls and denied that her clothing was her own. But, of course, it was the symptoms of the illness that was gradually and tragically taking Mum away from us.

In *The Pharmacist*, Rachel Roberts, a psychopath and consummate liar, abused her position and used readily available medication to confuse her mother and set the scene to prove Alice's demise. She was in the ideal position to take things from Alice's house and being an intelligent and articulate lady, Rachel too was convincing enough to be believed by the team who cared for her mother. Rachel may have been beautiful on the outside but far from it on the inside.

ACKNOWLEDGEMENTS

Once again, my thanks are due to Sean Jackson, friend and retired detective sergeant, for his help and advice on issues where I flounder. And to my ever-patient husband and family, who put up with the many hours I spend glued to my laptop.

Well-deserved thanks also go to the team at Bloodhound books for their amazing help in getting this book out into the world. I am grateful for their dedication, professionalism and guidance throughout the process.

A NOTE FROM THE PUBLISHER

Thank you for reading this book. If you enjoyed it please do consider leaving a review on Amazon to help others find it too.

We hate typos. All of our books have been rigorously edited and proofread, but sometimes mistakes do slip through. If you have spotted a typo, please do let us know and we can get it amended within hours.

info@bloodhoundbooks.com

Printed in Great Britain
by Amazon